D1647872

Thou Shalt Not Grill

Also by Tamar Myers in Large Print:

Between a Wok and a Hard Place
Eat, Drink, and Be Wary
The Hand That Rocks the Ladle
The Crepes of Wrath
Gruel and Unusual Punishment
A Penny Urned
Custard's Last Stand

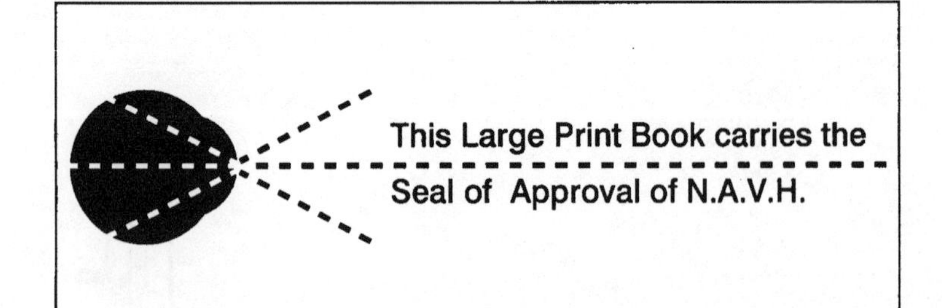

Thou Shalt Not Grill

A PENNSYLVANIA DUTCH MYSTERY WITH RECIPES

TAMAR MYERS

Thorndike Press • Waterville, Maine

This is a work of fiction. Names, characters, places, and incidents either are the product of the author's imagination or are used fictitiously, and any resemblance to actual persons, living or dead, business establishments, events, or locales is entirely coincidental.

Published in 2004 by arrangement with NAL Signet, a member of Penguin Group (USA) Inc.

Thorndike Press® Large Print Americana.

The tree indicium is a trademark of Thorndike Press.

The text of this Large Print edition is unabridged.
Other aspects of the book may vary from the original edition.

Set in 16 pt. Plantin by Minnie B. Raven.

Printed in the United States on permanent paper.

ISBN 0-7862-6407-1 (lg. print : hc : alk. paper)

For Genny Ostertag, with gratitude.

National Association for Visually Handicapped
serving the partially seeing

As the Founder/CEO of NAVH, the only national health agency solely devoted to those who, although not totally blind, have an eye disease which could lead to serious visual impairment, I am pleased to recognize Thorndike Press* as one of the leading publishers in the large print field.

Founded in 1954 in San Francisco to prepare large print textbooks for partially seeing children, NAVH became the pioneer and standard setting agency in the preparation of large type.

Today, those publishers who meet our standards carry the prestigious "Seal of Approval" indicating high quality large print. We are delighted that Thorndike Press is one of the publishers whose titles meet these standards. We are also pleased to recognize the significant contribution Thorndike Press is making in this important and growing field.

Lorraine H. Marchi, L.H.D.
Founder/CEO
NAVH

* Thorndike Press encompasses the following imprints: Thorndike, Wheeler, Walker and Large Print Press.

Acknowledgments

I'm a lousy cook. However, it is my pleasure to share the recipes included in this book. I am indebted to Sharon and John Wilkerson for their Grilled Grouper recipe and Jim and Jan Langdoc for their Beer Butt Chicken recipe. A special thanks goes to Damon Lee Fowler for the other recipes in the book, all of which came from *Damon Lee Fowler's New Southern Kitchen*, published by Simon & Schuster, New York, 2002.

1

I seldom discover feet protruding from the top of my washing machine. Forgive me, then, if I assumed the worst. Besides, jumping to conclusions is my only form of exercise.

My heart leaped into my mouth. Given the length of my scrawny neck, that is quite a trick. At any rate, there have been enough murders at my full-board inn to satisfy a multitude of morticians. Of course, murder is always tragic, but somehow it becomes even more so when it happens in your home. To put it plainly, a corpse in my Kenmore was not going to be good for business.

Forcing my heart back down my narrow gullet, I approached the machine for a closer look. The shoes were cheap. Some kind of shiny plastic. The pant legs looked plastic as well, and they didn't droop down the legs like real pants would. Then I noticed the little tube that protruded from one ankle. It looked just like the valve on the air mattress I sometimes use to float on when I swim at Miller's Pond.

"Buzzy Porter," I said through clenched teeth.

The man lived up to his name. He had been my guest for only an hour, and already this was his third stunt. The first was when we shook hands in my lobby and I got the shock of my life. I mean that literally. The little gadget hidden in his palm packed a punch that nearly lifted me out of my brogans. His second stunt was to take advantage of my state of confusion and slap a sign on my back that read KISS ME, I'M GORGEOUS. This gag might have worked on someone who is used to being manhandled. But I felt his hand, as hot as a branding iron, burning its way, first through the paper, then my dress, and finally my sturdy Christian underwear.

Perhaps I should have been flattered by the word "gorgeous," but it is so far from the truth as to not even be funny. Of course, my fiancé, Gabriel Rosen, would disagree with that, but he is blinded by love. My point is that I have no illusions about who I am.

One of the things that I am is opinionated — although I prefer to use the word "informed." I have been known to inform others of their failings, in hopes that they will mend their ways and in the end make the world a better place. It was high time Buzzy Porter did his share to help.

I found the prankster supine in the parlor, but hardly resplendent in faded shorts, a torn T-shirt, and bright orange flip-flops. In Grandma Yoder's day, there wouldn't have been a piece of furniture comfortable enough upon which to sprawl. Not only did Grandma believe that reclining was inherently evil, but it was her policy that guests — all of whom were friends and neighbors — should not stay more than two hours. Three straight-back chairs and one lumpy Victorian love seat enforced that policy.

My guests, on the other hand, pay through the nose for an "authentic" Pennsylvania Dutch experience. Some even take advantage of A.L.P.O. — Amish Lifestyle Plan Option — whereby they pay extra for the privilege of performing chores. None, however, are willing to risk hemorrhoids, and in recent years I've been forced to supply a comfy couch and several well-padded armchairs. But no *La-Z-Boy* recliners. Grandma's ghost wouldn't sit still for that.

"Mr. Porter," I said, after praying for patience, "you will find your toy in the kitchen trash can, should you wish to retrieve it."

He had the audacity to feign ignorance. "What toy is that?"

"On second thought, maybe I should keep it. I have a foster daughter who might get a kick out of it."

That got his attention enough to make him sit. "No, no, I'll go get it. But first, would you like a piece of gum?"

"No, thank you."

He held out a packet labeled Floozy Fruit. "Oh, come on, Miss Yoder. Take a piece."

"Mr. Porter —"

"For your foster daughter," he said. "Maybe she'd like a stick."

"All right," I said just to shut him up. Between you and me, I eschew gum chewing. It's not the substance itself I detest, but those people who chew like cows chomping on their cuds. Worse yet are the folks who attach used gum to the undersides of tables, or leave it to sizzle on hot sidewalks, where it invariably finds its way to the soles of my shoes.

I reached for the gum. But no sooner did my digits touch the pack, than a spring-loaded contraption came out of nowhere and snapped closed on my index finger. I felt like a mouse that had been trapped.

"Get this thing off me at once!" I roared.

"Gotcha!" Buzzy let go of the gum pack and slapped his thighs. At least he was entertained.

I ripped the offending gadget off my finger — it really wasn't on all that tight — and dropped it down the front of my dress. I have not been blessed in the bosom department, and where there was once room for a Siamese kitten, there was now plenty of room for a fake pack of gum. Frankly, if the little spring went off again, there was nothing for it to grab.

"Mr. Porter, one more prank, and you're out of here. And don't even think about asking for a refund. In fact, I have half a mind to charge you for what will surely be the onset of my first gray hair."

"Okay, okay, I hear you. But don't I at least get my trick back? It cost me twelve ninety-nine."

I may be a simple Mennonite innkeeper, but the Good Lord gave me a head for business. The Bible instructs us to nourish our talents, and I try to do so on a daily basis.

"Ten bucks even," I said.

"Aw come on, Miss Yoder. That's not fair."

"I'm going to count to ten, and then the price goes up to twenty."

"But, Miss Yoder —"

"You'll still be saving almost three dollars in the event you want to go out and buy yourself a new one."

"Miss Yoder —"

"That's my name all right. Don't wear it out. One, two, three —"

He whipped out his wallet so fast it was a blur. When my eyes had adjusted I studied the two bills he proffered. I even walked over to the window and held them to the light. They looked genuine, but I was, after all, dealing with an irrepressible jokester.

"If the ink on these disappears," I warned him, "I'll know where to find you."

"Yes, Miss Yoder," he said. Perhaps the smirk on his face was accidental.

My name is indeed Yoder — Magdalena Portulacca Yoder — although it won't be that way for long. Sometime next year I plan to marry Dr. Gabriel Rosen. Gabe the Babe, as I like to think of him, lives across Hertlzer Road in an old farmhouse. My intended is a retired M.D., an urban refugee from the Big Apple. For some reason he decided that my hometown of Hernia, Pennsylvania, population 1,978.5 (Selma Graber is five months pregnant) would be the perfect place to try his hand at writing mystery novels.

I, on the other hand, have local roots that extend to China. My Amish ancestors founded Hernia in 1804, my family having first settled in the eastern part of the state in the early seventeen hundreds. I am related to all the first families: the Yoders, of course, the Bloughs, the Hostetlers, the Seilers, the Zugs, and a host of others. In this south-central Pennsylvania valley we have inbred to the point that I am, in fact, my own cousin. Give me a sandwich and I constitute a family picnic.

However, I do not qualify as a family *reunion*, and that is a good thing. Hernia was about to celebrate its bicentennial — Hernia Heritage Days we were billing it — and Amish and Mennonite exiles were pouring into town like bees to the hive at dusk. My inn, The PennDutch, had been booked solid for more than two years in advance. This is not unusual, mind you, because the rich and famous have long used my establishment as a "quaint little getaway," to quote *Condornest Travels.*

In fact, it was in this very magazine that the town council had placed an advertisement, hoping to draw at least some of its dispersed back home to celebrate the birthday bash. For the record, I had been firmly against this ad, on the grounds that it might draw *too* many people, and as a result our hamlet would turn into another Lancaster. And judging from the buzz in the biz — and by that I mean other hoteliers in the county — we were in for quite a crowd. Of course, that didn't surprise me. What surprised me was that none of *my* expected guests appeared to be of the faith. They certainly didn't have the right names.

After I left Buzzy Porter — certainly not one of our kind — I mulled over this phenomenon. Perhaps this week's guests were merely run-of-the-mill tourists with exceptional foresight. I would have asked Buzzy his motive for visiting, had he not immediately given me the shock of my life. Oh well, the next guest to arrive was going to get grilled like a wienie at a Girl Scout cookout. A wienie that had broken off the stick and landed in the coals where it . . .

The jarring sound of my doorbell brought me back to reality. "Let the grilling begin!" I cried.

2

The couple that stood at my door looked as if they had already been grilled. Perhaps over a very hot fire. He was as bald as a cantaloupe, and his exposed skin, where not covered by freckles, was only a shade or two lighter than the poinsettia my sister gave me for Christmas. He wore faded overalls over a mostly white shirt. At least the yellow stains spreading from his armpits matched the clump of hair that sprouted above the top button of his collar and the eyebrows the size of sparrow wings.

She, on the other hand, was deeply tanned, but her blue eyes had faded to the point that their color was in question. Her sun-streaked brown hair was short and as dry and coarse as kindling. The hideous twigs were held in place by tortoiseshell barrettes that begged to be released from duty and thrown in the nearest garbage receptacle.

Because I charge exorbitant prices, I

normally get an exclusive clientele. After all, there is no limit to the amount of abuse folks will tolerate, just as long as they can view it as a cultural experience. The more you charge them, the better deal they think they are getting. At any rate, the couple standing before me didn't look like they could afford a night in a Motel 6, much less my esteemed establishment.

"May I help you?" I ask charitably.

He proffered a chapped paw. "We're the Nortons. Chuck and Bibi."

She nodded vigorously. I assumed it was in agreement, although it's possible she was trying to dislodge the ugly doodads from her do.

"You should have a reservation for us," he said. He spoke in flat tones that hinted of one of the square states far to our west.

While I like to think that I have a mind like a steel trap, it is more likely made from unadulterated iron. It seems to have been rusting up on me quite a bit lately.

"Ah yes, the Nortons."

"From Inman, Kansas," she said, sounding worried.

Inman, Kansas. That rang a bell. So it wasn't a square state but a rectangular one. Sort of like Pennsylvania, but a great deal flatter. My family is no longer Amish, but

Mennonite, and many of our number have migrated to Kansas, particularly to the Inman area. When I'd received the Nortons' request for lodging, I had made a mental note of their hometown, hoping to play "Mennonite geography" with them when I saw them.

Alas, Norton is neither an Amish nor a Mennonite name. But a buck is a buck, is it not?

"Koom on een, dears," I said. "Velkommen to zee PennDutch." Most guests, by the way, get a kick out of my fake German accent.

The Nortons showed no reaction, although Chuck did step aside to allow Bibi to enter first. She strode in on sturdy brown legs, but didn't give my quaint decor a second look.

"When do the festivities start?" she asked, preempting my grilling session.

Already it was time to ditch the accent. "The tractor pull and pig chase are tomorrow. The hay-baling contest and Bake-Off are the day after. So is the cow auction. And then Wednesday — well, that's the big day. The actual anniversary. At noon we dig up the time capsule. After that we have the town picnic up on Stucky Ridge."

"Fireworks?" Chuck Norton asked.

I shook my head. "We Plain People aren't really into that."

"How far is it back into town?"

"Four point two miles, but you're not going to find another place to stay. I'm the only game in town, and you won't even find a room over in Bedford, which is the nearest real city. Everything's been booked for months."

"Oh no, we're not looking for another place." The frumpy woman was as nervous as a mouse in a cattery.

"Mother likes to walk," Chuck Norton explained.

"Your mother!" I cried in amazement. "Why, she doesn't look but ten years older than you."

"She's my *wife*. Mother is what I call her."

Bibi Norton was too tanned to blush. "And I call him Father. We have twelve grown sons, you see."

Father Chuck slipped a thumb under an overall strap. "And all of them wheat farmers like Mother and me."

"You don't say." This is my newest response when, in fact, I have nothing to say. I'm sure the world can use twelve more wheat farmers, but for one couple to have a dozen offspring seems to be taking to excess the biblical commandment to be fruitful and multiply. Perhaps this is just sour grapes on my part, seeing as how I am forever doomed to be as barren as the Gobi Desert.

I checked in the Nortons. They declined A.L.P.O. and expressed no interest in the history of my charming inn or its engaging proprietress. In short, they promised to be as much fun as a mammogram. At least on the plus side, they were strong enough to carry their own luggage to the top of my impossibly steep stairs. Otherwise I would have had to schlep their bags up myself. My elevator, which is barely larger than a bread box, has been on the fritz ever since two contestants from a pie-eating contest decided to do the mattress mambo in that minuscule space.

"Third room on your right," I called after them.

They didn't even have the courtesy to respond.

I was still filing the Nortons' paperwork when the front door slammed open. Without looking up I knew exactly who it was and had a pretty good idea what had happened. My foster daughter has at least one hormone-related crisis a day.

"Boy trouble?" I asked.

"I hate him!" But instead of stomping off to our room — we share one when we have guests — Alison collapsed on the floor like a winter coat that had slid off its hanger.

"Jimmy?" I asked, careful to keep my tone neutral. Jimmy was her boyfriend du jour, and I did not approve of him in the least. She had just turned thirteen, and he was seventeen. Of course, she wasn't allowed to date, but I couldn't stop them from seeing each other at school. What's a pseudomother to do, except pray that they broke up?

"Don't be a dingus, Mom. Of course it's Jimmy. Do you know what he had the nerve to do?"

"What?" It was all I could do not to jump and shout for joy. Because the check-in counter hid my feet, I did a little shuffling dance. Yes, I know, it's a sin to dance. I would just have to repent of it later.

Alison pulled herself up into something resembling a sitting human being. "He went out with Carrie Sanders, that's what. On a real date! In a car and everything. And you know what?"

"What?"

"It's all your fault."

"Mine?"

“ ’Cause you won’t let me date. Carrie’s mom lets her.”

“How old is Carrie?”

She shrugged. “Who cares? I hate her.”

“Is she older than you?”

“Okay, so she’s a junior, but so what? Jimmy is the only man I’ll ever love — except that now I hate him.”

The parlor door opened and Buzzy stepped into the foyer. When he saw Alison, he smiled. In those few seconds he was transformed from a clown into a rather handsome young man.

“Sorry, Miss Yoder,” he said. “I didn’t know you had company.”

I shook my head. “This is my daughter, Alison. She lives here. Alison, this is Mr. Porter.”

“Hey,” she said.

“Care for a piece of gum?” he asked.

“Yeah.” She looked at me defiantly. Alison has a habit of discarding her used gum wherever she happens to be when she tires of it. Usually it ends up on the floor or, at best, stuck to the bottom of a piece of furniture. Pleading and scolding have had zero effect on her, so lately I’d been making her chew it outside.

Buzzy winked at me and held out the bogus pack. Apparently that old gag isn’t popular in Minnesota from whence Alison hails, because she shrieked in surprise. When she saw that it was just a trick, she shrieked with laughter.

"What else do ya got?" she asked. From the look on her face it was clear my newly dumped daughter had developed an instant crush on the bothersome Buzzy. Needless to say, I was about as thrilled as I'd be if my prize hen, Pertelote, took up with a fox.

My next guests, Buist and Capers Littleton, more than made up for the Nortons' lack of social graces. This couple hailed from Charleston, South Carolina, which is the nation's capital of good manners. I know this for a fact, because I've been there. The folks in that fair city are always polite to your face, even if they hate your guts. While this isn't my style, I appreciate being the recipient of consideration, no matter how insincere.

The Littletons had driven twelve hours just to attend our bicentennial. Even though they must have been as tired as hookers after a Shriners' convention, they trotted out their good manners the minute they set foot in my inn.

"Oh, what a lovely place," Capers cooed,

adding two syllables to the final word.

"But it isn't half as lovely as you," Buist purred. He appeared to be looking at my feet.

I beamed. "And for only twenty dollars more a day, you can experience an authentic Amish lifestyle by pitching in with the chores."

"Oh what fun," they exclaimed in unison.

I doubted, however, that Capers was capable of any real work. She was a tiny thing with lacquered nails. Her bottle-blond bob was lacquered as well. Her dress was linen, that curious choice of the idle rich, who claim to like this fabric for its cooling properties, yet invariably wear outfits lined with some man-made unbreathable material. The end result is that folks who could well afford a maid, walk around as wrinkled as a Chinese shar-pei, and smelling like a wet dog too.

Buist Littleton wasn't nearly as rumpled in his blue and white seersucker suit, although his jacket was undoubtedly lined as well. In fact, he looked rather dapper, what with his bow tie and white buckskin shoes.

The couple appeared to be in their mid-thirties, although their driver's licenses pegged them at a full decade older. A good sunscreen, I've learned through observation, can do almost as much to preserve the appearance of youth as can a surgeon's scalpel.

As it turned out, I need not have worried about carrying their cases upstairs. Buist was far too much of a gentleman to have allowed that.

"Miss Yoder," Capers said, as she turned to follow her husband, "do we dress for dinner?"

Needless to say, I was properly shocked. I had to catch my breath before answering, during which time I couldn't help but picture Buist in the buff. Frankly, it was an intriguing sight.

"Of course," I rasped. "I do not allow naked people in the dining room. Or in my inn altogether, unless, of course, they're bathing —"

"Ma'am," Buist said with a twinkle in his eye, "I believe what my wife meant was, do we need to change into evening wear?"

I must confess that I learned one of life's most useful lessons not from kindergarten, but from my cat. Alas, I had to give my poor pussy away on account of my foster daughter's allergies, but not before the feline had a chance to teach me the importance of staying cool. Whenever you miscalculate a distance, or commit some other attention-grabbing blunder, just pretend you *meant* to do it.

"Gotcha!" I said, borrowing from Buzzy.

"Very good," Buist said, and then he and Capers pretended to laugh. Like I said, the folks from Charleston are nothing, if not polite.

"By all means, put on the dog."

"I beg your pardon?"

"Dress to the nines. Even the tens, if you want."

They smiled happily. I smiled as well, knowing that I would encourage all my guests to gussy it up, except for Buzzy. That would fix his wagon good.

I know, a good Christian should be above such spiteful thoughts, but I am only a saint-in-training. In fact, every now and then I find myself in sinners' rehab. With any luck Buzzy Porter was going to get a taste of his own medicine come dinner.

3

I had good reason to believe that at least one from among my next batch of guests would need no coaxing to play dress up. The trio arrived in a stretch limousine. Luxury cars are not unusual in Hernia, thanks to the caliber of my clientele, but they impress no one. Amish are known as the Plain People, and most Mennonites I know run a close second in the race for modesty. True, we have a few Methodists and Presbyterians in town, as well as two Jews — even a lone Episcopalian — but over the years folks have become blasé about celebrities roaming our streets.

The locals certainly were not going to drop their teeth over an actress like Octavia Cabot-Dodge. When her manager, a Ms. Augusta Miller, had called to make the reservations, she'd made a point of emphasizing the woman's stardom. Now, I don't watch movies, and gave up on TV when *Green Acres* reruns went off the air, but even I knew that Ms. Cabot-Dodge was a has-been. I remembered reading an article — *Peephole* magazine, I think — that said the actress's biggest achievement was staying in seclusion for forty years. Before going into hiding she'd managed to do three movies, one of which won her an Oscar, and two that were complete bombs. She might still have succeeded as an actress, but she was reportedly impossible to work with. According to the magazine — and I read this rag only when I'm in the checkout line at the supermarket — the fallen star was hoping to gain notoriety by her absence. Apparently she'd succeeded to a point, or the editor at *Peephole* would have passed on the piece.

While I, for one, wasn't going to open my peephole and spill the beans, I doubted that she really wanted her privacy. If that was the case, why had she shown up in a limo? My hunch — and a hunch from a woman is worth two facts from a man — is that the faded film star had run out of funds and was planning to stage a comeback. Whatever her reasons for her ostentatious arrival, just as long as she cooperated and dressed for dinner, her secret was safe with me.

When she stepped out of the stretch she was already dressed to the eights. From her narrow shoulders hung a green satin creation that fell just short of being a ball gown. It went too far to qualify as a mother-of-the-bride dress at a formal wedding, yet atop her head perched a very matronly, not to mention dated, green pillbox hat. Even from a distance I could see that her face was swathed in green netting. It may be true that rolling stones gather no moss, but apparently stagnant stars do.

Trailing behind the down-on-her-luck diva was a frumpy woman of advancing years and a bespectacled chauffeur in an ill-fitting uniform. I pasted a cheery smile on my face and opened the door.

"Gut marriye," I brayed. "Velkommen to zee PennDutch."

"Good morning," Octavia said in a voice a full octave lower than mine. "I suppose you know who I am."

"Well, you must be —"

"Octavia Cabot-Dodge." She said this loud enough so that the Babester, had he been standing on his porch across the road, could have heard it.

"Magdalena Yoder," I said. "I'm the proprietress."

She sniffed. "I hope this festival of yours is all it's been cracked up to be."

"Of course, dear. Folks in Hernia love a

good time. Just last month we had a mock funeral for Orville Humpheimer's two-headed calf. There was even a drawing — the winner got veal chops — but I didn't win, which was fine with me, since I don't eat veal on principle. Except that Orville's calf died of natural causes. Seems it got one head stuck in a barbed-wire fence —"

"Is there a porter for my bags?"

"At your service, dear. Although I'm sure your chauffeur would do a far better job. Last time I dropped one of the cases down the stairs and it split wide open, like a melon on a sidewalk. You wouldn't believe what that woman had inside."

"Stanley," she said, without turning her head. "Get the bags."

The chauffeur, who was barely more than a teenager, stepped forward boldly. "I'm not just a chauffeur," he said, looking directly at me. "I also rappel."

"Don't be so hard on yourself, dear," I said kindly. "Nobody gets to choose how they look."

The lad rolled his eyes behind his wire-rim frames. Besides being repelling, he was impudent.

I might have said something to correct the young man, but the dowdy diva did it for me. He rolled his eyes again, but sauntered off to do as he was bid.

It was time to drop the phony accent. "Come on in," I said, "before the flies do."

Octavia Cabot-Dodge placed a tiny foot on the first step leading to my porch, but then removed it. She immediately put the other foot on the step and removed it. She repeated this behavior seven times. It was like watching someone do step aerobics. Finally she put her first foot on the second level. From then on she progressed normally. In the meantime I observed that her shoes, which had at one time obviously cost a great deal, were rather scuffed.

"This is my personal assistant, Augusta Miller," she said, upon reaching the porch.

Assistant? I was sure Ms. Miller had introduced herself as the actress's manager. Well, perhaps a personal assistant and a manager were one and the same. Despite five years of dealing with the herd from the Hills, the ways of Hollywood remain beyond my ken.

The woman whose job description was in question mumbled something unintelligible. I thought best not to pursue the matter and attempted to usher the ladies in, but again, Ms. Cabot-Dodge did her little dance. This time over the threshold. I pretended to look away, but you can be sure I counted. As before, eight was the magical number.

Once inside both ladies scrutinized the foyer, which, by the way, does double duty as my office. "This floor looks new," Augusta said. "The wallpaper too."

"Well, they are," I said. "Relatively."

"Either they are, or they aren't," Octavia said.

"They're less than two years old," I wailed.

"How old is the inn? Your brochure said it was a historical Pennsylvania Dutch farmhouse."

My cheeks burned. "It is! I mean, almost. The original house was blown to smithereens by a tornado, but I rebuilt this place to look exactly like it was."

"Why, that's false advertising," Augusta muttered.

One thing I've learned from my teeny-bopper foster child is that when the going gets tough, change directions. "Would either of you like to avail yourselves of A.L.P.O.?"

Octavia recoiled in horror. "Dog food?"

"Oh, no. It's my Amish Lifestyle Plan Option. You see, for just twenty dollars more a day, you get to do chores — like clean your own room." No sooner had the words escaped my mouth, than I realized they were a mistake. Obviously the woman couldn't afford such an extravagance, even if she did arrive by limousine.

Much to my surprise, however, a glint appeared in her eyes, shining through the veil of green like twin beacons through fog. "Is that it? Just cleaning one's room?"

"By no means. There's the barn to muck, the chicken house straw needs replacing —"

"Sign up my assistant," she said, the glee in her voice quite evident. "The chauffeur as well."

Augusta gave her employer a look that would have turned grapes into raisins, had there been any lying around. I had the feeling she was going to give Octavia a piece of her mind as well, but Stanley the chauffeur stumbled up the steps under a load of suitcases that a dozen Sherpas would have been hard-pressed to manage.

I moved to help the lad, but Octavia stopped me by laying a withered hand on my bare arm. "Stanley can manage, Miss Yoder. If he needs help, my assistant will be glad to do it."

Her assistant shot her another glance capable of drying fruit. Since dried apricots are a favorite snack of mine, I made a mental note to tote some fresh ones with me for the next few days. Now that I no longer carry a kitten in my bra, there is plenty of room for goodies.

I smiled at Augusta, then turned my attention to Octavia. "Dinner is normally at six, like the Good Lord intended, but because today is Sunday, it will be a half hour later."

Octavia nodded. "Where does the help eat?"

"My cook, Freni, is an Amish woman. She prefers to eat in the kitchen."

"I meant *my* help."

"Why, in the dining room with everyone else."

"Well!" Octavia said in a huff, but Augusta was grinning like the Cheshire cat.

It was time to hustle their bustles through the registration process before it came to fisticuffs. I even risked Octavia's wrath by helping the hapless Stanley schlep the rest of the mountain of suitcases up my impossibly steep stairs. To be honest, I did it just because I knew it would irk her. You see, I had already made up my mind I was going to side with the help this time.

When one is as successful a proprietress as I am, one can afford to make up any rules that one wishes. Therefore, I choose not to rent my rooms by the day, but by the week. Guests must arrive on Sunday between the hours of three and six. Theoretically this gives them plenty of time to attend the church of their choice earlier in the day, but the truth is most of the folks, all of whom are blessed just by virtue of the fact they can afford my rates, have not darkened the door of a church or synagogue since they were children. At any rate, guests must check out by noon the following Saturday. They may, of course, leave earlier, but they will not get any money refunded. To the contrary, those who depart before the agreed-upon date are subject to a fine. S.A.L.E., I call it. Suckers Always Leave Early.

In fact, I have a whole string of fines that I am free to impose at will, because they are all delineated in the fine print on my brochures. Guests arriving after the six p.m. Sunday deadline are charged a late arrival fee. And believe you me, I was extremely irritated at twenty after six when all but one of my guests had gathered in the parlor, waiting to be ushered into the dining room. The holdout had yet to arrive on the premises. Never mind that we were all dressed in our best clothes. I, for one, was looking pretty spiffy, if I must say so myself. I'd polished my brogans, put on a freshly laundered prayer cap, and my blue broadcloth dress was one that I'd worn only a handful of times. Much to my disappointment, even Buzzy had cleaned up pretty well.

"You certainly look handsome," I said. I was not being flirtatious, mind you, merely kind. Compared to the Babester, Buzzy at his best looked like a comic strip character with his finger in a socket. According to my sister, Susannah, some men actually work at getting their hair to stick out in all directions.

"Thank you, Miss Yoder. Do you like my flower?"

I didn't. It was obviously a fake. But a compliment is a blessing one bestows upon another person, and should not be construed as a lie.

"It's lovely," I said graciously.

"Smell it," he said.

"I beg your pardon?"

"It's a gardenia. It has a really nice scent."

I decided to bless Buzzy further by pretending to smell his flower. "Mmm," I murmured, but all I could smell was the odor of Buzzy's aftershave.

"You need to lean closer, Miss Yoder. This is a new variety. They say it smells like lemon."

I leaned closer. "Smells just like Pledge," I said, to show that I was a good sport.

"You really think so?"

"Aack!" I shrieked, as Buzzy's blossom squirted water directly into my left eye.

Buzzy roared with laughter. He even slapped his thighs — although he should have been slapping his own face. The only thing stopping me from doing so was my genes. My Amish and Mennonite ancestors have been professing pacifists for almost five hundred years and it's all I can do to swat a fly.

Fortunately Buist Littleton was not a pacifist. Au contraire, I hear that the Civil War is still being waged in his fair state.

"Apologize to the lady," he said in a quiet, authoritative voice.

Buzzy appeared puzzled. "Excuse me?"

"You heard me, sir. Apologize to her."

Buzzy stopped laughing. "All right, you don't need to make a federal case out of it." He looked at me with all the sincerity of a televangelist. "I'm sorry, Miss Yoder. That was childish of me. Will you forgive me?"

The Bible says to forgive seventy-seven

times, and Buzzy had offended me only fourteen times since setting foot on my property — not that I was counting. The only other human being to irritate me so many times in such a short space of time was my brother-in-law, Melvin Stoltzfus.

"Sure," I said, to set a Christian example.

"Shake?" He offered me his right hand, which looked to be empty of battery-powered devices, but my parents didn't raise a complete idiot.

"How about we just nod our heads, dear?"

"Yeah." He seemed actually eager for the change of custom.

I nodded my head, and he nodded his head. But he didn't stop. He nodded faster and faster until his noggin was vibrating like the paint mixer at the Home Depot over in Bedford. Then — and if swearing wasn't against my religion, I'd swear this was true — his head spun all the way around, as if it weren't even attached at the neck. So bizarre was the sight that both Octavia and Augusta gasped like drowning turkeys — I've heard a few of those, by the way. Even Buist was shocked into silence, but Capers, bless her genteel heart, almost gagged. Apparently Chuck and Bibi Norton were used to such sights down on the farm, because they barely blinked.

Stanley Dalrumple, the youthful chauffeur, scowled behind his wire-rimmed glasses. "The guy's a show-off," he said as Buzzy Porter's head shimmied to a stop.

Buist found his tongue. "It was just an illusion. The human body is not capable of such movement."

"Linda Blair did it in the *Exorcist*," Augusta ventured.

"That was a movie," Octavia snapped. She licked her lips, which, although painted, were as dry as cornflakes. "Did you know they wanted me to play her part?"

Augusta snorted. "Nonsense. Linda Blair was a teenager and you were —"

Octavia had changed to a forest green satin gown. She was hatless and therefore without a veil. Her dark eyes bored into her assistant.

"Too good for the part," Augusta said, finishing her sentence.

I glanced at my trusty Timex. "Dinner is now served. Our one remaining guest will just have to fend for himself when he arrives. The rest of you will find place cards at your assigned spots. Of course, none of us will begin eating until after grace has been said." I glared at Buzzy. "And you, young man, will behave yourself. Is that clear?"

"As clear as your best crystal," he said with a smirk.

Since I don't own any crystal, I found that to be a strangely foreboding remark.

4

My cook is also my kinswoman. Although she is eighteen years my senior, a cursory glance at our tangled family tree could produce the conclusion that she is my very much older, identical twin sister. Never mind that we look nothing alike. While I am tall and skinny enough to be a cell phone tower, dear Freni Hostetler is short and squat. She wears glasses, not to mention the fact that as an Amish woman, she dresses in distinct garb. Although my modest dresses and white organza cap set me apart from most of our tourists, I am clearly not of her faith.

The word Mennonite is derived from the name of a Roman Catholic priest, Menno Simons, who became a fervent supporter of the Anabaptist movement and formally left the Church in 1536. The Amish are named after Jacob Amman, who believed the Mennonites were too liberal, especially in regards to the doctrine of shunning unrepentant members. Amish who leave their church will often, but not necessarily, end up as Mennonites. This is what happened in my family two generations back.

Freni's interpretation of scriptures is, in a word, more strict than mine. She refuses to work on Sundays, and I respect that. As a consequence, our dinner that night had all been prepared the day before. It was not, however, a repast to be sneezed at.

My massive dining-room table groaned under the weight of food: platters of cold roast beef and smoked ham, bowls of chicken salad, tuna salad, potato salad, three-bean salad, green pea salad, and tossed salad, deviled eggs, chunky apple sauce, corn relish, pickled beets, pickled cauliflower, watermelon rind pickles, dill pickles and sweet pickles, and homemade bread. In the kitchen waited two shoofly pies, an apple pie, a custard pie, and a chocolate cake with fudge icing. Except for the tuna, none of the victuals came from a can. Any guest who went hungry was too picky for his or her own good.

When I threw open the pocket doors that opened to my dining room, Chuck and Bibi Norton's sun-faded eyes lit up at the sight of my bountiful table. "My, my," Bibi said, "someone has certainly gone to a lot of trouble."

"It all looks absolutely delicious," Capers said.

Everyone else nodded, including Buzzy. "Looks just like the salad bar at Shoney's," he said. I think he meant it as a compliment.

There was a bit of milling about as the guests found their seats. The handsome and mannerly Buist was seated on my right. Stanley Dalrumple had the honor of sitting on my left. Bibi's place was next to Buist and across from Augusta Miller. Chuck, alias "Father" Norton, was on her left. Buzzy was to sit on Bibi's right, and Alison had whined her way to Buzzy's right, which put her on Capers's left. The end of the table was reserved for the declining diva.

As for the missing guest — I still didn't know if it was male or female — he or she would sit across from Alison on Chuck's left. If the mystery diner didn't show up before the food was gone, he or she was just plain out of luck.

At any rate, Buist, ever the Southern gentleman, pulled out my chair for me. To my amazement everyone waited until I was seated before following suit. My point is, I was safely ensconced in my seat when the puerile prank was pulled. I am merely an opinionated woman, not crude, so I shall not describe the noise I heard in detail. Suffice it to say, it was as if one of my guests had already consumed an entire bowl of three-bean salad. By the look of surprise on Augusta Miller's face, followed by one of utter mortification, my guess is that Buzzy had left a whoopee cushion on her chair.

Of course, Alison howled. Her high-pitched yips would have summoned dogs from three counties if I hadn't given her the business. She shut up immediately, but reserved the right to glower back at me.

The second Alison shushed, Chuck Norton scraped his chair on the floor. I wouldn't have thought a sturdy, beef-fed farmer like Chuck could think so fast — I certainly couldn't.

"Miss Yoder," he said, louder than normal conversation would require, "if you put some little rubber tips on these chair legs, they wouldn't make this noise. Save them from getting worn, too."

I smiled. "Really? Well, I'll have to look into that." Alison fought to stifle a giggle, while both Buzzy and young Stanley grinned behind their napkins like foolish schoolboys. "Mr. Porter, dear," I said, without missing a beat, "would you like to say grace?"

The grin widened. "Excuse me?"

"Thank the Good Lord for providing us with this food. And for making it so available to us, that we don't have to drive all the way into Pittsburgh in search of a Shoney's."

"Can do," he said, which was not the answer I was expecting.

He started to say something else — perhaps he even began his prayer — but I interrupted him. The Good Lord expects us to pray with our eyes tightly closed and our hands folded. Not like the Episcopalians. I know for a fact that at least one of them prays with her eyes wide open. The Lord also expects us to offer prayers, the length of which are in direct proportion to the time it took to prepare the food. The minimum requirement is that the blessing be long enough to allow hot food to become cold and cold food to warm up to room temperature. Anything shorter than that smacks of ingratitude.

When I was sure everyone had their eyes tightly closed and their hands folded, I ordered Buzzy to begin. However, to enforce the Lord's rules, I kept my peepers open. Just as Buzzy began his second attempt, I saw Octavia and Augusta exchange glances. Since both women were emitting icy stares, I felt confident that Buzzy's prayer, no matter how interminable, would not contribute to our food spoiling. Still, I had no choice but to clear my throat and force the women to behave.

"Go ahead now, dear," I said to Buzzy, when the women were under control.

Eyes tightly closed, he smiled. "Rub-a-dub-dub. Thanks for the grub. Yay, God!"

All eyes flew open, all mouths as well. Stanley Dalrumple snickered, but Alison had lived with me long enough to be properly shocked. If not, she faked it well.

"Mr. Porter," I said sharply, "what kind of prayer was that?"

"The kind we used to say in college."

"Was this a school for heathens?"

Stanley snickered again.

"Mr. Porter, I asked you a question."

"It was a state school," Buzzy mumbled.

"Why am I not surprised?" It was a rhetorical question, meant to buy time while I considered my options. What if the prankster's prayer hadn't taken, like a vaccine gone bad? In that case we would be eating unblessed food. Yes, I know, folks do it all the time, but look at the state the world is in.

On the other hand, I couldn't very well ask the man to pray again, because that would be like second-guessing the Good Lord. In the end I decided to leave the problem in God's capable hands, but just to let the Lord know I didn't approve of Buzzy's irreverence, I sighed loudly. Meanwhile my guests waited with their forks poised.

"Dig in," I finally said. "Bon appétit!"

They dug, some much deeper than others. In fact, the way Chuck Norton helped himself to the meat platter, I was afraid I might have to run out and kill the fatted calf. I mean that literally.

But poor Chuck had taken only one bite of ham when his face turned the color of a good pickled beet and his eyes began to bulge. "Brrrgh," he said, his mouth quite full.

"What was that, dear?"

"Auugh."

Bibi sprung to life. "Father is choking! Please, somebody, do something."

My heart pounded. "Does anyone know the Heimlich Maneuver?"

The rest of my guests shook their heads in horrified amazement as Chuck tried futilely to dislodge the ham. Thank heavens I had read enough books to have a basic understanding of what needed to be done. There are perhaps better teachers than fear, but no better motivators. Fearing that Chuck might actually choke on my ham and die — not to mention a potential lawsuit filed by his devoted wife, Bibi — I flew into action.

I may be tall, but I'm scrawny. Still, I had enough adrenaline coursing through my veins to hoist an elephant and fling it over my shoulder. I yanked the farmer out of his chair and squeezed his middle like I was a python and he was my dinner. Of course, I did it a lot faster than a real python would. The upshot was that Chuck's dinner shot across the room, barely missing Octavia's head, and landed on the floor with a splat.

Chuck gasped a few times, as he fought for words. "Why, that's not ham at all. That's rubber."

So much for gratitude. "Mr. Norton, I assure you that this establishment serves only the finest cuts of meat."

"No!" He coughed. "I don't mean that it's tough — it's rubber."

I raced over to the regurgitated repast and prodded it gingerly with the toe of my brogan. It had the same texture as my shower mat.

"Buzzy Porter!" I bellowed.

The wise guy winced. "He was supposed to chew it — not inhale it."

"That's beside the point." I gestured to Chuck Norton. "Do you wish to press some sort of charges?"

"Well, I — are you a police officer, Miss Yoder?"

"Gracious no. But the Chief of Police is my brother-in-law." There was no need to tell him that my sister's husband and I get along as well as children and bathwater.

"I'm sorry," Buzzy blurted. "Like I said, he wasn't supposed to swallow it."

I nodded to Chuck. "It's your call, dear."

Bibi Norton looked anything but dowdy when she was angry. "Let's do it, Father."

Buzzy blanched. "Hey, wait. Maybe we can make some kind of a deal."

"You could have died," Bibi reminded her husband.

Buzzy turned to me. "Please, Miss Yoder."

I have a kind heart, but I'm about as sentimental as a Chinese snakefish. There was, however, something in the young man's voice that made me believe him. *This* time.

"Okay, let's say we cut you a deal. You'd have to stick to it, or suffer the consequences."

"Sure, anything."

Bibi's faded eyes grew bright with emotion. "But we didn't agree to a deal."

I gave her a patient smile. "If your husband presses charges, Buzzy here could end up in the slammer. But it would probably be for only a few days — maybe just overnight, or until someone bails him out. In the meantime, who knows what little gags he has already laid in place. It's more than likely he has already short-sheeted your beds. There could be spiders in your showers, water balloons above your doors — this young man is capable of anything."

"Miss Yoder, are you suggesting we just let him go? My husband could have died."

"No, I'm not suggesting that — although I might suggest your husband cut his food into bite-size pieces and chew first. Now, where was I?"

"You were about to cut a deal with this hooligan," Octavia Cabot-Dodge said. Since grace, she had opened and folded her napkin eight times.

"Ah yes. I suggest that we require young Buzzy here confess to everything he has done, in exchange for immunity. Because I assure you, there are things we don't know about that will rear their ugly heads. Then we give him exactly half an hour to undo his dastardly deeds."

"And if he doesn't?" Plain Bibi Norton was out for blood. Seeing as how I didn't have an electric chair at my disposal, perhaps I could let her throw my toaster in Buzzy's bathwater.

"Then it's back to plan A. We call the cops."

"Man, that's no fair," Alison said. She stamped a foot under the table.

I swallowed back my irritation. "It's quite fair. It's all up to Buzzy, isn't it?"

Everyone nodded except for Alison, Stanley, and Buzzy.

"Mene, mene, tekel, parsin," I said.

They stared at me like I was missing grain in my silo, prompting Alison to come to my defense. "That's Pennsylvania Dutch, ya know."

I thanked her with a smile. "Actually, it's Babylonian. It's from the Bible. It's the handwriting on the wall." I mustered a stern look for Buzzy. "The writing is for you, dear. You have exactly one hour."

Buzzy didn't even excuse himself from the table. He just got up and slunk from the room. I would like to say that the rest of the meal was enjoyable, despite Alison's accusing stares. Alas, that is not the case.

Augusta and the diva conducted their own ocular warfare, while Chuck continued to inhale his food without chewing. Stanley smirked his way through dessert. Had it not been for a smattering of pleasant conversation between myself and the cultured Capers, we might well have resembled your typical American family.

As for Buist — he jumped to the top of my short list the second time his foot made contact with mine. The first time he did it, I passed it off as an innocent mistake. I have long legs, and given the size of my tootsies, you can be sure that I have, at times, strayed into someone else's territory. But this was no accidental touching. Buist Littleton's foot was pressed firmly up against mine, and whenever I moved mine, his followed.

Perhaps then you can understand why a confirmed pacifist would slide her fork under the protective cover of the tablecloth and give him a gentle jab. Unfortunately, the Southern gentleman's only response was a grin. Well, a gal's gotta do what a gal's gotta do, so I made like I was testing one of Freni's roasts for doneness.

Buist gasped and his eyes glazed over, but this time he moved his foot. The rest of the guests were too caught up in their own scenarios to notice our little drama — except for Capers.

"Darling," she drawled, "remember the vacation we took to Aruba?"

Buist paled as the glaze left his eyes. "Yes, of course, sugar."

"Keep remembering, darling." The ice in her voice could have cooled a Charleston summer.

For a moment neither of them spoke. "Aruba?" I prodded. "I have always wanted to go to Aruba. Please, tell me more."

"It's a lovely island," Capers said, and then cleverly put a piece of shoofly pie in her mouth.

Dinner was essentially over. Before I excused the guests I invited them to help me clear the dishes and, should they be feeling stressed, contribute a few stitches to a quilt I keep stretched across a frame in a corner of the room. The quilt is generally a big hit with guests, and it is a win-win situation, because the subsequent sale of their handiwork adds coins to my coffers. This particular evening there were no takers for either task.

Theoretically I could have forced the A.L.P.O. guests to help me with the dishes, but I was suddenly in the mood for solitude. I let the guests drift off to the parlor, where they waited out the appointed hour, while I labored and contemplated a new wrinkle in my life.

5

John and Sharon Wilkerson's Grilled Grouper

1 cup olive oil
2 tablespoons minced onion
3 tablespoons grated Parmesan cheese
1 1/2 teaspoons dried basil leaves
1 1/2 teaspoons dry mustard
1 1/2 teaspoons dried oregano leaves
1 1/2 teaspoons sugar
4 teaspoons salt
2 teaspoons pepper
1/2 cup red-wine vinegar
2 tablespoons fresh squeezed lemon juice
4 grouper steaks or 2 large grouper fillets

Combine first nine ingredients in a blender and process for 30 seconds. Add vinegar and lemon juice; process for an additional 30 seconds. Transfer sauce to a large bowl.

Dip fish into sauce to generously cover.

Grill fish over hot coals 10 minutes on each side or until fish flakes easily when tested with a fork. Baste frequently with prepared sauce.

Remove fish to a warm serving platter and serve immediately.

SERVES 4 TO 6

6

Actually, the new wrinkle in my life was a face full of wrinkles. Gabriel Rosen, my gorgeous hunk of a fiancé, had surprised me on my birthday by announcing that his mother would be living with us — after the wedding, of course. For the record, I don't do the horizontal hootchy-kootchy unless I'm hitched. And please, no reminders that I was an inadvertent adulteress by virtue of unwittingly marrying a bigamist. That was then, and this is now, as Alison is fond of saying. Besides, Aaron, snake that he was, talked me into doing far worse things than the mattress mambo. Once we even danced — standing up!

Now where was I? Oh yes, Gabe's mother. Don't you agree that he could at least have discussed his intentions with me first? But no, he announced this arrangement right in front of her. What was I to do? Grin and bear it?

Well, I'd grinned until my face nearly

split in two. Frankly, I didn't know how much longer I could take it. Ida Rosen was opinionated, demanding, overbearing — at least that's how she treated me. Gabe she treated like he was still a little boy. In the blink of an eye my dearly beloved went from batching it to living a life of pampered ease. Ida did all his cooking, cleaning, and laundry. That I could almost understand. But whenever he went out she insisted on knowing where he was going, and why. In cool weather she made him wear a jacket. Once I even saw her cut his meat!

I had to quit obsessing about Ida Rosen. Just thinking about her was making my skin itch under my sturdy Christian underwear. To take my mind off my misery, I washed the dishes by hand in scalding water. Still unable to rid my brain of frightening images of my future mother-in-law, I started to scrub the kitchen floor. This was, of course, an exercise in futility, since Freni keeps the place so clean that germs die of starvation. Nevertheless, I had worked my way halfway across the room, when the doorbell rang. That's when I discovered, much to my dismay, that I had trapped myself by an expanse of wet floor.

“Would someone please get the door?” I hollered.

No one responded, and the bell rang again.

“Doesn’t anyone hear the doorbell?” I bellowed. After all, the front door is much closer to the front parlor than it is to the kitchen.

The bell rang a third and fourth time in rapid succession.

“Darn,” I said, which is as bad as I can swear.

Because I was still expecting one last guest, I had no choice but to answer it myself. I was not, however, a happy hostess when I flung open the door. In my mind I saw Ida Rosen, her face screwed up in a disapproving look. It took me a few seconds to adjust to reality. Unfortunately my mouth works faster than my mind.

“Now what is it?” I snapped.

“Is this the PennDutch Inn?” a small voice asked.

I stared. Standing on the porch was a beautiful Japanese girl. I knew her nationality because it was written on the reservation card. What I hadn’t known until then was her gender, thanks to a rather difficult name.

“Miss Mukaisan?” I did the best I could

with the pronunciation.

She bowed from the waist. I followed her example, which prompted her to bow again. After the fourth round we both gave up.

"My name is Teruko Mukai," she said, "but everyone calls me Terri."

I hate being wrong. "Are you sure? I know there was a 'san' in there someplace."

She smiled. " 'San' is a title — like mister or miss. We attach it to the end of the name. But in English, I think, you would hyphenate it."

"Then you may call me Yoder-san. Velkommen to zee —" I stopped my silly charade. After all, the girl spoke perfect, unaccented English, and she hailed from the other side of the globe. "Yes, this is the PennDutch Inn. And you're a mite late, dear."

She smiled again. "I'm sorry Yoder-san, but this is a very big country. I had no idea Pennsylvania was such a long state. And the traffic out of New York City —"

"New York? Is that where you drove from?"

"Oh no. I took a cab from Kennedy International Airport."

"You *what?*" But there it was, pulling out

of the driveway and onto Hertlzer Road.

"I'm afraid he was not happy with my tip, but that was all the cash I had."

"Don't worry, dear. I take most credit cards, and there are banks over in Bedford." She was a mere slip of a girl, so it was easy to glance behind her. "Where is your luggage?"

Terri's hands flew to her face. "The cab!"

I was faced with two choices: hop in my car and chase down the cab, or call the Hernia police. I'm a fast driver for a Mennonite, but what if the cabdriver refused to pull over? Or what if he did pull to the side of the road, and he was armed and still in a cantankerous mood? On the other hand, dealing with the local authorities was less appealing than a liver-flavored milkshake. The chief is my nincompoop brother-in-law, and the only other officer is his spoony sidekick, Zelda Root. Working together they could possibly find their way out of a paper bag — if given both directions and a string to follow.

"Darn," I said for the second time that night, and ran inside to make the call.

No one answered at the station, so I called Melvin at home. My sister, Susannah, picked up.

"Susannah! Put Melvin on the phone,

please. This is an emergency."

My sister giggled. "I can't, Mags."

"Is he there?"

"Oh, he's here all right, but he can't come to the phone."

There was no time for nonsense. "Then take it to him."

"We don't have a portable, silly. You know that. Besides, he hates being disturbed when he's — uh — you know."

"Put him on *now*."

Susannah sighed loudly and let the phone drop. Then I heard her voice in the background, followed by a whoosh of water. Finally Melvin picked up.

"Yoder, this better be good. I still haven't read the comics."

"Melvin, listen to me. You need to take the cruiser and chase down a cab."

"You're nuts, Yoder," he said and hung up.

I know I should make allowances for Melvin, given that he was kicked in the head by a bull when he was a teenager — one that he was trying to milk — but not only is he a nincompoop, he's arrogant. Besides, I'm not really sure he's human. He looks just like a praying mantis, with eyes that move independently of each other and a bony carapace. The Bible commands us to love our neighbors, but it says nothing about loving insects.

Still, the man wields power in our small community, and one must give unto Caesar what is his. For the sake of Teruko Mukai I would grovel to the man who once sent his favorite aunt a gallon of ice cream by UPS. I punched redial.

My sister picked up after the first ring. "Susannah's house of perpetual love."

"Susannah!"

"Oh, Mags, I'm only pulling your leg. You know we have Caller ID."

"Put Melvin back on the phone."

"He doesn't want to speak to you."

"This is police business."

"But —"

"I'll cut off your allowance for a month." When our parents died — squished in a tunnel between a milk tanker and a truck full of state-of-the-art running shoes — they left the farm in a trust to me. I was instructed to make sure my sister was cared for, but she was not to be given her inheritance outright until such time that she proved she was a mature adult. That was eleven years ago, and Susannah is now thirty-six. Enough said.

Susannah didn't hesitate. "Melkins," she called, "Mags is insisting."

He got on the line with remarkable rapidity. "Is this extortion, Yoder? Because if it is —"

"Shut up, dear, and listen. One of my guests — a Japanese lady — took a cab from New York. He dropped her off here, but then drove away with her luggage. He was angry at her for not tipping well, and I think he means to keep her stuff. By now he's probably halfway to Bedford."

"But, Yoder, I'm in my pajamas."

"Then throw a coat on. Just think, this time you'll have a good excuse to drive fast with the siren on."

"Hmm. Okay, but you better not be making this up."

It was my turn to hang up. Then I comforted Terri Mukai. The poor woman had been privy to my conversation, and being somewhat brighter than my brother-in-law, she was clearly concerned about his competence.

I'm convinced the Good Lord doesn't mind a white lie if it's meant to comfort someone. "Don't worry, dear," I said. "The man's an expert at what he does." An expert at irritating me, that's what.

The reason there hadn't been a helpful response from the parlor when the doorbell rang is most of my guests had gone to bed early. Freni's cooking has a tendency to produce that effect. Plus, as I've observed, traveling can be very tiring. What surprised me is that Alison had hit the sack as well. I don't have a television — I have long since given away my black-and-white — but that doesn't stop her from begging to stay up late.

At any rate, the Littletons were still awake; I could tell by the light under their door. When they heard me show Teruko Mukai to her room, they popped out to say hello. The Charlestonians were still dressed, by the way. Even though it wasn't their business, I shared with them the sad fate of Miss Mukai's belongings. I thought of it as a preemptive strike, lest the new arrival put an even worse spin on the story. It wouldn't do to have my charming Southern guests think that we Yankees were nothing but a bunch of cutthroats and thieves.

Upon hearing the sad tale, Capers Littleton gave Miss Mukai a hug and then held her at arm's length. "You know, darling," she drawled to the new arrival, "you and I are about the same size. I'm sure I could find a few things for you to wear."

"Please, Mrs. Littleton," the young

woman protested, "I do not want to trouble you."

"Oh, it is no trouble. I insist. I always travel with twice as many clothes as I need. Don't I dear?"

Buist nodded vigorously. "That's a fact."

"There then, it's all settled," I said.

Teruko Mukai bowed deeply to show her appreciation. "Americans are very kind," she said.

I waited patiently while Capers retrieved a fresh nightgown and a set of casual clothes for the following day, and then I showed the girl her room. Her basic toiletries I supplied myself. Half my guests leave their brains at home when they go on vacation, along with half the things they mean to pack, so I am well stocked with the essentials. Usually I charge my guests by the item, but in Teruko's case I decided to make an exception in the interest of international goodwill. Finally, the girl was settled in and I was able to totter off to bed myself.

Although Alison complains loudly when she has to share my room, the child is starved for affection and doesn't really mind. Many times she stays in my room a few extra days on her own volition. I enjoy her company too. The only real downside is that she somehow manages to hog my king-size bed — oh, and she thrashes about like a shark out of water.

Sure enough, the girl was sprawled across both sides, snoring as loud as a chain saw. "Move over, dear," I said and pushed her to the halfway mark.

She rolled back to where I'd found her. I pushed her again, and before she could react, I threw myself on the empty spot. A moment later the back of her hand connected with my nose. I have the prominent Yoder nose — one deserving of its own zip code — and I know it's an easy target, but it's just as sensitive as any other schnoz. Being bonked on it hurt like the dickens.

Because I knew the child meant no harm, I gently moved her arm away and then protected my face with my pillow. That turned out to be a good move, because four inches of feathers helped to muffle the sound of her snores. Eventually I fell asleep, although I dreamed I was on the *Nina* with Christopher Columbus. The ship was pitching, and every now and then the yardarm would smack me on some vulnerable part of my body. Just as I was lecturing the famous explorer on how to provide better guest services, his cell phone rang. And rang.

"Chris, dear, pick it up."

"But Magdalena, carina, it's your phone you hear."

"It is?"

That's when I awoke to find my bedside phone ringing. I glanced at my alarm clock. Five a.m. on the dot. Unlike my sister, I do not have Caller ID. Since the only folks who have my private number are family or close friends and they would all be asleep now — well, except for Babs who, given the time difference, could still be partying — I panicked.

"What happened?" I blurted.

"I didn't catch the cabdriver, that's what."

"Melvin! You woke me at five in the morning to tell me you failed at your job?"

"I didn't fail, because there never was a cab. It's time to face it, Yoder, you're getting senile."

"Good night, Melvin."

"Yoder, I'm not calling about the stupid cab, anyway."

"Susannah? Is something wrong?"

"Something's wrong, all right, but it has nothing to do with my Sugar Boo."

"Spit it out, dear. You've got to the count of three. One —"

"There's been a murder."

7

"What?" I sat up straight in bed.

"Yoder, are you getting deaf now too?"

"I heard what you said. What does it have to do with me?"

"The name Buzzy Porter ring a bell?"

"Loud and clear. What about him?"

"He's the victim, and I found one of your room keys in his pocket."

"But that's impossible. Mr. Porter is upstairs — asleep."

"He's sleeping all right. The kind you never wake up from."

"Stay right there. Don't hang up!"

I thundered up my impossibly steep stairs and pounded on the prankster's door. "Mr. Porter, are you in there?"

There was no answer, so I tried the knob. It was locked. This meant I had to thunder back downstairs and grab my key ring from atop my bureau. I took a second to holler into the phone.

"Stay!"

By the time I got back to Buzzy's room, every other door along the hallway was opened. Glassy-eyed guests stood mutely on their thresholds, waiting for the night's entertainment to continue. Ignoring them, I fumbled with the keys, and when I got the door unlocked, I flung it open with such force that the stopper broke, allowing the doorknob to punch a hole in the wall. If by chance Buzzy was still among the living, he would pay for the repairs.

And the nerve of the guy. He was lying in bed, sleeping as peacefully as a teen-ager — Alison excepted. I ripped off the lazy man's covers.

"Pillows!" I roared. There was nothing in the bed but pillows and bunched-up clothes.

"Yoder-san," Terri said, appearing suddenly in the doorway, wearing Capers's nightgown, "is there a problem?"

"Not now, please!"

I pushed past her and thundered down the stairs yet one more time. "Melvin," I barked into the phone, "you still there?"

"No, Yoder. I'm in Las Vegas."

"Spare me the sarcasm and describe the corpse."

"You didn't say please, Yoder."

"Please. Pretty please with sugar on

top," I added to appease him.

"That's better. Okay, the guy's about five ten — dark hair. His driver's license pegs him at thirty-five."

"That old, huh?" The Buzzy I knew had appeared younger than that, but his juvenile personality might well have contributed to the illusion of youth. "Melvin, where is he?"

"Stucky Ridge."

"What?"

"I swear, Yoder, you need to get your hearing checked."

"I can hear just fine, thank you. But what would someone from out of town be doing up on Stucky Ridge at this hour?"

"Beats me. Ron Humphrey found him about half an hour ago."

"What was Ron doing up on the ridge? It's still dark, for crying out loud."

"Jogging. He's practicing for some kind of marathon. Says running up the ridge is the best kind of training."

"That figures." Ron is Hernia's sole Episcopalian and, next to the Babester, our most liberal resident. It is no secret that he drinks wine and other alcoholic beverages. He even has a satellite dish. I'd heard rumors that he belongs to a gym over in Bedford, an idea which, frankly, baffles me.

I am convinced that the Good Lord programmed each of us with a finite number of heartbeats at birth. Use them all up, and you die. Exercise, then, is a waste of heartbeats. Unfortunately, I'd just wasted an inordinate number of heartbeats going up and down the stairs.

"Yoder, you know I never ask for much —"

"Beans, Melvin."

"You swore!"

"So I did. But you're always asking for favors."

"Yes, but the election is only weeks away. I don't have time to work on this case. You know that."

My brother-in-law has delusions of grandeur. He's running for a position in the state legislature, but with at least one of his eyes on the White House. Susannah is already planning what color to wear at the inauguration. The style of the dress is the same as every other one in her closet: Fifteen feet of filmy fabric draped loosely around her rail-thin body. One's first impression is not of a sari, but a half-wrapped mummy. Of course, Melvin will never make it that far, but in the event he does, my biggest fear — besides the ruination of our country — is that my beloved sister will catch her death of cold on the reviewing stand.

"Melvin, dear, I'm not a police officer. Assign the case to Zelda."

"Yoder, you've helped me before. Besides, Zelda is going to have her hands full directing traffic for Hernia Heritage Days."

"I'm afraid that's your problem, not mine."

"Magdalena, please."

I couldn't believe my ears. This was the first time the miserable mantis had ever used the *M* word. As long as I've known him, which is to say his entire life, he has called me Yoder. Okay, so maybe he didn't call me Yoder when he was a baby, but as soon as he learned to speak — about age six — he's used only my last name, and always with a hint of derision.

"What did you say?"

"You heard me."

"Say it again if you want my help."

"M-m-magdalena."

I sighed. "Okay — but I'm only going to *help* you. You have to do the bulk of the work yourself."

"Sure, Yoder. Anything."

"Ah, ah, ah!"

"I mean Magdalena."

"That's better. But get this straight, dear

— I have official duties to attend to in the next few days, and I plan to keep my commitments."

"Whatever you say, Magdalena."

"And you're going to have to take orders from me. Do you think you can handle that?"

During the ensuing pause my beloved country elected its first female President — a black Jewish woman with a Spanish surname. "Yeah, yeah," he finally grumbled. "I can handle it."

"Good. Because my first order is that you don't touch anything until I get there."

"But I —"

"Already did?"

"You hadn't given me any orders yet."

I sighed again. "Well, stop touching. Have you called the coroner?"

"No."

"The morgue?"

"The morgue?"

"Never mind. I'll be right there."

One can see Stucky Ridge from my front porch, but getting there took me fifteen minutes. That's because I had to first put on some clothes, and then I had to parry anxious queries from my guests. Also, this local landmark is more of a mountain than a ridge, and the road to the top winds like an uncoiled Slinky.

Melvin hadn't said where the murder had occurred, and I was hoping against hope that I would find him on the picnic table side and not the cemetery. Settlers' Cemetery is where my parents are buried, and it's spooky enough at high noon on a bright summer day.

To my immense relief my nemesis was on neither side of the ridge, but in a copse that straddles the middle and serves as a divider between these two key areas. I could see the flashing blue lights of the cruiser as soon as I crested the ridge. What I couldn't figure out was how he had managed to get the car into the dense woods. I cruised down the road that leads past the picnic area, and finding no access, started down the cemetery lane. That's when Melvin came charging out of the trees waving a flashlight.

I rolled down my window. "How on earth did you get the cruiser in there?"

"You go past the cemetery — all the way to the end, and make a sharp left. But don't worry about that. Leave your car where it is and follow me."

I did as I was bid. "What's with the road back there? I never knew it existed."

"It's not a real road, Yoder. It's a way the teenagers get their cars in the woods."

"Why would they do that?"

"To have sex, Yoder — and to drink. You should see all the empty beer cans and discarded condoms."

That was a shocker. I knew that amorous couples parked in the picnic area — the Babester and I once exchanged a chaste smooch there — but it never occurred to me that someone would go all the way, so to speak, in a public place. Stucky Ridge was beginning to sound a lot like Sodom and Gomorrah.

I trotted gingerly behind Melvin. Should I accidentally step on something unpleasant, the Hernia Police Department was going to owe me a new pair of brogans. When we'd gone about thirty yards I could see Ron Humphrey standing next to the cruiser. A few more yards and the corpse was visible, facedown and illuminated by the headlights.

"Hi, Ron," I said. But I was looking at the dead body. Even from the back I could tell it was Buzzy.

"Hello, Miss Yoder. Just so you know, I had nothing to do with this."

I nodded. The young man is a computer programmer who lives in Hernia but works in Bedford. Other than the fact that he drinks alcohol — in church, no less — and believes in infant baptism, and is a fairly recent arrival in town, I have nothing against him. By all accounts he's a hardworking, taxpaying citizen, who involves himself in civic affairs. He isn't married, but the grapevine has it that he's heterosexual. My hope is that he will marry a Mennonite woman who can show him the error of his ways.

Now, where was I? Oh yes, Buzzy Porter's trunk and extremities appeared to be unmarked. However, the back of his head was covered with blood, and there seemed to be a slight depression at the crest.

"Has either of you touched the body?" I asked.

"I already confessed, Yoder. Of course I touched the body. How else could I tell if he was really dead?"

"Good point. But did you move it?"

Melvin's left eye was trained on the corpse; his right eye stared into mine. It gave me the willies.

"Yoder," he snarled, "what was I supposed to do, run over him?"

"I beg your pardon?"

"You can't back up in here. You've got to make a loop to get out, and he was right in the way."

There is no use in beating a dead horse — or a rationally challenged arthropod. "Show me exactly where you found him," I said to Ron Humphrey.

He led me about ten feet past the cruiser. "Here, I think."

I studied the surrounding area with a flashlight I borrowed from Melvin. As Melvin had warned, the ground was littered with empty cans, bottles, and unmentionables. There was even a brassiere hanging from a bush. Size 36C.

There was, however, no indication of a struggle, although I did find splotches of dark blood on fallen leaves. Most of it was concentrated where Ron had pointed, but there seemed to be a trail as well. In my opinion there was nothing more I could do until the world below awoke. But since the sky to the east was beginning to brighten, it wouldn't be long.

"Melvin, did you call the sheriff?"

"You know I can't do that."

There was no need for him to elaborate. Sheriff Hobson thought the same way I did about Melvin's investigation skills. Besides, due to the optimistic attitude of the founding fathers, Stucky Ridge was well within the city limits. Technically, it was Melvin's bailiwick, unless he sought outside help from the county. With the election three weeks away, that wasn't going to happen.

"But you finally called the coroner?"

"Yes. He should be here any minute."

"Good. I'm going to give Ron a ride home, then I'm coming right back. You wait here for the coroner."

"Alone?"

I couldn't blame the guy for sounding nervous. "Play the radio."

Melvin followed us to the edge of the copse. When I looked in the rearview mirror he appeared poised, as if at any second he would break into a run and beat me down the mountain.

"So, Ron," I said in a voice as smooth as Freni's chocolate silk pie, "do you often jog up the mountain in the dark?"

"Yeah."

"No kidding? Why?" Perhaps it was some weird Episcopalian ritual.

"I'm practicing for a marathon."

"That's what Chief Stoltzfus said. But why in the dark?"

"Because then I don't have to worry about cars. It takes me thirty-five minutes to get up here, twenty to get down. By then it's just starting to get light, so I run around the high-school track fifty times."

I gasped. "Don't you realize you're using up all your heartbeats?"

"Excuse me?"

"Never mind, dear. So tell me about this morning. What time did you start?"

"I keep my alarm set at four thirty — except for this morning. I got up a little earlier on account I have to get to work early because of a virus that's shut down two of our biggest clients."

"Feed a cold and starve a fever."

"This is a computer virus, Miss Yoder."

"I knew that." Show me where it's a sin to lie in one's own defense. "So, dear, do you normally run through the woods?"

"No, ma'am. I run to the end of the picnic area, touch the last table, and then start down. But tonight — I mean, this morning — I saw a light in the woods, so I decided to investigate."

"You didn't think that could be dangerous?"

He chuckled. "Miss Yoder, I moved here from Boston. What could possibly be dangerous in the woods out here?"

"Too bad you can't ask the victim that."

"Yeah, well, that definitely changes things. Anyway, I was hoping for a sighting."

"Of what? Teenagers doing the — never you mind."

"Trust me, Hernia kids never stay out that late. I was hoping it was an alien spacecraft."

That didn't surprise me coming from an Episcopalian. If he read his Bible — the King James version, of course, because that's what the Good Lord Himself reads — he wouldn't find anything about little green men from Mars. Come to think of it, he wouldn't find anything about computers either. I squelched my impulse to lecture the lad by stepping on the gas.

"Miss Yoder, you really know how to drive."

We squealed around a turn. "So you entered the woods. What happened next?"

"The light went out and I heard a thud. Then someone running through the brush. There must have been a car parked on the cemetery side, because the next thing I heard was a car tearing down the mountain — about as fast as you're driving now."

I took that as a compliment. "Tell me about the thud. Do you think that was the sound made when Buzzy Porter was hit on the back of the head?"

"No, ma'am. This was off to the side, and it sounded more like something hitting a tree."

I shuddered. How could the boy possibly discern between the sounds of something whacking a skull, as opposed to a tree? Perhaps it was knowledge he picked up playing those video games young folks are so fond of.

"Then what did you do, Ron?"

"Well, I have this little flashlight I take with me when I run in the dark" — he held up an object no larger than a pen — "and I picked my way over to where I thought I'd seen the light. That's when I almost stumbled over the body. Man, it was awful. I couldn't believe what I was seeing at first. But as soon as I got it together, I called Chief Stoltzfus on my cell phone."

"You carry that with you wherever you go?"

"Doesn't everyone?"

Cell phones. That's another *c* word you won't find in the Bible. I always leave my cell phone in the car.

"Weren't you scared," I asked, "waiting alone there for Chief Stoltzfus to arrive?"

"Not really. Like I said, the car took off. If it came back I would have made a beeline straight down the side of the mountain. Sure it's steep, but the car couldn't follow."

I wouldn't want to stand guard over a

corpse in a copse, especially one so close to a cemetery. No doubt about it, I would have hoofed it back down the mountain to meet Melvin halfway. One had to admire the young man in spite of his bizarre belief in aliens.

"Thanks for your help in this matter, dear."

"No problem. And if you want to know who did it, just ask."

8

It's a good thing I make my passengers wear seat belts. I braked so hard my probing proboscis came within a millimeter of reinventing itself on the steering wheel. But instead of my past fleeting before my eyes, I saw my future. With a bit less beak, and in the right light, I could pass for Meryl Streep. Then think of all the opportunities that would lay before me. I could leave my sheltered life in the hills of Hernia and move to the hills of Hollywood. Of course, I'd have to give up my religion, and maybe the Babester, but if Mel Gibson or Harrison Ford came along . . .

"Miss Yoder, you all right?"

I shook myself into reality. "I'm fine, dear. I was just lost in thought. It was unfamiliar territory. For a second there I thought you said you knew who killed Buzzy Porter."

"Drug dealers, that's who."

I stared through the easing darkness.

"You know that for a fact? How?"

"It just stands to reason. A man, alone, gets murdered in a remote location, it's night — what else could it be?"

I felt as let down as Susannah must have felt when she discovered the truth about Santa Claus. At least I was a mature woman with a job to do, whereas she was barely out of her teens at the time.

"I'll keep your theory in mind," I said charitably.

"Oh, it's a fact. You'll see."

I didn't have much to say to him the rest of the way to his house, except to inform him that I would probably be in touch with him again soon. The second he hopped out, I pressed the pedal to the metal. And why not? The town's only squad car was up on Stucky Ridge. Besides, there still wasn't a soul stirring — if you discount the mob of marauding raccoons that were just getting off work. Somehow I managed to miss all of them.

When I got back on top it was barely light enough to read a newspaper. Melvin was standing in the open, silhouetted by the rising sun. His arms and legs looked unusually spindly, and his head was enormous. Perhaps Ron's original theory of aliens had been the correct one. If so, our town's theological pundits were going to have to do some quick thinking. Because God had only one son to sacrifice for the sins of the world, any visitors from outer space were either sinless, or doomed. No matter how you looked at it, it was a sticky wicket.

I rolled the window down. "You looking for a ride, mister?"

"Very funny, Yoder. You bring me coffee and doughnuts?"

"No."

"Then what took you so long?"

"You didn't want me to speed, did you?"

He waved aside my question with a sticklike arm. "Bad news, Yoder. The coroner called. There's been a pileup on the turnpike. We have to handle this ourselves."

"You call Hernia Hospital?"

"The ambulance is on its way. They've agreed to let us keep the victim in the morgue."

That was a minor miracle. Hernia Hospital is a private institution and really nothing more than a glorified clinic run by the autocratic Dr. Luther and his imperious sidekick, Nurse Dudley. If I were asked to rename them I would pick Dr. Mean and Nurse Meaner. I much prefer to drive the twelve twisting miles into Bedford for my medical care. And yes, I would still feel that way if I wasn't banned from the premises.

"What are the strings, dear?"

"No strings."

"Beans."

"There you go, swearing again. Okay, so I promised to take the ambulance in for a tune-up and lube job. You happy, Yoder?"

Of course I wasn't happy. A man had died, for pity's sake.

Now that it was light I could see just how much Melvin had destroyed the crime scene by moving Buzzy's body. Still, it appeared to my untrained mind that the prankster had not been killed at the site where he was found, but moved there afterwards. Or least he had been badly wounded at some other location. I found a streak of blood on a low-hanging leaf about a yard away, and a splotch of blood on the ground about ten feet from that. Then the trail, if that's what it was, disappeared.

"Melvin, you wait here for the ambulance. I'm going to get help."

"Don't be crazy, Yoder. That boyfriend of yours is a doctor, but he can't work miracles."

"The help isn't for Buzzy," I said through clenched teeth. "It's help with the investigation."

I didn't stick around to hear Melvin's ranting. No doubt he felt threatened, but he'd only feel foolish when he saw who I had in mind.

Doc Shafor is a retired veterinarian. He is also an octogenarian whose libido got stuck on high sometime during his twenties. But most important, he is the only person I know in Hernia who owns an honest-to-goodness bloodhound.

As I suspected, he was up and about at that hour. In fact, he was in the process of cooking breakfast and had a hard time hearing my knock over the sound of sizzling bacon. When he finally opened the door, his face lit up.

"You're just in time, Magdalena."

"Doc, I can't stay for breakfast. I just —"

"Sure you can."

"No, really. There's —"

He grabbed my arm with gnarled fingers that had not lost their strength. "Whatever the problem is, it will keep until after we eat. I've made scrambled eggs with cheese, bacon, two kinds of sausage, hash browns, fried apples, and biscuits from scratch. And not drop biscuits either, but rolled."

"Man does not live by bread alone," I said and sailed into the house on a wave of aromas.

"Good call."

"But I'll have to eat and run. I'm here on police business."

I followed Doc into the kitchen. There were two place settings on the table, but I knew the extra one was not intended for me. Although Doc's been a widower for thirty years, he hates to eat alone. He even cooks like he's cooking for two. After we'd loaded our plates, I could have fed the guests back at the inn with what remained on the stove.

"Magdalena," he said when we were seated, "you're still a fine-looking woman."

The way his eyes appraised me, I felt like a horse. I suppose that was fitting, because after the Good Lord made me He didn't break the mold. Instead He made an exact copy, slapped a saddle on its back, and yelled giddyap.

"Thanks, Doc — I think. You're looking pretty good yourself."

"Is that a come on?"

"Gracious, no. You know I have a beau." I knew Doc too well to be shocked.

"I hope you realize that if this thing with that New York doctor doesn't work out — well, I'm willing to be more than friends."

It was time to switch to the world's second most deliberated topic. "These are the best biscuits I've ever eaten."

"It was my wife's recipe. After Belinda passed, I had no choice but to learn how to cook. Say, you in the mood for some scrapple?"

"I'd sooner eat ground glass. Doc, I have a question to ask you."

"Ask away, but I have a hunch the answer is going to be eight inches."

"Excuse me?"

"You want to know how far I keep the biscuits from the top of the oven, so they don't burn on top. Right?"

"It's a favor, Doc, not a cooking tip. You still own that bloodhound?"

"You mean Blue? Yeah, she's out back. I have to keep her outside full-time now because she's incontinent."

"Does her sniffer still work?"

Doc winked. "She let me know you were coming, Magdalena. That's how I knew to set two plates."

"Right. Doc, you think I could borrow Blue?"

"Don't see why not. This the police business you were talking about?"

"Yes. There's been a murder up on Stucky Ridge."

"Anyone I know?"

"I don't think so — he was a guest of mine. There seems to be a trail of blood. I was hoping Blue could follow it."

"Have another sausage link, Magdalena. You can't do police work on an empty stomach."

I did as my mama always told me and listened to my elders.

There was nothing wrong with Blue's sniffer. She tore through the woods like a hyperactive child on an Easter-egg hunt. I needed that extra sausage just to keep up. Her first stop was the spot where Melvin had found Buzzy. By then both the body and the bumbling chief were gone.

Blue snuffled the saturated ground and then charged off on the trail I'd begun. She, of course, had much better success. She led us out of the woods to the picnic side of the ridge and didn't stop until we'd reached a place that is popularly called Lovers' Leap. Believe me when I say no lovers have ever leaped to their deaths from that spot. There is a sheer vertical drop of about fifty feet to the closest ledge, but the enormous trees below would prevent anyone from falling more than twenty feet without being snagged by branches.

About the best a forlorn lover could expect is a slew of broken bones and multiple abrasions.

This is the highest spot on Stucky Ridge and is marked by a concrete pillar that notes the elevation — a mind-boggling 2,801 feet. I know that sounds puny by Rocky Mountain standards, but for us Hernians it's a nosebleed height. At any rate, the numbers on the pillar are almost illegible, thanks to the graffiti painted on it by generations of expressive teenagers. Because this is our town's most significant landmark, it is also where the time capsule is buried.

No one knows for sure how deep the metal box lies, or even whether it is under the monument, or just next to it. All that is known for sure is that the box was buried in 1904 and was meant to be dug up a hundred years later. Because the marker is in such bad shape, it is the town council's plan to replace the old one after the successful retrieval of the capsule on Wednesday.

"Land o' Goshen," I panted as we neared the spot. "Would you look at that!"

Doc moves sprightly for a man his age and caught up with me seconds later. Together we stared at the scene of devastation.

The marker had been toppled, its base broken into pieces by something — possibly a sledgehammer — and the ground where the pillar stood had been excavated to a depth of four feet. The hole had a diameter of a little more than two feet. At the bottom was a rectangular imprint. Clearly, whomever was responsible had gone straight for the treasure and gotten what they were after.

But Blue wasn't done yet. She stood at the edge of Lovers' Leap and howled like the hound of the Baskervilles. Doc had to pull her back and then temporarily muzzle her with his hands.

"Bet you anything," he said, "the tools are down there, below the trees."

"Yes. But why drag the body all the way into the woods? Why not just throw it over the edge too?"

"Don't have any idea," Doc said. "You're the expert."

"I'm not an expert," I wailed. "I am merely competent."

He winked. "I bet you're more than that."

"Doc, please, this is serious business. I need to think of possible scenarios."

He released Blue's muzzle and told her to sit. Having had a good workout, she lay instead on a pile of dirt.

"Okay, Magdalena, how about this? Your corpse — what was his name?"

"Buzzy. Buzzy Porter."

"Yeah, so Mr. Porter thinks the time capsule is worth stealing — maybe it contains some damning evidence that he's privy to — and so he comes up here in the dead of the night to dig for it. But someone else wants it too. They clobber Mr. Porter over the head and then plan to bury him in the woods. If they just threw him over the edge, he'd get caught up in the trees, but a shovel would most likely slip right through. Anyway, the murderer is about to dig a shallow grave when that Episcopalian kid — what's his name?"

"Ron Humphrey."

"Yeah, so that kid comes along and the murderer takes off. But first he throws the tools over the cliff."

"Why not just put them in his or her car?"

He shrugged. "Like I said, you're the expert."

I poked a finger under the organza prayer cap that covers my bun. My scalp was itching, which for me is either a sign of inspiration or untreated dandruff.

"But, Doc, it could also be that the killer

was here first, and Buzzy surprised him."

He grunted agreement. "Any idea how an out-of-towner would know where to look?"

"I haven't gotten that far." I peered into the hole. Its sides were absolutely vertical. "But I can tell you that it was a square-point shovel, not a round one."

He stepped closer, and Blue got up to look with him. "You're right about that. Now, who do you know in this county who owns a square-point shovel?"

I couldn't help but laugh. Looking for a square-point shovel in this county would be like searching for a particular fragment of fodder in a haystack. Virtually all the farmers, and half the townsfolk, own square-point shovels.

"My point exactly." Doc stepped sideways and draped an arm around my shoulder. In order to do so he had to reach up, so it wasn't the smoothest of moves.

"While we ruminate on the perplexities of this unfortunate incident, why don't we go back to my place? I'll make you lunch." He gave me a squeeze.

"Doc, it's only nine o'clock — oh my gracious! I'm supposed to announce the tractor pull at ten and I haven't even spoken to any of my guests today. Freni's going to be hysterical that I wasn't there for breakfast, and Gabe —"

He squeezed me again. "I've always liked a woman with purpose. Tell that people doctor of yours he's a lucky man."

We turned to go, but not before Blue took one last sniff of the breeze that was blowing toward us from Lovers' Leap. It was a cool morning, but that's not why I shivered.

9

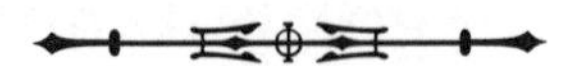

A fuming, flailing, frantic Freni is a fearsome thing. Although she's stout with stubby arms, when she becomes agitated she waves them so fast I'm afraid she'll achieve liftoff. Believe me, I have no desire to learn what it is Amish women wear under their skirts.

The moment I stepped through the outside kitchen door, Freni flew at me. "Ach, Magdalena, where were you?"

"I'm afraid it was police business, dear."

She flapped to a stop. "You got another traffic ticket, yah?"

"I'm afraid it's worse than that."

My friend and kinswoman stared at me through lenses as thick as the bottoms of Coke bottles — well, back in the days when they were made of glass. "Murder?"

"Yes, but —"

"English, yah?" To the Amish, anyone not of the faith is referred to as English. Even my Japanese guest would be considered English. No doubt this custom derives from the fact that it was the English who were in control of this country when the Amish first arrived in the early 1700s.

"So the victim was English, dear. What of it?"

Freni crossed her short arms beneath an ample bosom. Her stomach is ample as well, so it wasn't an easy position to assume.

"Was the English a guest?"

"Unfortunately, yes."

"Then I quit."

I struggled not to smile. Freni has quit her job as chief cook and bottle washer eighty-nine times in the last six years. When she reaches a hundred, I'm going to give her a plaque. It will read WORLD'S MOST FICKLE COOK. When she asks what "fickle" means, I'll tell her it is a synonym for "valuable." She'll think "synonym" is a spice and will be too confused to question me further.

"The murder didn't happen here at the inn, Freni. It happened up on Stucky Ridge."

"I still quit."

"But you can't! I have eight remaining guests to feed, the murder investigation to attend to, and my festival duties to perform." In addition to announcing the tractor pull, I was scheduled to award the prize in the greased pig contest. These honors were bestowed on me because I am the most inbred, yet articulate, resident of our burg. The prize, by the way, was two hundred dollars, and the winner got to keep the pig.

"Magdalena, these guests of yours are running me crazy."

"You mean 'driving,' dear."

"Yah, that's what I said. At breakfast, the old one who thinks she is a movie star wants her eggs poached, instead of fried. Then she wants me to put them on muffins with bacon and Holland sauce so they are a benediction."

"Ah, you mean eggs Benedict."

Her eyes, made all the more beady by the lenses, bore into mine. I knew when to quit.

"Tell me everything, dear."

Freni unfolded her arms so that she could take a deep breath. "Well, she is not the only one who gives me trouble. The Japanese English says she wants raw fish for lunch." She made a face. "Magdalena, who ever heard of eating such a thing?"

The Amish I know love fish, but it has to say Star-Kist on the label. "It's called sushi, dear. Did you tell them that you are in charge of the menus?"

"Yah, but there is much complaining." Now that her arms were free she untied her apron. "Magdalena, if I want this complaining, I can get it from Barbara."

Barbara Hostetler is Freni's daughter-in-law. Because the Bible commands it, they love each other in a general sort of way, but not a smidgen more. The truth is, Freni resents losing her only son to another woman's affections. Never mind that this woman, a "foreigner" from Iowa, has supplied the Hostetlers with three bouncing babies. And all in one fell swoop too.

I nodded gravely. "Yes, maybe it is a good idea for you to take some time off. Barbara was telling me just the other day how homesick she still gets. She's thinking of having her mother come and stay for a month."

"Ach! Then I unquit."

The best thing was to pretend our little tiff had never happened. "Where's Alison?"

"That nice couple from Charlesville, they take her to watch that silly tractor game."

I had nothing to gain by correcting her geography. Besides, it was already twenty to ten. If I didn't put my lead foot to good use, the tractor pull would be delayed.

* * *

I got there in the nick of time. The pull was to be held on Main Street, which really is the main drag in town. At the corners of Main and Elm sit the First Mennonite and Covenant Presbyterian churches. Across from them are the police station and Yoder's Corner Market, a small grocery selling dusty, overpriced goods. I don't own it, by the way. It belongs to my cousin Sam, who has the same designs on me that Doc Shafor has. Sam, however, lacks Doc's charm.

It is only a ten-minute drive from my inn to the center of town, but thanks to an overwhelming turnout of spectators, I had to park over on Kingdom Come. This is the name of a real street. It gets its moniker from the Baptist Church at the corner. At any rate, I was out of breath, and perhaps a mite out of sorts, when I arrived at my post. I certainly was not in the mood to be ambushed.

"Hi, babe," my fiancé said, as he appeared out of nowhere and grabbed my arm.

"Gabe!"

He hugged me close.

"Vell," somebody harrumphed, "this is certainly not the appropriate place for this kind of behavior."

At first I thought the disembodied voice belonged to my dear, departed mama. The poor woman is obviously not enjoying her stay in Heaven. If she was, she wouldn't find so much time to bother me. Perhaps the golden streets are too slippery — after all, Mama never did have a very good sense of balance.

"Really, dear," I whispered, "perhaps you should get back to your harp lessons." Mama also had a tin ear.

"You see what I mean, Gabriel? The voman's meshuga."

That's when I realized the voice was coming from below. Mama was definitely not spending eternity in that direction. My heart sank when I saw who it was.

"Mrs. Rosen, I'm afraid I didn't see you."

"That's because you're too tall, Magdalena. Like a bean stalk, if you ask me. But not to vorry. I hear they have surgery for that kind of thing nowadays."

"Somehow I don't think so."

"Tell her, Gabriel."

"Yes," I said, "tell *her* she's been reading too many tabloids."

My beloved didn't say anything, caught as he was between a stalk and a hard place.

"So," Mrs. Rosen said, putting her fists

on her hips — at least that's what it looked like from way up here — "you're not going to stick up for your mother?"

Gabe flinched, "Ma, I refuse to take sides. You know that."

"Then you're taking her side."

"Ma!"

I flashed Ida Rosen a triumphant look and made my way to the reviewing stand. There were three seats on the rickety wooden platform, and they were already occupied by the dignitaries of the day. Apparently I was meant to stand. Sitting ramrod straight in the middle seat was Sam Yoder, in front of whose store the event was taking place. To his right sat Reverend Richard Nixon, pastor of the First and Only True Church of the One and Only Living God of the Tabernacle of Supreme Holiness and Healing and Keeper of the Consecrated Righteousness of the Eternal Flame of Jehovah. The good man was going to open the ceremonies with an invocation. To Sam's left sprawled Betty Baumgartner, a Hernia teenager who had been asked to sing the national anthem. Betty's claim to fame is that she made it to the top one thousand finalists in a TV show called *American Idol.*

I've been blessed with a good pair of

lungs, so this was not my first time as an announcer. "Ladies and gentlemen, please bow your heads for a word of prayer."

Hats were doffed and heads were bowed, but the leader of the church with thirty-two names delivered more than a word. After asking God's blessing on the crowd, he prayed for the safety of the contestants, then launched into a long list of petitions that included requests for good weather, bountiful crops, and contrite hearts. So far so good, but unfortunately his mental needle got stuck in the repentance groove.

I gave the man a nudge to move things along, but the needle skipped and landed in the fire and brimstone band of his vinyl record. This is when the reverend, who evokes a taller and ganglier Abraham Lincoln, threw his arms in the air and waved them about with all the grace of a marionette manipulated by a drunken puppeteer.

"Repent!" he thundered, "or suffer forever the fiery horrors of hell. Behold, the last days are upon us —" I tugged on the tails of his frock coat. "A simple 'amen' would do nicely now, dear."

He pulled away. "— your throats will close up with unquenchable thirst, your lips will blister like the scales of a shed snakeskin —"

What was I to do? There were Presbyterians in the audience for pete's sake, and they might not appreciate the reverend's perspective on their future home — not to mention Ron the Episcopalian. Or Gabe and his mother for that matter. I was left with no choice but to punch the preacher in the soft spots behind his knees and watch him topple like the tower of Babel. Fortunately, Sam has good reflexes and caught the pontificating pastor before he could hurt himself.

I poked Betty Baumgartner. "Belt it out, dear."

Alas, the child was agog with wonder at what I had done, and when that finally passed she burst into shrill laughter. It was turning out to be a typical Hernia celebration.

"This may be your last chance at fame, dear. I hear there are talents scouts in the crowd."

Betty sobered instantly and grabbed the microphone. " 'Oh say can you see —' "

My mouth fell open. I assure you that I was not the only one to lose control of their jaw muscles. The girl was so off-key it would be impossible to find one note on a piano to match. I did the kind thing and prayed that she would forget the words and be forced to stop.

Half my prayer was answered. "— by the rocket's red glare in the dawn's early light —"

Just as I was leaning forward to give her a merciful punch behind the knees, somewhere across town a dog howled. It sounded a lot like Blue. Seconds later another dog joined in. Then another. It was the crowd's turn to laugh.

I grabbed the microphone from a blushing Betty. "Give the girl a big round of applause, folks."

Sam, bless his lecherous heart, clapped first. Then, one by one, the others joined in. A beaming Betty bowed dramatically before I pushed her gently aside. She plopped in her chair and picked up a pop she'd been guzzling.

"Everybody ready for the tractor pull?" I yelled.

The response was deafening. Hernians love their tractor pulls. Even the Amish, who eschew the use of such modern machines, seem to have no objection to observing this competition. The crowd was sprinkled with black bonnets and straw hats. In fact, some of the more enterprising women had set up stalls on the fringes where they sold homemade cheese and preserves. One entrepreneur had brought with her a small propane stove and was frying snitz pies, a greasy pastry filled with dried apples and a thousand calories.

I'm sure every community has their rules and regulations, but ours are simple. The contestants must be eighteen or over, and the machines they operate must belong to them. The playoffs are between pairs, who chain their tractors back to back and try to pull their opponent over a line. Think of it as a tug of war on steroids.

It can be a dangerous sport — chains sometimes snap, tractors rear like bucking broncos and can veer off course — and is normally not played on city streets. But deep down Hernians are a wild bunch, many of whom long to run before the bulls in Pamplona. Besides, Main Street is exceptionally wide, and the high-school stadium was being readied for the greased pig competition.

"First off we have Danny Gerber and 'Dirty Bob' Troyer. Danny — on my left — is driving the souped-up Massey Ferguson his dad gave him for graduation. Danny dear, did you ever finish your community service for having sprayed 'I Love Tina' on the overpass south of town?"

The crowd roared their approval and

Danny gave me the thumbs-up sign.

"Dirty Bob," I said, "time to pick on you next."

The crowd roared again.

I wasn't being nasty by any means. Everyone in town calls Robert Troyer by his nickname. In fact, he's proud of it. This rather handsome man dropped out of high school his senior year when his father died. In order to support his mother and two little sisters, young Robert got a job at a garden center over in Bedford. The place was called the Onion Patch at the time. The new employee was not afraid to get his hands dirty and today, ten years later, he owns the store. You guessed the rest — it's now called Dirty Bob's.

"If you win this round," I deadpanned, "you also win a free manicure at Selma's House of Beauty."

The crowd went hysterical. Even though he now has a dozen employees, Dirty Bob still digs with his hands. He feels he needs to set an example, and when one is transplanting delicate seedlings, that's the only way to do it. It's certainly no secret that Dirty Bob has dirt embedded beneath his nails that no soap and water will reach.

"Dirty Bob will be driving a John Deere that he rebuilt by himself and —" I gasped as a couple of dormant brain cells kicked back to life and I had a mini-epiphany. "Uh, ladies and gentleman, Sam Yoder will be taking over as announcer."

"What?" Sam was on his feet in a nano-second. "Magdalena, what the heck are you saying?"

Actually, Sam used a worse word, but as I already had a hand over the microphone, only belching Betty — her pop was long gone — heard him. "Sam, if you be a dear and do this one favor for me, I'll make your fondest wish come true."

"My house or yours? If it's mine, we'll have to pick a time when Dorothy's not there."

I was disgusted but not shocked by my cousin's proposition. He stopped being a Mennonite the day he married Dorothy, a liberal-leaning Methodist. I'm not saying that all Methodists cheat on their wives, merely that the town grocer's apple had fallen far from the tree. One might say that it rolled into another orchard altogether. In cases like that, one can expect just about anything to happen.

"Samuel Nevin Yoder, you should be ashamed of yourself. What would your mama say if she could hear you talking like that? More to the point, what will your wife say when I tell her?"

"You wouldn't dare tell Dorothy, because it would hurt her."

I sighed. "If you were a little boy, I'd turn you over my knee right now and spank you."

"I love it when you talk dirty, Magdalena."

The crowd had begun to buzz impatiently, and at least one of the contestants was revving his engine. I uncovered the mike.

"Hold your horsepower," I barked. I turned to Sam. "Look buster, what I had in mind was free advertising for your store. Between pulls you get to announce your overpriced specials. A head of wilted lettuce for one ninety-nine. That kind of thing."

"It's a deal," Sam said.

I practically threw the microphone at him. Thanks to Dirty Bob, all I needed to do was to make one phone call and I could prove whether Buzzy Porter had been the one to dig up Hernia's time capsule or had surprised someone else in the act.

10

Grilled Chicken Breasts with Eggplant, Creole Style

2 lemons
2 whole boneless chicken breasts, skinned, split, and trimmed
Salt and whole black peppercorns in a pepper mill
1 medium eggplant (about 3/4 pound)
1/4 cup all-purpose flour
1 large egg, well beaten, in a wide, shallow bowl
1 cup fine cracker crumbs or matzo meal, spread on a plate
3 tablespoons melted unsalted butter or extra-virgin olive oil
1 cup Creole Sauce
2 tablespoons chopped parsley

Grate the zest from 1 of the lemons and then juice them both through a strainer. Put the chicken breasts in a shallow nonreactive stainless steel or glass bowl and sprinkle them with the grated zest, a large pinch of salt, and several generous grindings of pepper. Pour the lemon juice over them, turning them several times to coat them, and set aside to marinate for 30 minutes (or as much as 8 hours or overnight, covered and refrigerated).

Wash the eggplant under cold, running water. Peel and slice it crosswise into $8^{1}/_{2}$-inch-thick slices. Lightly salt both sides of the eggplant slices and put them in a colander set in the sink or over a plate. Let them stand for 30 minutes. Meanwhile, prepare a charcoal grill with coals and light it. When the coals are glowing red and lightly ashed over, spread them and position a rack about 4 inches above them. Let the rack get very hot. Or preheat the oven broiler at least 15 minutes before you plan to use it.

Wipe the eggplant with a paper towel and pat dry. Lightly roll each slice in the flour, shake off the excess, then dip it in the egg, coating all sides. Lift it from the egg, allowing the excess to flow back into the bowl, and then roll it in the crumbs or matzo meal. Shake off the excess and put the breaded eggplant on a wire rack.

Lift the chicken from its marinade and

pat dry. Spread it on a platter in one layer and lightly brush it and the eggplant with butter or olive oil. Put them both on the grill (or on a broiling rack under the broiler), buttered side toward the heat. Grill/broil until the chicken breasts and eggplant slices are browned on the side toward the heat, about 3 to 4 minutes. Brush lightly with butter or oil, turn them, and grill/broil until the chicken is cooked through and the eggplant is tender and browned on both sides, about 3 to 4 minutes longer, depending on how hot the fire is. The eggplant may be ready a little before the chicken. Place the eggplant on a warm platter, lay a chicken breast over each slice, and spoon Creole Sauce (see Chapter 15) over them. Sprinkle with parsley and serve at once.

SERVES 4

11

Lucky for me Melvin has a perennial zit the size of Zimbabwe on his backside. Susannah has told me far too much about this condition, which she fondly refers to as "my Sugar Buns's auxiliary brain." Up until now I've been a good Magdalena and stifled my impulse to ask how she knows which brain is which. At any rate, after escorting Buzzy's body to the morgue, my nemesis hung out in the hospital waiting room until Dr. Luther had the time to lance the police chief's eruption. Dr. Luther may well be meaner than a tick-covered snake, but he's a competent surgeon, and my brother-in-law survived the operation with his real brain intact. He was, however, in a particularly foul mood.

"What now?" he shouted into his cell phone.

"How do you know it's me?"

"Yoder, I'm not in the mood to play your silly games. It's you, isn't it?"

"Yes, but — oh, never mind. Melvin,

dear, I need you to do me a big favor."

"I'm not going snipe hunting with you again, Yoder. Twice was enough."

"Melvin, I want you to look under Buzzy Porter's fingernails and tell me what you see."

"You're an idiot, Yoder."

"Just do as I say, or come election day you'll be lucky to get two votes."

"Like I said, you're an idiot. Susannah can't vote twice."

"Quit calling the kettle black and look under Buzzy's nails. Call me back the second you do so."

Melvin muttered something uncomplimentary, but I could hear him shuffle off to do as I'd ordered. On the way to the morgue he stopped for an ice cream — possibly in Beijing, China. When he returned my call he belched before speaking.

"So I looked at his nails. What about them?"

"Are they dirty?"

He sighed. "Now you tell me."

"Melvin, all you —"

"Hang on." He walked back to China for the chocolate syrup and whipped cream he'd forgotten. "They're clean, Yoder. So what?"

"Then he didn't dig up the time capsule."

"What time capsule?"

"That's right, you don't know. *The* time capsule — you know the one up on the ridge, by Lovers' Leap? The one we're supposed to open on Wednesday? Well, it's missing."

To say that Melvin was miffed at me for withholding information is an understatement. He ranted and raved and invented some curses that even a fallen Baptist is unlikely to know. He went so far as to suggest that I engage myself sexually in a position that is anatomically impossible to achieve (don't ask me how I know). Of course, Melvin was right for feeling this way. But did he have to be so rude?

In my defense, I hadn't intended to keep him in the dark. I'm so used to him being an utter incompetent, that it just didn't occur to me to fill him in. For that I ought to be ashamed.

"I'm sorry," I said for the zillionth time. "Really, I am."

"You ought to be, Yoder. Besides, why would anyone want to steal that thing?"

"Maybe if we could figure out the answer to that, we could figure out *who* took it. Oh well, at least we know it wasn't Buzzy."

"Oh yeah? How do we know that?"

"Because you can only dig so far with a shovel. Then you have to get down on your hands and knees and dig around the box with your fingers to get it loose."

Melvin snorted. "This Buzzy guy could have started the digging and then the other guy surprises him and finishes the digging. Clean nails don't mean nothing."

"Anything."

Melvin made another trip to Beijing — this time for nuts. "You have a hearing problem, Yoder? I said 'nothing.' "

"That's a double negative, dear. Anyway, I want you to check his pants. Especially the knee area."

"Check them yourself," he said and hung up.

My first impulse was to lose my temper. But fearing that I might never find it again, I wisely decided to take Melvin's suggestion. If you want something done right, do it yourself — even if it means scrutinizing a dead man's pants.

I was halfway back to my car, trotting past the gorgeous Victorian homes on upper Elm Street, when I ran into Stanley Dalrumple. I mean that literally. Arms and legs went flying in eight different directions, although all the limbs belonged to me. On the plus side, I learned that I could always have a second career, hiring myself out as a human threshing machine. The downside was that when I finally landed, I skinned both palms and the tip of my nose.

Stanley, who is slight of stature, appeared none the worse for wear. “Miss Yoder, are you all right?”

“No, I’m not all right. My hands hurt, my nose hurts — why weren’t you looking where you were going?”

“I was looking. You were the one who ran into me. You looked really zoned out — kind of like a zombie.”

“Well, I have important things to think about.”

Stanley snickered. “Yeah, I bet you do. Like what slop to feed us for lunch.”

“Excuse me?”

The young man knew he was no match for my lacerating lingua. “Never mind,” he mumbled.

But it was too late. My hackles were hiked and I needed to let off steam. Otherwise my eardrums might blow, taking half the town with them.

“For your information, buster, Freni Hostetler is one of the best cooks in the county. And not that it’s any of your business, but I had my mind on a murder case

I've been asked to solve."

The corners of his mouth twitched as he struggled to keep his sarcasm in check. It was a losing battle.

"Did the victim eat Miss Hostetler's cooking?"

"As a matter of fact, yes. The victim was Buzzy Porter."

Stanley Dalrumple didn't even blink behind his wire-rimmed glasses. "That figures."

"You don't seem surprised."

"The guy was a jerk."

"I seem to recall that you found him amusing."

"He was still a jerk."

"Mr. Dalrumple, I don't know about Hollywood, but here in Hernia being a jerk is not sufficient cause to murder someone."

He stared at me with all the emotion of a snake. "Miss Yoder, are you some kind of policewoman?"

"You might say that."

He showed no reaction. "I'm not a suspect, am I?"

"I never said you were. But until I can prove who the killer is, everyone is a suspect."

"I guess this means you're going to want

to ask me some questions."

"You guessed right. And now is as good a time as any."

He sighed. "Well, if you must know, I wasn't just at that stupid tractor pull."

The sound of the cheering crowd in the background made that obvious. Besides, he was headed from the opposite direction when I ran him down. While it is possible a man his age would be strolling about town to view all our fine architecture, it was about as likely as Freni dancing naked at Wednesday's picnic. I decided to return his blank stare and hopefully make him nervous enough to tell me the whole truth and nothing but. Alison says I give her the willies when I do this. Believe me, I've had plenty of practice.

Stanley Dalrumple caved like an over-mined coal shaft. "Okay, so I was out looking for some weed. Big deal."

It was my turn to snicker. "You won't find any weeds in these lawns. This is the high-rent district."

He had the audacity to laugh. "Not that kind of weed. I'm talking about pot. Cannabis. You know, the kind of weed you smoke."

I gasped. "You won't find that either. This is Hernia, not Harrisburg."

"Ha, you'd be surprised, Miss Yoder. I'm pretty good at sniffing it out — no pun intended. Had to learn how to find it quick after nine eleven, what with airport security being what it is. Was going to pick me up some in Pittsburgh, but the old bag didn't give me a minute to myself."

"Old bag? By that you would mean Octavia Cabot-Dodge, the down-on-her-luck diva?"

"Yeah, whatever."

I realized with a start that the upstart must have been successful in his search for illegal stimulants. Otherwise, he wouldn't be returning to the pull so soon.

"Where is it young man? Hand it over."

He finally blinked. "Do you have the authority to arrest me?"

"What if I said 'yes'?"

"You don't, do you?"

If Alison talked to me that way I'd ground her. Maybe even make her copy a page from the dictionary. The one on respect. Young people these days have no respect for their elders, which is one of society's major failings, if you ask me. In my day we had to respect even the people we loathed — which is not to say I hated Granny Yoder. It's just that I had great respect for her cane, which met my backside on more than one occasion. I know, today that would be called child abuse, and rightly so. But I don't think I'm any more screwed up than the average person, do you?

Lacking any way to discipline the impudent youth, I waggled a finger at him — presidential style. "You will not be smoking that stuff on my property. If I so much as smell one molecule of suspicious smoke, I'm calling someone who does have the power to arrest you. Is that clear?"

"Yeah, yeah. You done lecturing now?"

"Not quite. If you offer any drugs to my foster daughter, Alison, I'll see that they not only lock you up, but throw away the key."

"If you say so."

That last comment irritated me from the tips of my stocking-clad toes to the core of my bun. "I still have a hard time believing you found marijuana in Hernia."

Stanley's smile seemed almost genuine. "Met this kid in the crowd. Could tell right away he was a pothead. Followed him back to that house." He pointed at a yellow Victorian with white gingerbread trim. It's always been one of my favorites.

"That's impossible. That house belongs to Andrew and Lydia Byler. They're the salt of the earth. Their son, David, is — describe this kid, please."

"No prob. Red hair, a million freckles. Looks like he could open a bottle with his teeth."

"That's him!" I said in dismay.

To his credit, young Stanley did not rub it in. "Miss Yoder, I'd be happy to share my stash with you."

"What?"

"A couple of tokes and you'll be feeling real mellow. Come on, try it. You look like you deserve to chill out for a while. This stuff is guaranteed to make you feel like you're floating on a cloud."

"It really does that for you?" The truth is I'm so high strung I can fly a kite on a windless day. To my knowledge, the only time I've ever felt totally relaxed — and I mean all the way back to when I made my first appearance as a six-pound, seven-ounce, squalling bundle of annoyance — is when I inadvertently drank a pitcher of mimosas. What would be so wrong about feeling that way again? Perhaps the Good Lord created the cannabis plant so that we could enjoy its benefits.

Stanley dug into his pocket and withdrew a plastic sandwich bag filled with what looked like dried oregano. "Oh yeah, it really does that. When you're on this, you won't give a shoot about your problems."

He actually used a stronger word than shoot, and the shock of it brought me back to my senses. "Get behind me, Satan," I cried.

If someone from the *Guinness Book of World Records* had been watching, I would have earned a spot on those pages for having broken the land speed record for a human being. When I got to my car I was panting so hard I had to wait a full five minutes before I could drive.

As I've stated before, Hernia Hospital is a misnomer. Think of it as a twenty-four-hour clinic where Amish women come for births that are too complicated for midwives to handle, and where children receive stitches after falling off bicycles and skateboards. There is a small surgical unit on the premises, but the only time it was ever used was when Veronica Saylor had a bunion removed. That event made national news because the bunion was shaped like Elvis Presley's head, and Dr. Luther, who performed the operation, refused to turn the growth over to his patient. Veronica sued and won custody of her former body part. She later sold the hunk of inflamed tissue on eBay for eight thousand dollars.

Of course, I wasn't visiting the hospital to get my skinned palms and nose treated, but to get another look at Buzzy Porter. Well, at least his clothes. At any rate, you can imagine my surprise when I entered through the front door and found Alison and the Littletons sitting in the minuscule lobby.

"What's wrong?" I demanded.

The Littletons jumped to their feet, but Alison remained seated, just as pale as Granny Yoder's ghost.

"I'm afraid she has stomach pains," Capers said. Her charming Charleston accent failed to make the words less frightening.

I flew to my foster daughter's side. "Where, exactly?"

Alison groaned and pointed to the lower right quadrant of her abdomen.

My darling, and only sometimes obnoxious, child had appendicitis. I was beside myself with concern. Fortunately, I am bean-pole thin, and two of me occupy very little space.

"Has the doctor seen her?"

Buist Littleton shook his head. "There was a nurse — Dudley, I think her name was. Said she'd be right back, but it's been almost fifteen minutes."

I glanced at the receptionist on duty — Thelma Umble. Bless her heart, the poor gal has the intelligence of a gerbil and the personality of an artichoke. Or is it the other way around? I had always hoped she would catch one of Melvin's eyes and that he would marry her instead of Susannah. After all, the hospital receptionist and the Chief of Police were not only double first cousins, but third cousins five different ways — or was *that* the other way around? Anyway, when my sister's marriage to the mantis became a fait accompli, I had to adjust my thinking. The descendants of this Umble-Stoltzfus union would have been genetic wildcards that might have eventually threatened national security.

Pasting a friendly smile on my mug, I waltzed over to the receptionist's desk. I don't mean that literally, mind you, ever aware that dancing is a sin.

"Thelma, dear, what's keeping Attila the Hun so long?"

Perhaps I should mention that Thelma is a natural blonde who dies her hair brown. "Ooh," she squealed, "is this a riddle? I just love riddles."

"Sorry, but this isn't a riddle. I just want

to know what's taking that battle-ax of a nurse so long."

"I heard that!" Nurse Dudley has a voice that can be picked up by a seismograph — one all the way out in California. She also possesses the stealth of a Siberian tiger.

I am not exaggerating when I say I jumped out of my shoes — well, one of them anyway. A word of advice: a snoop should be just as careful about mending her stockings as she is about wearing clean underclothes.

"Nurse Dudley," I gasped, "how very nice to see you."

"Miss Yoder! Didn't I tell you to never set foot on these premises again?"

"Well, technically, it's only one foot. And then just my big toe, which is unfortunately poking through that hole." I shoved the offending foot back into its brogan.

"Get out of my hospital," the battle-ax bellowed, as fine cracks appeared in the plaster on the walls.

"Not until Alison gets help. And besides, I came here on police business. You don't want to be cited for obstructing justice, do you?"

Nurse Dudley knew that I often functioned as the mantis's mind, but she didn't have to like it. She scowled so deeply one could have planted corn in the furrows of her brow.

"Very well. I'll have the doctor see her in a minute. But first, what is this police business all about?"

"I need to see the corpse that was brought in this morning."

The furrows grew so deep I could have planted onion sets in them. "This better be on the level."

"As level as my chest." I said it soft enough so that Buist Littleton wouldn't hear. Of course, it's no secret that I'm a carpenter's dream, but why advertise it to men, even if I am engaged and he's married?

Nurse Dudley saw her opportunity to pounce and grinned in triumph. "You are as flat as a board, so I'll take that as a yes." You can be sure she didn't whisper.

I blushed as I addressed the Littletons. "Please stay with Alison for a minute." I turned back to Nurse Dudley. "How do I get to the morgue?"

She handed me a ring with just one key on it. "You'll need this. Go through those swinging doors, make a left, and it's the door at the end of the hall. The storage unit has only three drawers and he's in the middle one. There's a box of surgical gloves just inside the door if you need to touch him."

I shivered at the thought. I shivered again when I entered the ice-cold room. But I went numb with shock when I opened the middle drawer.

12

The body before me was not only stark naked, but it had once belonged to someone other than Buzzy Porter. As soon as I could react, I closed the drawer and mumbled an apology. Nurse Dudley was going to pay for her practical joke. I didn't know when, but I did know how. She and Dr. Luther liked to golf together. I'd seen the pair on many occasions, whacking the little white balls early Sunday mornings at the Bedford Country Club. At that hour they were the only ones on the course. I didn't belong to the club, by the way, but had to drive by it on my way into town to buy doughnuts for the Sunday school class I teach. (There is nothing wrong in bribing fifth and sixth graders into being cooperative.)

At any rate, I would make it a point to get up extra early one Sunday. A couple of bags of marshmallows scattered about the greens should prove frustrating, especially if my hunch was right and the confections swelled up from the dew. Then we'd see who laughed last.

Still mumbling, I opened the top drawer, which slid out far too easily. It was empty. I jerked open the bottom drawer, and it came nearly all the way out, knocking me flat on my bony behind.

"Ding dang darn!" I said. If I didn't mend my ways soon, I would surely turn into a potty mouth.

The drawer had come at me so fast because, like the top one, it was empty. I glanced around the room, which was barely more than a cubicle. An icy cubicle. There was nowhere else to look for a corpse. I tugged the middle drawer open again, and risking blindness, scrutinized the body more carefully. Primarily the face.

I had been able to immediately discern that the body wasn't Buzzy's, because the last time I saw him he had dark hair. The body in front of me was blond — everywhere, including the eyebrows. The eyes were closed, but the patrician shape of the nose was familiar. In fact, it looked a lot like Ron Humphrey's nose. I leaned in closer, breathing in the sickly sweet smell of death. It *was* Ron Humphrey in the drawer.

Anticipating my collapse, I voluntarily connected my derriere with the concrete floor. I don't know how long I sat there — maybe five minutes — as I screwed up my courage to continue my investigation. When the time was right I struggled to my feet, all the while giving audible thanks to the Good Lord for creating me with such big ones. With enough warning, and if I planted my tootsies just right, I could fall asleep standing up. Anyone who doubts my ability to do so should ask Reverend Schrock. It's been said that even the Almighty falls asleep during his lengthy prayers.

But before taking my lock-kneed position, I did something I never would have imagined. I donned a pair of the surgical gloves. Alas, there were no masks visible in the room, or else I would have worn one as well.

A closer look involved the support of every inch of my tootsies. Ron Humphrey's body was a waxy blue-gray, almost translucent in appearance. If it weren't for his distinctive proboscis and somewhat unusual hair color, I would have never recognized the man. Death is more than the absence of life; it is the absence of essence.

As an Episcopalian, Ron had existed on

the fringes of our close-knit community. He and I had locked horns on a few occasions, mostly over alcohol-related issues, but we were not enemies by any means. I found him to be affable and generally very well informed. To my knowledge, everyone in Hernia regarded the young man as a hardworking citizen, deserving of the same respect afforded everyone else. He had no enemies that I knew of.

I gingerly touched one arm in a farewell gesture. It felt cool through the thin layer of latex. This meant nothing from an investigative point of view, especially since I had just taken the corpse out of cold storage.

"Good-bye, Ron," I said, since I was totally alone with the body. "I'm sure some Episcopalians find their way into Heaven, and if you're one of the fortunate ones, please say hello to my mama and papa. But if you run into Granny Yoder — well, even up there I suggest you run the other way."

Of course, Ron didn't respond, so I got right down to business. There appeared to be no unusual marks on his head. His chest looked fine as well — wait a minute. There was a small dark gray hole just below his left nipple. I hadn't spotted it at first, given that it was hidden by a mat of curly blond hair. If my hunch was right, the lad had been killed by a bullet through the heart.

Dead folks seldom cooperate when you try to turn them, and Ron was no exception. I managed to pivot him onto his right shoulder so that his back was off the floor of the drawer at a forty-five-degree angle. There didn't seem to be an exit wound, although his dorsal skin was a pale purple, a sign that blood had begun to collect there. I poked his shoulder blade with a gloved finger. Ron's skin blanched at the point of contact.

I set him down and removed the gloves. I am not skilled in forensics, but I had learned all I needed to know. At least for now. After saying a prayer for wisdom — and a second, backup prayer for patience — I strode off to find the two people who could give me some answers.

It was a slow day at Hernia Hospital, and I found the first of my targets in the staff lounge, polishing off a glazed doughnut. Nurse Ratchet — I mean Nurse Dudley — looked a bit glazed herself. It was a pleasure to disturb her sugar-induced reverie.

"You've got the wrong body in there," I barked.

Nurse Dudley fumbled with her doughnut before dropping it in the lap of her pristine uniform. As any sensible person would do, she snatched up the morsel and popped it in her mouth. She also swore at me, which is just plain not nice.

"What are you doing in here anyway?" I said. "Where is my Alison?"

It was no surprise that she spoke before swallowing. "The brat's gone home."

"Home? But she had appendicitis!"

"She had a bad case of indigestion, that's what."

"Indigestion?"

The ill-tempered woman arranged her sugar-coated lips in what was supposed to be a triumphant smile. To me it looked more like she was trying to imitate a cat swallowing a canary. Unfortunately, the poor bird was still visible in her mouth.

"Dr. Luther knows how to deal with snotty delinquents. Right away he got her to confess that she'd eaten six fried apple pies and two funnel cakes. Miss Yoder, don't you believe in teaching your foster child the basics of nutrition?"

Alison has more faults than the State of California, but nobody gets to criticize her except for her birth parents. And, of course, me. My hackles were hiked so high at that point, I could have won a Louisiana cockfight with a ten-foot rooster.

"She is most certainly not a delinquent! There is no school until Thursday." I prayed for more patience before continuing, but I've learned that it is best not to wait too long after that prayer, lest it really come true. "You'd know that little fact, dear, if you had a child of your own. Oh, and one more thing — apple pies *are* a balanced meal, just as long as you drink plenty of milk."

The nasty nurse has enviable bosoms — actually, she is top-heavy altogether — and she had to struggle to maintain her balance as she stood. "Get out of my hospital, Yoder!"

"*Your* hospital? I was always under the impression that Dr. Luther was in charge."

"Out!" she bellowed through a spray of sugar flecks.

Although she was advancing on me like a bull in heat, I did the knee-lock thing again and stood my ground. "Well, since it is your hospital, maybe you can explain why you have the wrong body in your matchbox-size morgue."

Some people can feign bewilderment, but I honestly think Nurse Dudley lacks the guile to do so — although she definitely has the bile. She scrunched her forehead in genuine astonishment.

"What do you mean the wrong body? There is only one in there."

"I know that. But the body in there belongs to Ron Humphrey, not Buzzy Porter."

"Hernia's Ron Humphrey? That cute Episcopalian boy?" That was, by the way, the first nonconfrontational sentence I'd ever heard her speak. Her sudden passivity, and the fact that her skin was as pale as Buzzy's when I first saw him in the woods, confirmed my hunch. The woman was rude and incompetent, but she wasn't hiding anything.

"Follow me," I said.

It was a silly thing to say. Nurse Dudley bolted for the morgue, with yours truly close on her thick foam rubber heels. When she stopped in front of the drawer, I nearly ran into her. Her rear end is very well upholstered, so I wouldn't have been hurt by the collision, but there is no telling what she might have done to me afterwards.

She panted like a spent sprinter for a minute before finding a voice. It certainly wasn't hers. Nurse Dudley sounded like a grade-school girl in a screaming contest.

"It *is* Ron Humphrey!"

"That's what I said."

"But it wasn't him when they brought him in. I mean —"

"I know what you mean. Somebody switched bodies, right?"

"Right. Magdalena, you do believe me, don't you?" It was the first time she'd ever used my Christian name. This was turning into a banner week for me.

"Let's say I believe you, what possible explanation could there be for this?"

She shrugged shoulders that would have looked at home on a quarterback. "I just know I had nothing to do with this, and neither did Dr. Luther. We've been together all morning — well, not *together* together, but when we didn't have patients we were taking advantage of the lull to take inventory."

"Are doughnuts on the list?" I know that was wicked and unfair of me, but the woman had been a thorn in my side for many years.

"One has to take a break sometime."

The tiny room had two doors. I pointed to the one I had yet to use.

"Where does that go?"

"That's our rear exit door."

"But it isn't marked. And what kind of

cockeyed committee would issue a permit for a building in which one has to exit through the morgue?"

She didn't hesitate. "You should know. You were on it."

I swallowed my irritation. It's one of the ways I maintain my weight.

"You should have that marked," I said. "And you know, don't you, that it needs to be unlocked at times when people are in the building?"

"It is unlocked — that's why I gave you a key. We only lock the inside door to the morgue."

I sighed. Nurse Dudley and her doctor compatriot both had the reasoning power of teenagers. On the other hand, their illogical minds had given me the edge that I needed to secure their cooperation. At least for the near future.

"I hope you realize, Nurse Dudley, that if someone reports this violation, the county can shut you down."

"It can?" Her tone was actually respectful.

"You bet your bippy, dear."

"What do we do about it?"

"Either leave this door unlocked" — I pointed to the door that led back into the hall — "or have a contractor put in a new outside door somewhere else. But if that's the case, clear the plans first with the planning committee. In any event, you'll need to erect a proper exit sign."

"That's it?"

"Pretty much — oh, but I need to speak to the ambulance crew before I leave."

"You just did."

"I beg your pardon?"

"Magdalena, you know that we're not really a hospital — not in the traditional sense."

"You mean not accredited."

"Whatever. But we do the best we can to meet the needs of the community. Why, next year we're thinking of hiring another doctor and maybe two more nurses."

"Good for you, dear. But what did you mean by saying I'd already spoken to the ambulance crew?"

"Like I've been trying to explain, we can't afford to keep a standing crew. When the call came in this morning we hadn't opened yet, so Dr. Luther and I answered it ourselves."

"Isn't that illegal? Aren't paramedics supposed to be specially trained?"

She snorted, then caught herself by clapping a man-size mitt over her mouth. "You can't get any more trained than Dr. Luther," she finally said.

"Nurse Dudley, in addition to contacting the planning commission, I'd contact a lawyer and ask him or her to check on all the necessary regulations for running this sort of enterprise."

"That means you're not going to snitch?"

"No, I'm not going to snitch."

"Promise?"

"I promise."

"Then get out of my hospital, Miss Yoder!"

I held up my skinned hands. "But I'm wounded. I need medical care."

"Out, before I throw you out!"

"Promises are made to be broken," I said over my shoulder. It was wise to retreat while I still had the upper hand — even if it was missing part of its epidermis.

I tried calling Melvin on my cell phone. While I despise it when other people steer with one hand, I always seem to have a good excuse. And what could be more important than a body switched in a mini-morgue? Besides, I have exceptional hand-eye coordination, if I must say so myself. The only person who ever beat me at jacks when I was a little girl was Gertrude Plank

— and she had seven fingers on her right hand.

But our Chief of Police was simply unavailable. Even the 911 number didn't work. I had no choice but to swing by the station and wait for a warm body to show up. In the meantime I dialed home.

"Jimmy, is that you?" a girl's voice said.

"Alison?"

"Mom?"

"Sweetie, you're supposed to answer 'PennDutch.' "

"Sorry mom. Hey, do ya mind getting off the phone, because Jimmy said he was gonna call right back."

"Are we talking about Jimmy Mast, who, as we've discussed a million times, is far too old for you?"

"He's seventeen, which is only four years older than me."

"Yes, but at your age you have to figure the difference out in dog years. Think of Jimmy as being twenty-eight years older than you. That would make him forty-one."

"Gross. That's ancient. No way I'm gonna date anyone that old."

There was no point in reminding her just then that she wasn't going to date anyone — period — until she was older. At least not for another two dog years.

"Sweetie," I said as sweetly as I could, "did you have anything to eat at the tractor pull this morning?"

"Man! Somebody busted me, didn't they?"

"I'm afraid so."

"And them Southerners seemed like such nice people."

"It was Nurse Dudley, dear."

"Figures. Oh well, go ahead and yell at me, Mom."

"I'm not going to yell, Alison. I think you already learned your lesson. Now, put Freni on the phone, please."

"I can't."

"Why can't you?"

"She quit."

"What? She just unquit a few hours ago."

"Yeah, but you see, that nice Japanese lady and them farmer hicks —"

"You mean the Nortons, dear."

"Whatever. They went into Bedford and came back with fancy groceries and the Japanese lady is going to make everyone lunch. Something called terry yucky. Oh, and she had to buy herself some new clothes too, on account of you."

"It's not my fault that cabdriver hasn't

been caught. And by the way, that's teriyaki, dear."

"Whatever. Mom, do I have to eat it?"

"No." Normally I would have said "yes" — both to teach her a lesson about gorging on pastries and to expose her palate to a wider range of tastes, but I was miffed that my guests had commandeered the kitchen.

"Cool. Mom, you're the best."

"Remember that the next time you're tempted to say I'm the meanest mom in the whole wide world."

"Yeah, yeah, whatever."

"Alison, dear, did you still want to go to the greased-pig chase this afternoon?"

"Nah. I want to hang out here. My stomach still hurts."

"Okay, but Jimmy does not come over. Is that clear?"

She mumbled something un- intelligible.

"I said, is that clear?"

"I heard ya. And anyway, he can't come over because he's going to be in that stupid pig race."

"It's not a race, dear. It's a chase."

"Whatever. Can I go now?"

"Yes, dear," I said. My tone was still sweet, even though my patience had been stretched as thin as phyllo dough.

Frankly, I was glad my charge had decided to stay home. It was time to take my investigation of Buzzy Porter's death to the next level. I decided to skip the police station and go straight to the heart of Hernia's law-enforcement team.

13

Zelda Root is our only full-time police officer other than Melvin. She's a short thing with enormous breasts, no hips, and matchstick ankles. In other words, the poor woman is shaped vaguely like a rooster, except that a cockerel has only one breast, and Zelda has almost no feathers. But few people ever notice Zelda's intriguing physique, not if they get a gander at her head first. Her bleached hair is short and worn in spikes, like greasy porcupine quills. As for her face — don't get me wrong; there is nothing inherently homely about it. The fact is Zelda applies her makeup with a trowel, making even Tammy Faye seem like a minimalist. For years there were rumors that Jimmy Hoffa was alive and well and living in Hernia, disguised by layers of Maybelline.

Since there had been no sign of Zelda downtown, I had a hunch I'd find her at home. Sure enough, her beat-up 1978 blue

Oldsmobile was parked in the carport adjacent to her vinyl-sided bungalow. Zelda never uses her front door, so I knocked on the side kitchen door. Almost immediately I could see Zelda through the unobstructed pane. She was teetering toward me on heels as spiky as her hairdo. The second she saw who it was, her puttied face began to crumble.

"Now what?" she said, opening the door just a crack. I could barely fit my nose through the space, for crying out loud.

"Zelda, dear, aren't you going to invite me in?"

"Magdalena, this is my day off."

"It is? Melvin said you would be directing traffic, and whatever else it took to keep those unruly Amish and Mennonites in line."

She shrugged, precipitating a shower of spackle speckles on her broad shoulders. "I put in my application to take today off last year. Melvin okayed it."

"I'm not questioning that, dear. But he probably wasn't remembering the festival. It's been planned for years. A hundred years to be exact."

"That may be, but I'm not working today. I have more important things to do."

"Like what? You're not even enjoying the

festivities. Why, the tractor pull must be half-over by now."

"Yes, but the pig chase isn't until this afternoon."

"And you plan to watch that?"

"I don't plan to watch, Magdalena. I plan to win the competition. The price of meat has been skyrocketing lately."

"Get out of town!" I have my sister, Susannah, to thank for that worldly expression.

She sighed, and I had to dodge a minor dust storm. "Okay," she said, "you might as well come in. You're like a bulldog, Magdalena, you know that? Once you get your teeth into something, there is no shaking you loose."

"I'll take that as a compliment, dear."

She opened the glass storm door and I sailed in. I'd been in Zelda's house dozens of times, so I didn't even wait for the invitation to plop my bony behind in one of her neon orange beanbag chairs. Just as quickly, I hauled my patooty out of the legumes.

"Zelda, do you have company? I hear voices in another room."

Zelda blushed. I could tell, because the cracks on her face, the ones from which putty had fallen, were red.

"That's the radio you hear."

"I don't think so. One sounds a lot like Mary Lehman."

"No, it doesn't."

"And the other one sounds like Esther Rensberger."

"No, it doesn't."

"Zelda," I said sternly, and gave her my best "mom" look.

"All right, I give up. But you had no business stopping by here without calling." Without further ado she led me to her guest bedroom.

The two aforementioned ladies were seated cross-legged on the floor in front of an open closet. A long low table occupied this narrow space. Atop the table was a framed photograph of the menacing mantis, Melvin Stoltzfus, flanked by two flaming candles. Three yellow roses, laid in a straight line, defined the front of this makeshift altar.

Esther Rensberger was the first to her feet. "This isn't what it looks like."

I gave her the look. "Oh?"

"We weren't actually worshipping him."

Mary Lehman is on the heavy side and had to kneel before standing. "She means we don't pray *to* him. We just pray for him."

"But we do sing hymns," Esther said. Although she's in the choir at my church, Beechy Grove Mennonite, her singing voice has been known to make tomcats commit suicide. Reverend Schrock insists that she has a right to be in choir and cites Psalm 100 to support his stand.

"Just not church hymns," Mary said, between pants.

A glance at Zelda's crumbling facade confirmed that our town's policewoman was mortified. She knew I was aware of the shrine she maintained in my brother-in-law's honor, but that was all. Trust me, I wouldn't have dreamed — not in a zillion years — that there could be three people in Hernia this kooky.

I was both appalled and intrigued. "Ladies, please sing one of your hymns."

"They're not really hymns," Zelda muttered. "They're more like odes."

"Then honor me with one of your odes."

"Magdalena, you're mocking us, aren't you?"

"*Moi?* How can I mock unless I have all the facts? What exactly goes on in this room?"

Zelda and Mary exchanged meaning-packed glances, but Esther stepped right up to the plate. "We affirm that Melvin

Stoltzfus," she said, as if reading from a document, "is the most handsome, charming, and intelligent man in the Commonwealth of Pennsylvania."

"You really believe that?"

"He's God's gift to women," Mary cooed.

Zelda uttered a soft "amen."

I treated them all to my most withering look. "God gave that gift to my sister, Susannah. If you want to be recipients, you need to find yourselves another man. Besides, you've got it all wrong. Melvin Stoltzfus is the *least* handsome, charming, and intelligent man in the state."

"Infidel!" Mary shouted, shaking a pudgy fist in the air.

"Blasphemer!" Esther grabbed a rose and hurled it at me. Her aim, like her voice, was far off the mark.

I pinched one of Zelda's elbows with my talons and hauled her back to the kitchen. "Your friends are nuts, you know that?"

"Magdalena, don't be rude."

"Keep them away from caramel, because they could easily end up as PayDay bars."

She glared at me through faux lashes so thick I couldn't see the whites of her eyes. "Why did you come here anyway?"

"Police business, dear. I'm afraid there's

been another murder in town. Two murders, actually."

"The PennDutch?"

"No! Why does everybody assume that?"

"Face it, even Jessica Fletcher wouldn't spend the night there."

"Who is she?"

"Never mind. Who are the victims?"

"Well, a man named Buzzy Porter, for one. He was a guest of mine — but the murder happened up on Stucky Ridge. The second victim was Ron Humphrey."

Zelda teetered on her stilettos. "*Our* Ron Humphrey?"

"I'm afraid so."

"Where did that happen?"

Although Zelda has a decade on Ron, they were well acquainted. Our town has a small closely knit singles group with the disgusting name of Hernia Hotties. When Zelda isn't mooning after Melvin, she attends the functions and, I am told, can be quite the flirt. It was obvious from her fractured face that the news of Ron's death was hitting her hard, so I guided her to one of the beanbags and pushed her gently down. She offered no resistance.

"I don't know where it happened, dear, but I found him in the morgue at the so-called Hernia Hospital. It was supposed to be Buzzy's body in that drawer, not Ron's. I can only conclude that somebody switched them."

"Dr. Mean and Nurse Meaner?"

You see? I'm not the only one who feels this way about the malevolent duo who run our town's only health care facility.

"Yes, but Nurse Meaner swears they know nothing about the switch. Zelda, this time I'm inclined to believe her."

She shook her head in dismay, and chunks of foundation — one the size of New Jersey — flew in my direction. I deftly dodged the Cover Girl comet.

"But he was such a nice young man," she sobbed.

I squatted beside her and patted her awkwardly on the shoulder. I am genetically incapable of displaying any more affection. Seeing how Zelda is a distant cousin of mine, I'm sure she understood.

"Yes, he was. And even though he was Episcopalian — well, I'm sure the Good Lord makes exceptions from time to time."

Zelda turned to look at me. The Jamaican bobsled team could do their practice runs in the ruts she presented.

"Does Melvin know about this?" she asked.

"He knows about Buzzy. I've been trying

to reach him to tell him about Ron — but I can't locate him. That's why I'm here."

"Do you know where *she* is?"

"I assume you mean my sister. And no, I don't know where she is. But she isn't home. I thought maybe the two of them were out raising campaign money, and had clued you in."

I had to dodge several asteroids when she shook her head again. And it may just be my imagination, but I thought I heard the faint cries of miniature Jamaican bobsledders as they plunged to their deaths.

"We never speak about what he does with *her.* Magdalena, you're always coming up with bizarre theories. Do you have any idea why somebody would kill Ron Humphrey?"

"He was the one who discovered the first body. Maybe the killer was hiding and saw Ron Humphrey at the site — although why he or she didn't just kill Ron then . . ." I shrugged. "Murder never really makes sense."

"Yes, it does."

Oh yeah, smarty-pants? That's what I *wanted* to say. Instead I arranged my equine features into what approximated a smile.

"Would you like to explain this murder, dear?"

"I'll give it a try," she said, without batting a false eyelash. "But first you have to start at the beginning."

I pointed with my chin to the guest bedroom. It sounded like a hive of bees had invaded Zelda's house.

"Oh, don't worry about them, Magdalena. Now they're reciting the One Hundred and Seventy-seven Virtues of Melvin the Magnificent. It usually takes us an hour."

I would have retched, had not my overtaxed nervous system already consumed all the fuel I'd stoked it with at Doc's bountiful breakfast. Instead, I rolled my peepers like a petulant teenager. If Mama were right, and one of them stuck in a strange position — well, at least Melvin the Magnificent and I might finally see eye to eye.

"Okay," I said, "I'll start from the beginning. But I'll need some snacks. Got any chips and dip? No pun intended."

"Very funny, Magdalena." But Zelda has Mennonite blood flowing through her veins, and a satisfying midday munchie was soon to follow.

"It's very simple," Zelda said, as soon as I was finished with my account. "The murder of Mr. Porter was not premeditated. The perpetrator didn't have a gun, so he or she sneaked up on this guy and bashed him on the back of the head with the most lethal thing he or she could get his or her hands on — in this case a shovel. But you see, even if the perpetrator was immediately aware that he or she had been observed, there was nothing they could do about it then. I mean, you can't sneak up on somebody when you've been spotted. Magdalena, even you should know that."

If Zelda's homemade molasses cookies hadn't been so good, I would have objected to her statement. "Yes, but the person who killed poor Ron Humphrey *did* have a gun. Are you suggesting there are two killers?"

"Of course not. The perpetrator *then* got a gun and shot Ron."

I cogitated on that while the cop cult in the next room chanted their ode. They were up to virtue number ninety-three, which was about Melvin having the wisdom of an owl. A bird brain beats an insect brain in the pecking order of intelligence, but sometimes one has to settle for the second-best insult.

"Amen to that!" I shouted.

Zelda snatched the plate of cookies away.

"Your sarcasm is not appreciated, Magdalena."

"Sorry, dear," I said in hope of more treats. "But even if your theory is right, what would be the motive? What is so special about a time capsule? Even if it were to contain some deep dark secrets of the past, well" — I laughed pleasantly — "that was a hundred years ago."

My hostess risked losing the rest of her makeup to give me a vastly overblown look of incredulity. "Some things can never be forgotten, Magdalena."

"No fair! I didn't know Aaron was already hitched when I married him."

"Maybe so. But the capsule didn't have to contain something negative to make somebody want to dig it up. Maybe there's something positive in there — like maybe a treasure map."

"Don't be silly, Zelda, we're hundreds of miles from an ocean." Too late I remembered the cookies.

"I didn't mean a pirate's treasure, Magdalena. But you've heard the stories."

"Stories?"

"You're being coy with me, Magdalena."

"But I'm not! I don't know what you're talking about."

She cocked her head, precipitating a

sudden shower of spackle. “Well, well, well. Imagine Magdalena Yoder not knowing about Hernia’s hidden treasure.”

14

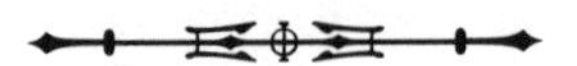

"So clue me in," I cried.

She took her sweet time in responding. Meanwhile the voices in the guest room informed me that Melvin's one hundred and thirteenth virtue was virility. They didn't stop there, but went on and on about what a studmuffin he was. After listening to this litany of lascivious praise, I would either have to poke out my mind's eye, or never look in my brother-in-law's eyes again.

"I can't remember any details," she finally said, "but it was something my grandmother prattled on about. Something about there being this enormous fortune hidden somewhere around town. I remember looking for it when I was a little girl — digging in the garden with my mother's spade. Of course, I never found it. Later on I learned that my parents thought it was all a bunch of hooey. Only the old folks took it seriously."

Zelda's parents, like mine, had long

since left their earthly bodies. There was no sense in talking to her mother. My mama on the other hand, does talk to me from her celestial perch — but she never says anything I want to hear. "Magdalena, are you still slouching? Put your knees together, child. Do you really think you ought to be driving such a fancy car? Don't marry that man, Magdalena — you'll regret it if you do." You see what I mean?

No, what I needed to do was to consult one of our town's old-timers. But who? Harriet Berkey was one hundred and four, but she suffered from dementia. Irma Yoder, a distant cousin, was almost that old, but she had a tongue that could slice cheese. Come to think of it, a lot of Hernia's elderly women had rapier-sharp linguae. Perhaps it was something in the water. Much safer to question an elderly gent.

But who? Wilbur Neubrander was pushing the century mark, but he had a reputation for letting it all hang out. Literally. I have not been privileged to witness this display, but from what I hear, I haven't missed much. Donald Rickenbach was ninety-five, but had already migrated to Florida for the winter season. That left Meryl Weaver, Doc Shafor . . .

"Toodle-oo," I said, springing to my feet.

Zelda scrambled to her feet as well. "You can't go, Magdalena."

"Of course I can. Oh, those cookies were delish by the way — although next time you might consider adding a tad more ginger."

"But Esther and Mary are just about to reach the one hundred and nineteenth virtue. That's when they have to do a little dance called the Shake-and-wag-your-heinie-poo."

It was the perfect excuse for me. "Dancing is a sin," I cried, and fled the den of iniquity.

Old Blue must have been on the ball again. Doc met me at the end of his drive. He had his thumb out like a hitchhiker. I stopped and lowered the passenger window.

"Going somewhere, mister?"

"Yeah, straight back up this drive, where we're going to have ourselves a nice lunch."

I gestured for him to get in. "Doc, I came to talk, not eat."

"There's no reason we can't do both, is there? I'm making pork chops, macaroni and cheese — not the kind from a box, but the real stuff with lots of extra-sharp cheddar — green-bean casserole, and wilted-endive salad with bacon dressing. And, of course, fresh-baked rolls. For dessert there's blackberry cobbler, or we can hand crank some ice cream. Better yet, we'll put the ice cream on the cobbler. What do you say to that?"

"Doc, do you always eat like this?"

"Folks as blessed as we are who only eat to live, and not the other way around, are missing half of life's pleasures."

I didn't dare ask what the other pleasures were. "Okay, count me in on lunch, just as long as I can ask you a serious question."

He made me wait on the shop talk — as he called it — until my second helping of warm cobbler. The mound of rich, high-in-butterfat ice cream was melting like an iceberg at the equator, and I tried in vain to catch all the sweet rivulets with my spoon. Finally I gave up and stirred them into the black goo.

"Doc, have you ever heard of buried treasure in Hernia?"

"You mean like a pirate's treasure?"

"Not a pirate's treasure, but nonetheless, something very valuable." I slurped a spoonful of blackberry cream. "Sounds silly, doesn't it? But Zelda Root claims it's true. Says the old folks — her grandmother, for one — used to talk about it all the time."

"Oh, that." He took a huge bite of his dessert just to torment me.

"Well? Speak with your mouth full if you have to. I won't fine you for doing so. I promise."

He chewed twenty times before swallowing. "It's not a buried treasure, it's a huge parcel of land back in the old country."

"Switzerland?"

He nodded. "You're a descendant of Jacob Hochstetler, the patriarch, aren't you?" He used the original German pronunciation.

"Of course. Mama was a Hostetler. You know that. And Papa was descended from Jacob in at least two ways."

"Do you own the bible?"

He didn't mean *the* Bible, by the way. The *Descendants of Jacob Hochstetler*, originally published in 1911, remains the most comprehensive genealogy devoted solely to the offspring of this important Amish settler. Written decades before the invention of the first computer, it lists nine thousand coded individuals, all of whom are cross-referenced. Jacob was born in 1704, but it has been estimated that now, three centuries later, close to a hundred thousand people can claim him as an ancestor.

"Yes, Mama passed her copy down to me. What about it?"

"It mentions the treasure."

"No kidding! I thought that book was just a bunch of begots."

Doc laughed. "There's a lot of interesting family history in there. But the treasure stories — and there are a number of variations — are conjecture. The version I heard from my daddy isn't even in the book."

"Tell it anyway!"

"Well —" He reached for his spoon, all the while grinning like a Cheshire cat on steroids.

I slapped the utensil out of Doc's hand. "Tell it now, or I'll never eat another bite of food in this house again."

Doc sobered instantly. "Daddy's version had it that our ancestor Jacob was forced from his land by the Swiss authorities, who considered him a threat because of his religious convictions. To avoid accusations of outright theft, they made Jacob sign a document that said they were leasing his land from him for the next two hundred and fifty years — a quarter of a millennium. At the end of that time his descendants were free to claim it, if they provided proof of kinship. Of course, poor Jacob had no choice but to sign the paper."

I sighed. "I'm sorry for what happened to Jacob, but I don't see of what importance that is today. I mean, how is a few acres of bucolic Swiss countryside such a big deal? It certainly isn't worth killing for — not that anything is."

Doc shook his hoary head. "And I always thought you were a dreamer. Well, let me tell you why this would be such a big deal — *if* it were true. According to the oral tradition in my family, those few acres were really hundreds of acres, and what's more, they were located in what is now the heart of Bern."

"Switzerland?"

"No, Berne, Indiana. Of course, Switzerland. Magdalena, the Hochstetler fortune, as described by my daddy, would be worth millions. Maybe even billions."

I pushed my lower jaw back into speaking position. "And all one has to do is show kinship?"

"That, *and* provide the lease."

"Which, of course, nobody can do — wait just a minute!" I had to wait as well, because my heart was pounding so hard Doc's pork chops were doing the rumba in my belly. I tried to breathe deeply, but couldn't get air past my esophagus. "What if," I finally managed to say, "the lease document has been buried in the time capsule all these years?"

Doc slapped his knee. "That's my girl. There's your famous imagination. Unfortunately, that scenario is just not possible."

"Why not?" The truth be told, the task of locating the missing time capsule had taken on an exciting new dimension. Yes, I am well-fixed financially, but one can never have too much moola. I mean, think of all the charitable donations I could make with that Swiss fortune. And so what if one or two of the donations were to myself?

Doc grinned. "I can read your mind, Magdalena. And that's what I like about you — you're honest with yourself. But it's not going to happen. If the lease document were buried in the time capsule, don't you think someone else would have dug it up years ago? Maybe even a century ago?"

"Poking pins in my balloons is not going to get you into my bloomers — not that anything would," I hastened to add.

"On the other hand," Doc said just as

quickly, "each branch of the family seems to have its own tradition. Local folks either discount the story these days, or assume that the document — if it ever existed — is lost in the annals of history. But it's possible that some of the family branches that moved away had traditions that involved the capsule, or they created their own stories. Family histories, if not well documented, tend to morph from generation to generation, and usually in a favorable direction. That's one of the reasons so many people claim to have royal blood."

"You'd think that trend would have reversed itself in recent years."

"Touché. Magdalena, was the time capsule mentioned in any of the ads the town council placed in magazines?"

"No. There wasn't room for everything. And we still managed to go over the budget. Although we did mention the tractor pull — but only because Sam insisted on it, since it was going to be held in front of his so-called grocery. We made him chip in some of his own dough for that."

"So any descendants that don't live around here, the exiles so to speak, had no clue we were going to dig up the capsule?"

"None." I caught my breath. "Uh, well, I

did send my guests an e-mail of the complete schedule and current weather conditions."

"When was this?"

"About three days ago. I wanted it to reach the Japanese guest, in case she didn't check her e-mail when she traveled. Except at the time I didn't know if she was a he, on account of the name."

Doc licked the last of the cobbler from his spoon. "This isn't much to go on, but you might take a closer look at your guests. Do you think any of them might own the bible?"

I had to laugh. "If any of them have even a drop of Hochstetler blood, I'll eat my prayer cap."

Doc scraped the empty spoon futilely around the inside of his bowl. "I'll make you a bet, Magdalena. If one of your guests turns out to be kin, you have to eat supper with me every Saturday night until Christmas. If they don't —"

"You know Mennonites don't wager."

"I'm not betting money. What's the matter, you afraid you're going to lose?"

Don't throw down the gauntlet in front of me unless you're prepared to lose. "You're on, buster."

"Good. And what is it you want from me

if you win — theoretically, at any rate, since it ain't going to happen?"

"You date Gabriel's mother."

The color drained so thoroughly from the octogenarian's face that I worried I'd gone too far. Three corpses in one day was more than even I, the doyenne of death, could handle.

"I beg your pardon?" he rasped.

"You heard me. You have to date Mrs. Rosen — and I mean take her on a *real* date. Maybe bowling in Bedford and then out to dinner. Or just a nice ride in the country. You could even show her the lights of Hernia from Stucky Ridge."

My friend shuddered. "You know I'm a ladies' man, Magdalena, but that woman is like a bucket of ice water. Make that a million buckets. Heck, the National Park Service ought to ship her out West to put out forest fires."

"Are you backing down?"

He shuddered again. "No. As a matter of fact, I've already started to plan the menus for our future feasts. Next time we'll start out with a nice oxtail soup —"

By the time I got to my car, he hadn't even gotten to the main course. Perhaps I should have lingered, because just hearing Doc talk about food can pack on the pounds, and the Good Lord knows I could use a little extra ballast.

I fled. If I lost this bet Gabriel was going to be jealous, which is not altogether a bad thing, but if I won, I might well be able to permanently pawn his mother off on the good-hearted veterinarian. She might have dampened his ardor with her abrasive opinions, but the woman could cook up a storm. Maybe even a tornado. If her flank steak didn't rekindle Doc's flame, then all his talk was just that.

If I hadn't been in such a hurry to purge my future mother-in-law from my life, I wouldn't have come so close to taking the lives of two pedestrians.

15

Creole Sauce

2 pounds ripe tomatoes (preferably plum or Roma type), or 2 cups canned Italian tomatoes, seeded and chopped, with their juices
2 tablespoons extra-virgin olive oil
3 large or medium shallots, or 1 medium yellow onion, split, peeled, and chopped
1 medium green bell pepper, stem, seeds, and membranes removed, chopped
1 small carrot, peeled and chopped
1 clove garlic, lightly crushed, peeled, and minced
1 small red hot chili pepper such as cayenne, serrano, or jalapeño
A bouquet garni made from 1 leafy celery top, 2 bay leaves, 2 large sprigs thyme, and 1 large sprig parsley
2 ounces lean salt-cured pork or

country ham, in one piece
1/2 cup dry white wine or medium dry sherry (such as amontillado)
Salt
1 large or 4 small scallions or other green onions, thinly sliced

Creole sauce is an important element of many cuisines of the African Diaspora of the Americas and comes in many variations, from the simple *salsa cruda* (raw sauce) of the Caribbean to the suave, complex *sauce creole* of New Orleans's French Quarter. It is an indispensable accompaniment for Grilled Chicken Breasts with Eggplant, Creole Style (Chapter 10), and enhances almost any fried vegetable, seafood, or poultry.

(If you are using canned tomatoes, skip to step 2.) Bring a large tea kettle full of water to a boil. Put the tomatoes into a heatproof bowl and slowly pour the boiling water over them until they are submerged. Let them stand for 1 minute, drain thoroughly, and refresh them under cold running water. Core them and slip off the peelings. Working over a wire sieve set into a large bowl, split the tomatoes in half crosswise, and scoop out the seeds into the sieve. Discard the seeds and roughly chop the tomatoes. Add them to the collected juices in the bowl and set aside.

Put the olive oil, shallot or onion, green pepper, and carrot into a heavy-bottomed sauce pan and turn on the heat to medium high. Sauté, tossing frequently, until the shallot is translucent but not colored, about 4 minutes. Add the garlic and sauté until fragrant, about a minute more. Add the tomatoes, hot pepper (left whole), bouquet garni, ham, and wine. Bring the liquids to a boil, then reduce the heat to medium low and simmer, stirring occasionally, until the tomatoes break down and the juices are thick, about an hour.

Taste and add salt if needed. Stir and let simmer for another minute or so to allow the salt to be absorbed into the sauce. Turn off the heat. Remove and discard the hot pepper, bouquet garni, and ham or salt pork. The sauce can be made up to this point several days ahead. Cool and refrigerate in a tightly sealed container.

Just before serving, reheat the sauce over medium-low heat. Stir in the scallions and serve at once.

MAKES ABOUT 2 1/2 CUPS

16

"I'm so sorry," I cried, mortified at what had nearly transpired.

"That's okay, darling," Capers Littleton said. "You sprayed us with a little gravel, that's all. It's really no big deal."

"But it is a big deal. I wasn't paying attention to the road. I may as well have been yakking it up on my cell phone. Ladies, again I apologize." It doesn't hurt to go overboard sometimes, especially if it can prevent lawsuits.

Terri Mukai bowed slightly. "Perhaps it is my fault. I am not used to cars driving on the wrong side of the road."

"This *is* the right side, dear, both literally and figuratively." I smiled pleasantly so as not to undo my apology. "May I offer you ladies a ride?"

They exchanged glances before Capers answered. "We're on our way to the pig chase."

"Great! So am I."

That was not a lie by any means. But since these two were on my list to interview, I would take a little longer to get there. And where they were coming from was the first question I'd ask. By my reckoning, they were less than a mile from the base of Stucky Ridge and on the side over which the murderer had quite possibly thrown the shovel. What's more, they were on the opposite side of town from Hernia High, where the pig chase was to be held.

"Thanks, Miss Yoder." Capers opened the front passenger door and gestured to Terri to get in, but the younger woman insisted that she would climb into the back. For several wasted minutes I was privy to a battle of manners: Miss Magnolia Blossom versus Miss Cherry Blossom.

We natives of the Keystone state have a different take on politeness. "Both of you hop in the back or you're going to walk."

They clambered in.

"Sorry, Miss Yoder," Capers panted.

"*Gomen nasai,* Yoder-san. I am sorry too."

"Think nothing of it, dears. Oh, by the way, what brought you to this far corner of Hernia?"

"The fall color," Capers said, without missing a beat. "I can't get enough of it.

Back home we get just a touch, and it isn't until much later in the season."

It seemed like a reasonable explanation, but I had a lot more to ask. Although shedding a future mother-in-law is not as important as finding a killer — possibly even a pair of them — it still ranked high on my list of priorities. I decided to drive slowly and make some unnecessary turns, in order to give me more time.

"Well, ladies," I said to my captive audience, "I'm sure you must find our ways very strange."

Terri nodded vigorously. "Yes, you Americans are very strange."

"I wouldn't be calling the kettle black, dear. I meant our Amish and Mennonite culture — not Americans in general. Mrs. Littleton, are there any questions you'd like to ask?"

"Why, yes," she said, stretching the two words into five syllables. "I was wondering what you thought of the movie *Witness*."

I clucked, not unlike my favorite hen, Pertelote. "I don't go to movies. Too much sin on the silver screen to suit me. The Amish don't watch movies either, but I heard that they hated this one."

"How could they hate something they hadn't seen?"

"Well, maybe hate is too strong a word. Anyway, they were very unhappy that Harrison Ford, who was dressed like an Amish man, committed an act of violence."

"Yes, when he struck the boy who was taunting them. I thought that might be the case."

"Ah, so you're familiar with our ways."

"Not really. Just what I've picked up from movies."

In desperation I resorted to trotting out the first thing folks asked me when I visited Charleston, South Carolina, on my vacation a year or two back. "Who are your people, dear?"

She smiled, grateful to be given the chance to impress me. "Well, my mama was a Capers — that's where I got the name, and her mama was a Rutledge, and her mama was a Pinckney, and her mama was a Moultrie and —"

"And your papa — I mean, daddy?"

"Daddy was a Calhoun, and his mama was a Hostetler —"

"Did you say Hostetler?" My heart sank. It's not that I minded eating supper with Doc all those times, but on whom was I going to palm off the pint-size pest that was my future mother-in-law?

Capers blushed. "Yes, just like your

cook's name. Miss Yoder, I can't help that I have some Yankee blood." She clapped a manicured hand over her mouth, no doubt thinking she had offended me.

"Don't worry, dear. We were not all lucky enough to be full-blooded Yankees. Please tell me about your grandmother who was a Hostetler."

"I'm afraid there isn't much to tell. She died before I was born, and Daddy never liked to talk about her — well, anyway, all I really know is that she was from up here someplace. When I saw the ad in *Condornest Travels* I thought this festival of yours would be the perfect opportunity for me to explore my roots."

"But you were too embarrassed to reveal your connection, am I right?"

"Guilty as charged, Miss Yoder." She hung her well-groomed head in shame.

I tried not to see red. It is, after all, the color of harlots. There is nothing wrong with Yankee blood, except when it recycles too often within the same circles. The exact thing, I've heard, happens some places in the South.

"How about you, Miss Mukai? Do you have local ancestors lurking in your family tree?" It was a long shot, I know, but I seem to hit my targets easier when I can't see them. And now that I'd already lost the bet with Doc, I had nothing to lose by her answer.

"I am afraid I do not understand the question."

"Are you somehow related to the Hostetler family, or any of its spelling variations?"

Thanks to the rearview mirror, I could see that my Japanese guest looked like she'd bolt from the car at any second. I pressed the pedal to the metal. With Melvin off doing who-knows-what, and Zelda taking the day off to practice idolatry, who was there to cite me for speeding?

"Miss Yoder," Terri said, after it was clear there would be no escape, "in my country it is best to be one hundred percent Japanese."

"That doesn't answer my question, dear. Do I call you cousin, or not?"

She squirmed. "Yes, I have this Hostetler blood."

"You don't say!"

Capers patted her companion's arm. "Darling, was your grandfather a GI?"

"Don't be silly, dear," I said on Terri's behalf. "Mennonites don't go to war."

Terri shook her lovely black hair. "Oh, but he was a soldier. However, he was not a Mennonite, but of the Amish faith."

I pulled the car over to the side of the road. "Why, that's just ridiculous. The Amish don't go to war either."

"That is true, Miss Yoder, but my grandfather left his people to join the American army. He believed it was not right for others to die in his defense, if he was not willing to help protect his country."

"He fought against Japan?"

"Yes. He was also part of the occupying force after the war. That is how my grandmother met him. When he was released from duty my grandfather remained in Kakogawa and taught English."

"So that's why you speak such lovely English," Capers cooed in her inimitable style. The next time I served squab, I would think of her.

"Yes, Capers, although I do not think my English is so hot — that is the word, am I right? It is my mother who speaks excellent English. I do not think you would tell the difference between her and Miss Yoder, although perhaps my mother is more gentle in her manner."

"Miss Mukai," I said irritably, "can we get back to the part about your grandfather being a Hostetler? Was he from this part of the state?"

She shrugged. "It was a place called Homes County."

"There isn't any Homes County — ah, *Holmes* County. That's in Ohio."

"But there are many Amish there, yes?"

"More than anywhere else in the world. Did he tell you any interesting stories?"

"Oh yes, Miss Yoder. He told me about the Indians who killed his grandmother of many generations. They stabbed her in the back and took her hair — I cannot remember the word for such a thing."

"Scalped, dear."

Capers patted her new friend's arm again. "Aren't these family legends fun?"

"Oh, but this is no legend," I assured her. "The Hostetler — only it was Hochstetler back then — family was attacked by the Delaware during the French and Indian War."

Terri cocked her head. "Were you there, Miss Yoder?"

"Not hardly, dear. It happened in the 1750s."

Capers winked at me. "I read someplace that the elderly are respected in Japan."

I glared at Capers. "I doubt if even in Japan folks live to be two hundred and fifty years old."

"I did not mean to offend, Miss Yoder.

Like Capers, I too have come to Hernia to learn my family's history."

I was at a loss as to how to proceed. I couldn't very well ask the women what they knew about a buried treasure and expect an honest answer. But I could create a legend of my own that would be too enticing for them not to pursue.

"Ladies, I'm sure you have both heard about the family treasure." I paused just long enough to be interrupted which, alas, I wasn't. "Personally, I think the legend is a bunch of hooey. And I ought to know. The treasure is really a large parcel of land in Switzerland, but the deed is supposed to be buried somewhere on my farm. When I was a little girl I must have dug up every square inch — except for under that pile of *haufa mischt*."

"What's *haufa mischt?*" Capers asked.

"Horse manure," Terri whispered.

I glanced at the girl through the rearview mirror, but already she was gazing out the window, looking every bit as composed as a geisha. Since I do indeed have a hefty pile of road apples, as the locals call them, to turn under the soil before the winter rains begin, I decided to carry my little deception one step further. And bear with me, please. Deceiving a murderer — and now that I knew both women had a local connection, they were as guilty or innocent as anyone else in the community — is not a sin. The sort of lying the Ten Commandments warned us about, concerns false testimony against neighbors, not against a pile of *haufa mischt.* Au contraire, the *haufa mischt* was in the middle of a clover field, and Psalm 23 says quite clearly the Good Lord Himself tells us to "Lie . . . in green pastures."

"I keep a pitchfork hanging on the wall just inside the barn," I said. "Along with my other tools. I keep meaning to turn all that potential fertilizer under so it can decompose, but something always comes up. Perhaps when I get around to doing my chores I'll find the deed to that Swiss property. Wouldn't that be ironic?" I laughed pleasantly. "The key to a billion dollars hidden beneath a dung heap."

"Miss Yoder," Capers said the second I closed my yap, "I don't mean to be rude, but it's only five minutes to three, and that's when the pig chase is supposed to start."

I responded by giving the ladies a taste of what Hernians are capable of, should they decide to really hustle. When we arrived at the stadium Terri was the hue of seaweed and Capers the color of cottage cheese. Together they averaged out to a nice mint green, just the shade I planned to paint my bedroom someday.

Of course I got them to the stadium on time. Never mind that they had to sit in the car until they stopped shaking before attempting to climb the bleachers. I had no problem vaulting up the steps to the announcer's box. The problem waited for me at the top.

"Well, folks, if it isn't our most illustrious citizen, Magdalena Yoder. Now that she's here I guess we can start."

There were a few guffaws and a smattering of applause before I got the crowd under control with a glare that would have shriveled Attila the Hun. Then I glared at Lodema Schrock, my pastor's wife. The woman was totally unqualified to announce a pig chase. The only reason we'd picked her to do the job is that the stadium's sound system is notoriously unreliable, and Lodema has a voice capable of waking the dead three counties over.

Reverend Schrock's wife is meaner than Attila and was unaffected by my glare. "Today we have twenty-three contestants — unless Magdalena wants to enter the competition instead of awarding the prize.

If so, you'll be *chasing* the pigs, right Magdalena?"

"Don't push your luck," I growled.

The preacher's pesky partner seemed oblivious to the fact that I donate more money to our church than anyone else. "Folks, she just said she'd enter. How about a round of applause for Magdalena Portulacca Yoder, pig chaser extraordinaire?" Not a soul dared clap, but Lodema dared push me further. "Oops, I just remembered. She can't be chasing pigs; she's engaged to a man of the Hebrew faith. Pork is forbidden in that religion, isn't it, Magdalena?"

I snatched the microphone out of her sweaty little hand. "For your information, Dr. Rosen's religion is the same one Jesus practiced. And Jesus, by the way, chased a whole lot of pigs."

"He most certainly did not!" Like I said, the woman didn't need amplification.

"Perhaps you should read your Bible, dear. In the Gospel of Mark, chapter five, Jesus chased two thousand pigs into the Sea of Galilee."

"Jesus didn't chase those pigs. They were possessed by demons."

"Which Jesus chased from a man. It's all the same."

"Are you trying to rewrite the Bible, Magdalena?"

The crowd gasped in unison. A hunch from a woman might be worth two facts from a man, but heresy from a woman — well, that was practically unheard of in Hernia. I was going to have to dance (and I mean that metaphorically) fast to save my reputation.

"Not only will I chase those pigs, Lodema, I'm going to win this contest. And I'm going to donate the prize money to the Hernia Widows and Orphans Fund."

"We don't have a Widows and Orphans Fund."

I fished in my otherwise empty bra for a handful of twenty-dollar bills. "We do now."

The crowd roared its approval.

Perhaps I've never been a people pleaser, but it's never too late to start. I thrust my hand into the other cup. Alas, my desperate digits encountered nothing but air. Not wanting to disappoint my fans, I held up my purse. It doesn't contain cash, since a bag can be snatched, but it does contain my checkbook.

"And I'll write a check for a thousand bucks as soon as this contest is over."

"Write it now," Lodema shouted.

The crowd cheered its support.

I whipped out my checkbook. "I'm sure Lodema will be happy to match this donation."

"How dare you?" she whispered. "You'll pay for this, you know." She raised her voice a zillion decibels. "I'm only a poor pastor's wife. You're on the church board. You know how much money my husband makes. We can barely afford to put bread on our table."

"Then why not eat cake?"

Please believe me, those were not my words. Okay, so maybe they were. But there were other words interspersed between them. Lots of other words. You see, the school's notorious sound system sided with Lodema and refused to amplify most of what I said, broadcasting only the offending words. Of course that didn't stop the crowd from turning on me. I even heard boos from the Who's Who of Hernia society.

"Shame on you," Herman Middledorf yelled. Because the man is the school principal, he was in the box with us. You can bet the P.A. system cooperated then.

"Yoder, you should apologize to the preacher's wife." The directive came from

Wanda Hemphopple, owner of the Sausage Barn out by the turnpike. She's kin to Lodema, and her lungs are the envy of scuba divers.

Lodema Schrock looked like she'd won the lottery. "What do you have to say now, Magdalena?"

I shoved a fist in my mouth in order to prevent a foot from going in. One can choke on size elevens.

17

Pig chase rules are very simple, but Lodema still botched them. Herman Middledorf had to explain everything to the crowd a second time, in his principal voice, which made the contest seem more like a punishment than a fun-filled event.

"There are now twenty-four contestants, and fifty pigs. When I fire the starter gun, the pigs will be released from that covered holding pen over there. The contestants must wait until they hear the gun before they can cross the ten-yard line — for those of you who don't bother to come and support our games, that's the third white line you see in front of the north goal."

Although his less-than-rapier wit drew only a few laughs — probably all from teachers — the principal beamed. In fact, he stood there so long, beaming silently, that I envisioned a new career for him. Herman Middledorf could be the world's first human lighthouse.

"Move it along, dear," I said kindly, when his audience began buzzing with impatience. "I, for one, don't have all day."

Herman cleared his throat loudly into the microphone in order to silence the throng. Since many of them had, at one time or another, been his students, most obeyed.

"There are two objectives in this pig chase. The first is to be the one who catches the first pig. The contestant who does that gets a hundred bonus points. The second objective is for the contestants to catch as many pigs as possible. And each pig is worth fifty points. When he or she has caught a pig, the contestant will carry it back to the holding pen — the gates will be closed again, although the cover will have been removed. The contestants are to lift their pigs over the sides of the pen and deposit them gently on the ground."

The crowd howled with laughter at this image, but I cringed. The term "pig" generally refers to younger swine, those not yet ready for the market, but even these can still weigh well over a hundred pounds. The last time I tried to lift something that weighed that much, I did not deposit it gently on the ground. Just ask my ex-pseudohusband, Aaron. He claims to have suffered from back pain the rest of our honeymoon.

Herman, energized by the crowd's response, resumed his lecture with vigor. "Coach Neidenmeir will keep track of each person's tally. When all the pigs have been caught and returned to the pen, the one with the highest score wins." He paused. "Oh, did I mention that the pigs just happen to be greased?"

By now the crowd had grown too impatient to give anything back. "Start the chase, start the chase, start the chase . . ."

"You better get down to the starting line," Lodema hissed. "You don't want to miss this chance to play with pigs."

I shot her a new look I'd recently learned from Alison and then hustled my bustle down the bleachers to take my place at the far end of the starting line. The contestants were much friendlier than the spectators, and for good reason. I was, after all, no competition. The others were all high school and college kids — well, except for Zelda Root and Chuck Norton.

Zelda and I didn't exchange words because she was in the middle of the lineup, busily tying her shoes. I was dumbstruck yet pleased to see that she was wearing high-heeled platform shoes that laced up her sinewy calves, almost all the way up to her much-abbreviated skirt. But the second the cat let go of my tongue, I had a question for Chuck.

"What on earth are you doing here?"

His broad freckled face widened even more as he grinned. "Howdy, Miss Yoder. Thought I'd have me a little fun this afternoon. Being a farmer, I've had me some experience chasing pigs."

I glanced at his trademark overalls. "No doubt you have. Where's your lovely wife? Doesn't she want to try her hand at catching a pig or two?"

"Nah. Bibi had her some shopping to do."

"You old farts need any help?" an impertinent youth yelled down the line at us. I recognized the voice as belonging to Jimmy Mast, Alison's recent beau — the one she'd decided she hated.

Of course, all the young contestants thought Jimmy's remark was hilarious and whooped it up like a flock of cranes. Even Chuck chuckled. So as not to be seen as the elderly flatulence I'd just been accused of being, I forced my lips into a lopsided grin.

"It might be you needing the help,

Jimmy Mast. One of my great-grandpas was struck by lightning one day when he was feeding his hogs. Fell right into the pen. By the time my great-grandma found him, the hogs had eaten away his face and one of his ears."

"Ooh, gross!" A teenage contestant by the name of Brandy bolted for the safety of the stands.

"She's just putting us on," Jimmy yelled, but the girl ignored him.

"She's talking smack," a boy said. His accent identified him as Lenny Coldiron, a recent emigrant from the big city with no farming connections.

"Actually, she's got a point," Chuck said, much to my surprise. "Them animals can be dangerous. Especially if they're scared. I once seen a —"

"Take your marks," Herman hollered, and held the gun aloft. The P.A. system was working just fine at the moment, by the way. When Herman finally fired the pistol — I'm convinced he was torturing us in the interim — the amplified explosion sounded like one of the cannons in the Overture of 1812. It's a wonder I was the only one who screamed.

At least I wasn't the only one who stayed put. No one, not even Chuck, put as much as one toe over the line until Coach Neidenmeir opened the gates. Even then only a few of the older boys inched cautiously forward. Jimmy Mast was not among them.

"Here them pigs come," Chuck said. "You better brace yourself, Miss Yoder. Them porkers can weigh a fair amount."

The brave boys stepped back in unison.

I steeled myself for the onslaught of swine. Although the gates to the pen had been flung open, I didn't see any pigs. Finally Coach Neidenmeir tore the canvas top off the pen. A split second later the crowd exploded with laughter.

"Why, them aren't nothing but farrow pigs."

"I beg your pardon?"

"Baby pigs. Just look at them."

I looked. Even though I always ate my veggies, especially carrots, I must have been the last person in the stadium to see the small swine. Finally I got my peepers to focus that far.

Chuck was right. They were no bigger than large house cats. Spotted things that didn't even come up to my knees. They clustered nervously, unwilling, or unable, to face their would-be captors.

"This is ridiculous," I said.

No sooner were those words uttered than the unexpected happened. Coach Neidenmeir, using a push broom, literally swept the piglets out into the open stadium. Once in the open and separated from their litter mates, the little ones panicked and darted, squealing, in fifty directions.

Simultaneously, the contestants diverged in twenty-three directions. Some of them were squealing as well. I was a late bloomer, which is the only reason I can offer for why I was so late in getting started. Most of my competitors were over the fifty-yard line and in contact with the little critters, before I even moved. But believe me, I wasn't scared.

I was, however, annoyed. Zelda's disciples had infiltrated the stands, and had apparently brought reinforcements.

"Zelda! Zelda! Zelda! *Melvin!* Zelda!"

"Cut it out!" I hollered, although it was just a waste of breath.

Turning my attention back to the contest, I noticed that while the others had no trouble catching up with the piglets, once they grabbed the squealing tikes, they were unable to hold on. Of course! The babies had been greased. By this point the crowd was laughing so hard they mercifully drowned out the cult of Melvin.

I pondered the situation. What could I possibly do different? I wasn't young and lithe like the kids. I didn't have the strength of Chuck, or the moral support Zelda had. But surely I had some small advantage — besides my schnoz (I certainly wasn't going to spear the little darlings).

Then it hit me. I'm not claiming the answer came straight from the Lord, but it did come out of the blue, and after all, that's where Heaven is. And by the way, Heaven is directly over North America, quite possibly even centered over Hernia. I heard that straight from the lips of Reverend Schrock. When the Rapture occurs, faithful Christians in Australia and other southern hemisphere locations are going to have to do some fancy maneuvering in order to catch up with the main flock.

My revelation was simply this: I was wearing a dress. As every well-brought-up woman knows, a proper dress has a skirt that extends below the knees and does not fit tightly. Such a skirt can come in very handy for carrying things, although one must take care not to display one's sturdy Christian underwear.

The first piglet slipped through my hands like fog. But on my second attempt I managed to flip the little rascal into my skirt, gather the material into a sort of sack, and sprint to the enclosure — all without losing the precious cargo. The crowd started cheering just as I lowered the piglet, *gently*, into its pen.

By the time I deposited the third little pig, the good folks of Hernia were chanting: "Yoder! Yoder! Yoder!"

I waved to my fans.

The crowd roared in response, although I'm quite sure I heard two boos coming from the reviewing stand. But the latter only served to stoke the fires of my resolve. Within ten minutes I managed to catch and safely deliver every single piglet. By the time the last squealing swine made contact with the grass inside the enclosure, the crowd was on its feet, and the noise it made was deafening. A few folks even threw plastic cups and sandwich wrappers at me — in lieu of roses, I'm sure. For a few minutes I felt like I had single-handedly won a championship football game.

"Beginner's luck," Zelda shouted in my ear, before teetering off to an exit.

The din of the crowd abated only when the faulty P.A. system finally cooperated with Lodema's lungs. "Magdalena," she thundered, "seeing as how you're so rich, I'm sure you'll be returning your prize pig in order to save our beloved town a little money."

"In a pig's ear!" I shouted in return.

Alas, my response was almost as loud as her badgering. It might surprise you to know just how fast a crowd can turn, although no doubt they were egged on by the thumbs-down Lodema Schrock and Herman Middledorf were giving me. But despite the rain of lunch and snack accouterments, I took my time in selecting the perfect piglet — one that looked like it would grow into just the right combination of ham, bacon, pork roast, and chops. Oh, and four nice pickled feet.

Alison's jaw dropped when she saw the squirming youngster. "Oh, Mom, is that for me?"

"In a manner of speaking, dear."

"Donna Wylie has a pet pig, and it's just the coolest thing." My foster daughter threw her arms around me and the swine, dirt and all. "Thanks, Mom. This is the best present I ever had."

I struggled to disengage myself from her embrace. "But, dear, this little fellow is not going to be a pet. When he grows up he's going to be breakfast, lunch, and dinner."

It took a minute or two for my words to register. "Ya gonna *eat* him?"

"We both are. That's where bacon comes from, and you love bacon."

She stared at me. "Ya sure?"

"Positive."

"Man, then I ain't ever gonna eat that stuff again."

I couldn't help myself. "And veal comes from calves. And, of course, hamburger is ground up cow muscle, with some fat thrown in. Steak is —"

Alison clapped her hands over her ears. "Ya don't need to say any more, because from now on I'm a vegetarian."

"But you love hamburgers. And hot dogs."

Her hands weren't soundproof. "So? I still ain't eating them. And you can't make me."

I read somehow that the wise parent knows when to pick her battles. I'm sure Mama didn't teach me that lesson, because I didn't dare cut my hair or wear trousers until the day she died. I still don't do these things — Mama has a habit of turning over in her grave with such force that, if harnessed, the power could supply all of Pittsburgh's electrical needs. But I, Magdalena

Portulacca Yoder, was not about to follow in my mama's boat-size footsteps, even if they did match mine.

"Okay, you can become a vegetarian, but make sure you get enough protein."

Her eyes registered disbelief, but she shook her head in mock nonchalance. "No prob. Stacy at school is a vegetarian, and she gets all the protein she needs from peanut butter and eggs."

"Good for Stacy. But you might want to substitute beans for eggs." Perhaps it was mean of me, but I couldn't help it. You see, one of Alison's favorite foods was fried-egg sandwiches slathered with ketchup.

"How come I shouldn't eat eggs?"

"Because eggs come from chickens, and chickens are definitely meat."

"Yeah, but eggs ain't. They're just eggs."

"They're potential chickens, dear. You don't think they develop into cabbages, do you?"

She stomped her foot. "Ah, man!"

The piglet squealed loudly, startling me so much I dropped him. He wasn't hurt, mind you, because he landed on my foot. I hopped around on one size eleven while Alison chased my future pork roast around the ground floor of my inn. The two of them disappeared into the kitchen — an appropriate place, I thought — but when they emerged a few minutes later, Alison was cradling the pig like he was a baby.

"Oh, Mom, I just love him. I'm gonna name him Babe, just like that pig in the movie."

"But Babe is what Gabe calls me! And sometimes I call him Babester."

"Yuck. But that don't have nothing to do with this. *He*," she said, planting a kiss on the swine's snout, "is gonna be named after that movie. And, Mom, I promise to walk him every day. I'll even bathe him so he don't stink — although Donna Wylie said her pet pig didn't never stink. Please, Mom, pretty please? You'll make me the happiest girl in the whole world."

My heart has a higher melting point than most, but already I could feel it trickling down around my intestines. How could I refuse to give this child the gift of pet ownership?

"There will be no need to bathe or walk him, dear. He can have that paddock on the east side of the barn. The corner by the barn is always nice and muddy."

"But, Mom, he's gonna live inside."

"Over my dead body." Over my mama's dead body as well. I was surprised the ground hadn't started to shake.

"Hey, no fair! Donna Wylie gets to keep her pig inside."

"The Wylies aren't Mennonites."

"What's that supposed to mean?"

"They lack the clean gene," I said as kindly as possible. "Besides, you should be glad I'm even agreeing to let you have him for a pet at all."

"That mean ya ain't gonna kill him when he gets big?"

"Not so long as you take full responsibility for taking care of him. Because if you don't, I'm changing his name from Babe to Ham."

Alison's face went through multiple transformations. In the end she settled on a huge smile.

"You're the best mom I ever had, ya know that? I mean my real mom woulda never even let me keep him."

"Really?" Alison's "real" mom was the wife of Aaron Miller, my ex-pseudohusband. She lives in Minnesota with Aaron. The couple was unable to control the child, so a judge gave Alison the choice of living with me, or reform school. I got lucky. I would like to say that I never think of the woman, and that I certainly do not compare myself to her, but if I said that — well, I'd be lying. How can I not compare myself to the woman my Pooky Bear never divorced, and into whose perfumed arms he ultimately returned?

"Yeah, really," Alison said. "Mom, ya can be kinda dorky, ya know that?"

"I'll take that as a compliment."

"But I love ya anyway."

Before I had a chance to faint, she reached up and planted a kiss on my bony cheek. It may have been totally accidental, but I'm sure I felt a pair of whiskery pig lips as well. I managed to lock my knees into place.

"I love you very much too, dear."

"Gross, Mom, don't get mushy."

"But you just said —"

"Sheesh! 'Love ya' and 'I love you very much' — they ain't the same. The first one ya say to your mom, but the other one is for your boyfriend. Don't ya know anything?"

I shook my head. Not only was I feeling mushy, I was positively high on love — conditional though it may be. With the exception of Freni, the Babester, and my sister, I couldn't think of any others who truly loved me. So you see, it was euphoria that clouded my judgment, just as surely as if I'd drunk a pitcher of mimosas.

"Oh, what the haystack. You can keep

him inside — for now. But when he gets bigger we'll have to negotiate. In the meantime, ask the Wylie girl how she housebroke her pig, and I expect you to quickly and thoroughly clean up any mess."

Alison's eyes glowed with appreciation. Undoubtedly she would have slipped into pure mushiness had the front door not opened with a bang. While she tried to soothe the startled swine she cradled, I glared at the intruder.

"You better learn to knock," I growled.

18

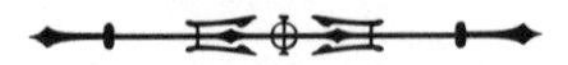

"Whatever you say, Yoder." But Melvin was not about to apologize. He swaggered up to us like he owned the place. I wouldn't be surprised to learn that he believes someday he'll own the inn, by virtue of his marriage to Susannah. If so, what he's forgotten is that arthropods — even extraordinarily large, two-legged ones — don't live as long as humans.

"What is it you want?" I snapped.

"See ya guys." Alison took the opportunity to flee the room before my irritation with her "uncle" escalated to the point that I took my feelings out on her and reversed my decision on the pig.

Melvin hadn't even bothered to greet his niece. "Yoder, I'm here on official business. We need to talk."

That was for certain. "Melvin, have you been drinking those garlic milk shakes again?"

"They're garlic soy shakes, Yoder. And I

just finished one. What about it?"

"Well, unless you want to be responsible for manslaughter, I suggest we repair to the parlor, and sit on opposite sides."

"For your information, thanks to those shakes, I haven't had a cold in three years."

"That's because the viruses die before they can even get close to you."

Without further ado I led the way into the parlor and closed the door tightly behind us. Then I straightaway picked the most comfortable seat for myself. My bony butt is far more sensitive than his crusty carapace — well, it usually is. Melvin winced when his newly recontoured derriere connected with the hard seat of one of Grandma's straight-back chairs. He ended up reclining on one buttock, which somehow caused him to look like he was sitting straight.

"Indeed," I said, "we do need to talk. I've been trying to reach you for hours. Where have you been?"

"Don't be a dingus, Yoder. I just said I was working on a case. In fact, I'm about to make an arrest."

"You are?" I was too astonished to be sarcastic.

"That's what I said. You deaf, Yoder?" He barreled ahead before my sarcasm gene could kick in. "Who's your worst enemy?"

"Melvin, I think you're capable of many things — perhaps even metamorphoses — but murder is not one of them."

"Not me, you idiot. I'm talking about Lodema Schrock."

My blood raced with excitement. Oh what schadenfreude I'd feel if only it were true. How sweet life would be once my pious pastor's partner was put in the poky. What joy to know that the tart-tongued gossip would never be free to harass me again. There was just one thing wrong with this picture — Lodema Schrock was even less likely to commit murder than Melvin. At least she had a modicum of brains to stop her.

"What's your evidence, Melvin?"

He arranged his mandibles into what approximated a sneer. "Well, I dropped by the reverend's house this morning. Wanted to ask him if he'd say a few words over the deceased — you know, like the Catholics do. Read him his last rites, that kind of thing. Anyway, the reverend was home, working on next Sunday's sermon, but Lodema was out."

"So?"

"So, she was out running. Practicing for the marathon — just like Ron Humphrey."

"Which means?"

He sighed, and the scent of garlic sailed across the room to assault my nostrils. "Yoder, it's a good thing you're not the one in uniform." He tapped his head with a hairless knuckle to indicate that I wasn't the brightest bulb in the chandelier. "It's as plain as day. The two of them were in cahoots. Together they killed Mr. Porter, and then while she made off with the time capsule, he distracted us by pretending to find the body."

"I see. You're saying that Lodema Schrock, who has all the upper-body strength of a rubber chicken, ran off with a chest that might well have weighed thirty or forty pounds? Perhaps even more, if all the things that are rumored to be in it really exist."

"Looks can be deceiving. I bet you some folks would be surprised to know that I can bench-press two hundred."

"Doughnuts?"

"Very funny, Yoder. I asked the reverend where exactly his wife was running, he said he thought she'd gone running in the direction of Stucky Ridge."

"I see. But tell me this, Melvin. Why would Ron and Lodema be in cahoots? They hardly know each other. And why would they wait until now to steal the time capsule? Why not take it a year ago? Or two years ago? Or in Lodema's case — since she's supposedly so strong — why didn't she swipe it ten years ago, before Ron moved here? Then she could have kept what's in it all to herself?"

Melvin's left eye was spinning like a pinwheel in a hurricane, while his right eye appeared to be studying a dust bunny under my chair. After all, I don't claim to be the most thorough of housekeepers.

"Yoder, consider this your opportunity to learn at the foot of the master. The two of them are lovers. She waited until now because — dang it, Yoder, I'm the one who's supposed to be asking the questions."

I disguised my smile by pretending to yawn. "Melvin, dear, what I was trying to reach you about is this — Ron Humphrey is dead."

Both eyes stared at me. "*Dead* dead?"

"Possibly even triple dead. I examined his body in the morgue myself."

While he processed this shocking information (a stranger might have concluded that he'd slipped into a coma), I wrote up a mental shopping list. With Freni in quit mode, I would have to dart into Bedford and pick up some of those frozen dinners I've heard so much about for the last forty years. The weather was still mild, and with any luck, my guests might not object to eating cold food. I also needed to buy some toilet tissue, laundry detergent, and bar soap. It might surprise you to know that finicky guests insist that their Lifeguard not have any previous lives.

Melvin groaned as he emerged from his reverie. "Yoder, these murders are going to ruin my chances of being elected to the legislature."

"Maybe, maybe not. It depends on how quickly we solve them."

"Believe me, Yoder, I don't want to move in with you any more than you want me to. Probably less."

"*What?*"

"Oh, didn't I tell you? I've decided to retire from the department at the end of December. Although, maybe I should resign right now, so I can throw all my energy into the election."

"Why on earth would you resign?"

"Susannah wants to start a family, and she doesn't want me in a dangerous job. So if I lose — well, there's no way we can afford our house payment. Because face it, Yoder, I don't have many other skills."

"Not to worry, dear. Your mother still lives on the family farm. She has oodles of room."

He shook his head so vigorously I thought sure it would snap free from his spindly neck and fly across the room in my direction. If so, I'd have to scramble to catch it. A noggin as hard as Melvin's can do serious damage to one's walls.

"Mama's selling what's left of the farm," he said. "She's says it's time for her to move into Rosewood Manor over in Bedford — that's if she can afford it. She's borrowed against the equity so many times there's almost nothing left. Heck, Susannah was supposed to talk to you about this. You know, about making up the difference in case Mama can't afford the rates."

His words sent a jolt of terror through me, one that started in the tips of my cotton-clad toes and ran to the top of my organza prayer cap. I'd be happy to pave the way for Elvina Stoltzfus in her so-called golden years, but I'd rather get hitched to Saddam Hussein than share my home with the mantis and his mate.

"Don't give up so soon, Melvin! Besides, you'd hate it here. We now have a pig in residence."

"Don't be so hard on yourself, Yoder."

He was deadly serious, but I chose to ignore the comment. I'd just had a brainstorm, and since that region is becoming increasingly arid, I needed to act on it as soon as possible.

"Why don't you two move in right now on a trial basis?"

"Uh —"

"I mean it. You'd have to sleep right here in the parlor on a roll-away, but that shouldn't be a problem. This batch of guests goes to bed early, and you two are night owls, right? Of course you'd have to do chores. I'm not a sexist, so I don't care who does what — but someone has to run into Bedford this afternoon and do the shopping. Meanwhile the other can be cleaning the bathrooms in the rooms of those who opted out of A.L.P.O. Oh, and you'll find a pile of dirty laundry in the —"

"Forget it, Yoder. My Sweetykins and I have far too much pride to be manual laborers."

"So you're not going to quit after all?"

"Don't be ridiculous. I was just kidding about moving in."

"Good. So maybe now we can talk about the switched bodies."

"You're nuts, Yoder, you know that?"

"Call me Macadamia, but if you don't

hush up and listen to what I have to say, you'll be scrubbing toilets before you can spell my new name."

The miserable mantis was suddenly as mum as a politician on a polygraph.

"So you're one hundred percent positive that the corpse you delivered to the morgue was Buzzy Porter?"

"Like I said, Yoder, you're nuts. From the time you left, until the ambulance arrived, I didn't leave the body alone for a second."

"Yes, but did you ride with it to the hospital?"

"Of course not. I drove the cruiser down."

"But you saw Dr. Mean and Nurse Meaner unload the victim, right?"

"Yeah." He shifted in his seat to alleviate the pain Granny's hardwood chair was inflicting on his bottom. "Yoder, we got ourselves a big problem on our hands, don't we?"

"The biggest, dear. Perhaps we should call the sheriff in on this one. Maybe even the F.B.I. I mean, kidnapping a corpse has got to be a federal crime."

The look of abject terror on my brother-in-law's face was almost touching. No doubt he believed that if we sought outside help, his reputation would suffer. But au contraire. The good folk of Hernia have no delusions about their chief's competency. If he asked for outside assistance, the majority of us would view it as a sign of latent intelligence.

"Okay, okay, we don't need to call the sheriff — at least not yet. I believe that both murders are tied to the time capsule box, and" — I lowered my voice so that there was no chance Alison could hear us, should she be trying to listen in — "I think that at least one of my current guests might be involved."

He rolled an eye, but refrained from commenting.

"I'm also convinced that the motive is a treasure — in a manner of speaking — the key to which is a document that has been in that box all these years."

"You mean the Hochstetler fortune?"

It's a good thing I don't wear dentures, or I would have had to waste precious time rinsing them off.

"You know about this fortune?"

"*Supposed* fortune, Yoder. Anyone with any brains knows that it's crap."

"Do tell."

"It's supposed to be in a cave, you know.

I looked for it all the time when I was a kid. Been inside every cave and abandoned mine shaft in Bedford County but never found a damn thing. Nothing, zilch, nada."

"Don't swear in this house, Melvin." My words may have been chiding, but my tone wasn't. Frankly, I was intrigued. I'd known the police chief his entire life, and I had never pictured him doing childlike things. Childish, yes, but not childlike. The image of a large-headed little boy tramping around in the woods looking for caves was almost endearing. "Did you do this by yourself?"

"Don't be mean, Yoder. You know I didn't have many friends. Of course I was alone. Almost died one day too, on account of those caves can be dangerous. Once, when I was about nine, I slipped inside a cave on some mud and knocked myself out. I have no idea how long I was unconscious, but when I came to I was seeing double and had a lump on my head the size of my fist. It wasn't until the swelling finally went down that the doc noticed an actual depression. Here, you can still feel it."

He was out of his chair and headed my way before I could stop him. "Bull!" I shouted.

He retraced his steps. "I'm not lying, Yoder. Susannah sometimes parks her gum there when she goes to sleep."

"I believe you have the dent, but it was caused when that bull kicked you. You know, the one you were trying to milk."

"Don't be ridiculous, Yoder. I didn't milk the bull until high school."

I smiled, vindicated. "Melvin, did your family tradition mention a specific cave?"

He gave me a look that would have withered a water-logged cactus, had there been one in the room. "There is only one tradition, Yoder. You ought to know — seeing as how you think you know everything. Mama said the right cave was the one at the bottom of Stucky Ridge. Her mama's mama's mama told her that. I only looked in the other caves because I couldn't find —"

"There's a cave at the bottom of Stucky Ridge?"

Melvin smiled, looking rather vindicated himself. "So you don't know everything."

"Quel surprise." I glanced at my watch, which, by the way, is a conservative Christian model. "Do you know what time it gets dark now?"

"When the sun goes down, of course. Although in the summer it sometimes stays light a while longer."

"Stay right where you are," I ordered.

"Can I at least sit in your chair?" he whined.

I said he could. Then I hurried off to find Alison. Alas, the child was happily bathing the pig named Babe — in my bathtub! I made a mental note to invest in Purell stock, but refrained from lecturing her just then.

"I'm leaving a note on the dining room table. The guests are supposed to make their own supper, but they have to pay extra for the privilege. You, of course, don't have to pay. In fact, if you cook something for them — like maybe scrambled eggs and toast — I'll double your allowance this week. And in case I'm not back at your normal bedtime, put yourself to bed. And no, you may not go over to a friend's. I need you here tonight. Any questions, dear?"

Alison seemed remarkably unperturbed by my instructions. She kissed Babe on his pink, plasticlike snout before answering.

"Can Donna Wylie come over to see him?"

"If one of her parents does the driving. I don't want to come back and find Jimmy here."

"Mom, you're so silly. Who needs boys when I've got him?"

Oh, the wisdom of youth. I planted a kiss on the back of Alison's head and sized Babe's head up for head cheese — it would take a few years — and then skedaddled. My bothersome brother-in-law just might have accidentally babbled some useful information. It was time to go spelunking with the Stoltzfus.

19

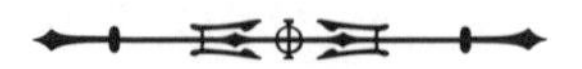

Tourists like to think that Hernia is all gingerbread Victorian houses surrounded by neat Amish farms. The truth is we have a slum, albeit a rather small one. There are two streets on the south end of the town that we locals shamefully refer to as Ragsdale. I know it's a sin to judge others on their lack of material possessions, and I promise to repent for even sharing this bit of information. And not that it's a valid excuse, but the habit was ingrained in us as children.

When Susannah and I were girls (at separate times, of course), our school bus used to stop in this part of town to take on students. It was common knowledge among us children that the Ragsdale kids were a breed apart. Some of them sported tattoos, many of them smoked, and on at least three occasions Miss Proschel, our bus driver, had to confiscate knives. Like many other stereotypes in this world, Ragsdale's reputation was based on both fact and fancy.

The neighborhood remains poor, but frankly, today I feel safer walking through it than I do visiting Foxcroft, our newest subdivision. Foxcroft, by the way, is where Susannah and Melvin live, in a house that can be distinguished from its neighbors only because my sister ignores the covenants and hangs scarlet drapes at the windows. Anyway, in the last five years since its establishment, Foxcroft has seen a homicide, eight cases of nonlethal domestic violence (that have been reported), four break-ins, and a rash of mailbox bashing. In that time period Ragsdale has been virtually crime free.

Melvin and I drove separately, agreeing to park in front of the "Block House." This residence is locally famous because the Strubleheimers, who own it, have eighteen wheelless vehicles up on concrete blocks. Most of the cars lack glass panes and are therefore home to numerous small mammals. When this unsightly collection began, the animals were primarily mice and rats. Over the years the rodents have been replaced by cats. At one point the feline population was so large that it rivaled that of the Roman Coliseum, or so experienced travelers tell me. Recently some of our more wealthy citizens, yours truly included, have been sponsoring the spaying and neutering of these mousers. The furry explosion has halted, although occasionally one still sees a kitten or two playing in the shade of the mounted wrecks.

One might think the town could do something about this eyesore, but alas, the Strubleheimers have a grandfather clause that dates back to the days when a Struble-heimer ancestor ran a repair shop for Model A Fords. It is said to have been the first in the county. And anyway, the sad truth is that as long as the mess doesn't spill out of Ragsdale and into Hernia proper, most folks don't care. The only complaints we on the town council get are from tourists who accidentally stray from the official sightseers' route, the one marked Highway to Heaven on our give-away maps.

Melvin and I picked this spot to rendez-vous because the Block House sits at the end of Tar Shingle Alley, the closest one can drive to this flank of Stucky Ridge (the portion directly below Lovers' Leap). My brother-in-law assured me that there was an actual path that wound among the rusting hulks and into the tangle of woods that hugs the base of this outcrop. As a boy, bent on discovering treasure, he was forced to run through the maze of vehicles, and not because the supposed Ragsdale bullies were after him, but because of the giant rats. If he is to be believed a rat the size of Robin Williams — but not quite as hairy — knocked him down one day, bit his ears, and probably would have eaten them had not our hero remembered that he had one of his mother's cookies in his pocket. He fed the confection to the rodent, which immediately toppled over dead. *That* part of the story I believe.

As soon as I got out of the car on that otherwise pleasant September afternoon, the scent of ammonia nearly overwhelmed me. I would either have to beef up my contributions to the spaying fund or start feeding the cats Elvina Stoltzfus's cookies. Of course I am joking, but it was no wonder that Blue's sniffer had gone berserk when he stood at the edge of Lovers' Leap.

"Melvin, do you think any of them have rabies?"

"Don't be such a scaredy-cat, Yoder. I got bit by a rabid rat once, remember? Didn't even get any treatment for it — and look at me."

"That's why I asked, dear."

The cats were obviously used to being

fed, and the real danger came from tripping over them as they vied for our attention. By the time I got halfway to the woods, I had a live leg warmer wrapped around each ankle. A few of the persistent pussies even followed us into the dense undergrowth at the woods' edge. Finally the going got so tough, even they became discouraged and turned back.

"Melvin, you said there was a trail."

"There is, Yoder. Can't you see it?"

"I can barely see you — not that I'm complaining."

"See that? I carved that notch into that tree when I was just a kid. That was over thirty years ago and it's still there. Look, there's another."

I didn't see a thing except dying leaves and brambles. At one point, while trying to protect my face, my still-sore right hand snagged on a blackberry vine. If Melvin hadn't sounded so cocksure, I would have turned back and joined the pussies. A bird in the hand might be worth two in the bush, but a hand in a bush — well, that can be mighty painful.

There simply isn't all that much woods between the Block House and the ridge, so Melvin must have led me in concentric circles. It got to the point where I wouldn't have been surprised if we suddenly stumbled onto the Pacific Ocean. A sweating Stoltzfus and a scratched Sacagawea, that's what we were.

The panting mantis finally stopped, and I came within inches of smacking into him. "It used to be right there."

"What? Where?"

He pointed at the ground just in front of him. "The cave, you idiot. I swear that's where it was."

That's when I first noticed that we were standing at the base of a sheer rock wall. Funny how I hadn't noticed the ridge through the trees. At any rate, there was nothing to see where Melvin pointed except leaf clutter and a few half-rotted branches. It was what one might expect on the floor of any dense woods.

"How can you be sure this is the spot?" A terrifying thought had just occurred to me. Sure, Melvin had managed to find the cliff, but by way of San Francisco. No doubt it would be ten times harder to find our way back to the Block House. We might even get so lost we could wander over the border into Maryland, a situation for which we were not prepared. After all, one should never venture into Maryland without provisions.

"I'm positive this is the right spot, Yoder, because there're my initials again. I carved them into the rock with the knife Mama gave me for my ninth birthday."

"Elvina Stoltzfus gave *you* a pocket knife?" It's a good thing nobody else knew that at the time, or Melvin's mama would surely have been cited for child endangerment.

"Don't be ridiculous, Yoder. It was a table knife — but it did have a serrated edge."

I shuffled through the leaves and sticks to get a closer look. While I couldn't be certain Melvin had carved them, there were indeed initials.

MS loves MY.

"Who's MY? Mabel Yutzy?"

Unable to decipher Melvin's low mumble, I guessed again.

"Marilyn Yost?"

"Don't be mean, Yoder. I was just a kid."

"I'm not being mean. Marilyn Yost is a beautiful, talented woman. It's too bad she can't seem to stay married. And just in case you're getting ideas — remember that you're married."

"It wasn't Marilyn Yost, damn it, it was you!"

I recoiled right into a veritable thicket of

blackberry vines. So shocked was I that I forgot to chide Melvin for swearing. In fact, I didn't even feel the pain of a thousand thorns.

"What did you say?"

"You heard me. But like I said, I was just a kid, and you were so — uh, well, magnificent."

I thrashed free of the thorns. Try saying that five times in rapid succession. Perhaps then you can imagine what it was like for me to spit out anything coherent.

"B-but I'm eleven years older than you. I would have been a twenty-year-old woman."

"Yeah," he said, sounding wistful. "And what a woman. Smart, funny, sexy —"

"Aack!" I clamped bloody hands over my ears, but a fat lot of good that did.

"I mean it, Yoder. You are — I mean, were — everything I wanted in a woman."

"A carpenter's dream?"

"I like flat-chested women. I married Susannah, didn't I?"

Oh what a laugh the Good Lord must be having. The same Magdalena Portulacca Yoder who never had a date in either high school or college, and who had come to think of herself as the poster woman for maiden ladies everywhere, was really a sex goddess.

"Melvin, please tell me you no longer feel that way about me."

He brayed like a donkey, which was, to say the least, disconcerting. There are no wild asses in Pennsylvania, and it was still a good two months until deer season, but some hunters break the rules. And neither of us was wearing red — although one of us was starting to see that color.

"What's so funny?" I demanded.

"You got to be kidding. Of course I don't feel that way now."

"Oh?" It's much nicer to be lusted after than laughed at.

"It's because you've gotten arrogant, Yoder."

"That's not true! I've always been conceited."

"You think you're so much smarter than me. You're always putting me down. Susannah, on the other hand, builds me up. Makes me feel like a man."

"I never realized she was such a hard worker."

"You see what I mean?"

Sometimes I think I'm diagonally parked in a parallel universe. Even just this morning I would have thought this entire scenario was about as likely to happen as — well, me allowing a pig to live in the inn.

And almost as surprising was the fact that I wanted to argue with Melvin, to convince him that I was still worthy of his affection. Not that I was attracted to him, mind you, but isn't it human nature to want to be liked? Yes, I'd detested the man all these years (in a loving, Christian sort of way), but I hadn't known there was a time when we could have actually been civil to each other.

But instead of making a fool of myself, or lapsing into familiar sarcasm, I decided to practice random acts of intelligence and senseless acts of self-control. At least until we got back to the safety of civilization. And believe you me, eighteen wheelless cars and a hundred-odd cats were starting to seem pretty normal.

"Melvin, dear, perhaps the cave and your initials are farther apart than you remembered. After all, you were a little boy."

He grunted, which I took as agreement. I began to follow the cliff face in one direction, and he in another. After about fifty yards I gave up, but only because the sheer wall had given way to a steep, but wooded slope. The terrain no longer jibed at all with Melvin's description.

When I returned to our starting point, I learned that he had not been successful either. "It's a trick, Yoder."

"What is?"

He nodded in the direction of the initials. "I know I carved them above the entrance, so this isn't the place. Must have been Buffalo Mountain I was remembering — like you said, I was just a kid back then. Must have carved my initials in two places."

"Melvin, only a goat kid would confuse Buffalo Mountain with Stucky Ridge. Even you —" I've bitten my tongue so many times, that I have permanent indentations for my teeth. In fact, it doesn't even hurt anymore.

"You see, Yoder? This is what I mean. When you were twenty, you weren't mean like this."

That, however, hurt. "I wasn't trying to be mean. I was backing you up. If you remembered there being a cave here, there must have been one.

He snorted, sounding more like a horse now than a donkey. "Caves don't just disappear," he said. "It's not like there was a magic rock you rolled over the opening."

"Yes, but there could be another explanation." I stared at the rock face and the ground in front of it. Just a solid expanse of rock and wet leaves — suddenly my heart was beating even faster than it had on my wedding night to that cad Aaron Miller. "Melvin, when is the last time it rained?"

"How should I know? I'm not a meteorologist."

"You'll be seeing stars if you don't give me a quick answer."

"August — but I don't know when. Like I said, I'm not a weatherman."

"Are you sure it hasn't rained since August?"

"Positive. Every Labor Day my Sweetie Pot Pie and I spend the night in the backyard. It's kinda a tradition, I guess. We put up our pup tent just in case it rains, but if it's really nice we — well, some things are more exciting if they're done outside. Not that you'd understand, Yoder. "

"And I don't want to," I wailed. "Now, can we get back to the task on hand?"

"You're the one who asked."

"Look at those leaves," I ordered. "The ones by the wall, just below your initials. Do you see what I see?"

"You mean ugly wet leaves?"

"Exactly. But if it hasn't rained for at least a couple of weeks, how did they get wet?"

I may as well have been asking sheep geometry questions. The mantis's minuscule brain couldn't even begin to think of an answer. His left eye stared at me balefully, while his right eye studied the tops of his shoes.

"I give up, Yoder. How?"

"Because those leaves were on the bottom of the forest litter until very recently." I found a sturdy stick and turned over a patch of dry leaves some distance from the cliff. Sure enough the leaves next to the ground were wet and clumped together like cold broad noodles. "See what happens?"

One of the lights went on in my nemesis's noggin. "Yeah, I see what you mean. But what does it prove?"

I strode back to the cliff. "The leaves here are a bit deeper. It's a wonder we didn't notice it before, but they look as if they've been piled up. See how they slope away from where I'm standing?"

Another light switched on. "But, Yoder, the entrance to the cave wasn't just a crack along the ground."

"It might not have seemed that way to a little boy. Here, help me." I started to push leaves aside with hands that felt like I'd run them through a blender. Unless you tried it yourself, you wouldn't believe the number and variety of creepy crawly things that inhabit piles of rotting vegetation.

Melvin just stood there.

"Help me," I said.

"Can't, Yoder. I have allergies. Leaf mold exacerbates them."

"If you don't help, you won't get any credit for what we discover."

He dug like a dog that smelled a bone — one with a three-pound steak attached to it. Because the leaves had recently been disturbed and the heavy wet bottom layer redistributed, we cleared the ground at the base of Lovers' Leap in no time.

"Still no cave," Melvin moaned, as we used our feet to scrape away the last of the fallen foliage.

"But look — fresh dirt! There definitely is something here that's been covered."

Because my modesty precludes the wearing of fingernails that resemble painted claws, I had nothing to lose by digging in the soil with my hands — except for my last remaining shreds of skin. Melvin, who does wear clear polish — thanks to Susannah's influence — was again reluctant to dig.

"Melvin, you have to help me."

"Your shoes are the size of boats, Yoder. Why don't you use one for a shovel?"

He needed incentive. "When I describe this to the newspapers, I might accidentally refer to you as a sissy."

He dug like a dog again. Within minutes we had uncovered what was indeed the entrance to a small cave. At least a small entrance to something. It was perhaps six feet long, but only eighteen inches high. When I stepped back a few paces, it appeared to be nothing more than a dark gash at the cliff's base.

"Oh yeah," Melvin said, in a maddeningly offhand manner, "it was kind of a tough squeeze at that. Funny how your mind plays tricks on you."

"I guess it has to amuse itself somehow in all that empty space." I got down on all fours and peered into the darkness. Darkness was all I saw. "What does your mind have to say about the size of the cave itself?"

"You don't need to be rude, Yoder. That I remember as clear as day. It may not be the biggest cave around, but it's plenty big enough for a bear to hibernate in."

"Bear?" I backed away from the opening and struggled to my feet. Thank heavens I realized my foolishness before Melvin did. "The entrance was disguised, dear. Do bears generally do that before, or after, they crawl in?"

"How should I know?"

Bears, or not, we were running out of daytime. September sunsets can take one by surprise, especially on mild days like this. But we weren't going to get any more work done here without a light source.

"By any chance would you happen to have a flashlight on you?"

"Of course not."

"Me either," I grumbled. "How stupid could we have been?"

"Speak for yourself, Yoder. At least I have one back at the car."

"Be a dear and get it, will you please?"

My gallant brother-in-law charged into the trees. I tapped a long, slender foot — more like a canoe than a boat — as I counted. Before I got to five, he'd returned.

"Very funny, Yoder."

"I do my best. How about matches? Do you have any of those? Or better yet, a cigarette lighter?"

"You know I haven't smoked since I've been married."

"That's right. Since you set Susannah's veil on fire. Well, we're just going to have to come back tomorrow with flashlights."

"Guess again, Yoder. We have a job to do. And anyway, there's no point. I searched all over that cave — even took a pickax to the floor. Read my lips: There isn't any treasure."

"But there could be a body," I said quietly.

Melvin stared at me. Then he stared at the mouth of the cave. In the deepening shadows it looked as if someone had painted the rock face with a swath of India ink.

"Let's get the heck out of here, Yoder."

20

Grilled Breaded Veal Chops

4 veal rib or loin chops, each about
 3/4-inch thick
Salt and whole white pepper in
 a pepper mill
Whole nutmeg in a grater
Grated zest from 1 lemon
1 tablespoon chopped parsley
1/4 cup all-purpose flour
1 egg, lightly beaten
1 cup dry bread crumbs
4 tablespoons butter, melted
1 lemon, cut into 8 wedges

If you are using rib chops, scrape the meat and fat from the long end of the bone, leaving only the meaty eye of the chop attached. Set the scraps aside for broth. With a mallet or scaloppine pounder, lightly beat the chops until the meat is about 1/2-inch thick. (If you are using loin chops, beat the tougher loin side well to tenderize it.) Sprinkle both sides liberally with salt, several grindings of white pepper, a generous grating of nutmeg, lemon zest, and parsley. Lightly press the seasonings into the meat.

Put the flour, egg, and crumbs into separate shallow bowls. Lightly roll each chop first in the flour, then dip it in the egg until it is well coated and roll it in the crumbs. Lay the chops on a wire rack and let the crumbs set for at least 30 minutes.

Prepare a grill with hardwood coals or preheat the broiler for at least 15 minutes. When the coals are glowing red but lightly ashed over, spread them and position a rack about 5 inches above them (in the broiler, about 5 inches below the heat source). Brush one side of the chops lightly with the butter and put them on the grill, buttered side toward the heat. Grill/broil until the crumbs are toasted golden brown, about 3 minutes. Brush the uncooked side with butter, turn, and grill until they are evenly browned, about 3 minutes more for medium rare. If you prefer the veal more done, move the rack a couple of inches away from the heat and grill/broil about 1 to 2 minutes more per side for medium. Don't overcook them or they will be tough. Serve hot, garnished with lemon wedges.

SERVES 4

21

Melvin and I agreed to meet at the Block House at seven in the morning. We would both bring flashlights. In addition, he would bring rope and I would bring provisions. I wanted to be prepared in case the cave was larger inside than he remembered, and we accidentally ventured over the state line into Maryland. I was, however, anything but prepared for what greeted me at the inn. The second I set foot over the threshold of the kitchen door, Gabriel grabbed me by an arm and pulled me the rest of way in.

"Where have you been?" he demanded.

"Gabe! What are *you* doing here?"

"You want someone should starve?" a raspy female voice answered.

I glanced around the room, seeing no one. Then I lowered my eyes a few feet. Ida Rosen was standing at Freni's stove, her back turned to me. She appeared to be stirring something. If it hadn't been for that movement, I would have dismissed her as an apron, or a tea towel, tucked dangerously into the handle of the oven door. Even I know that a talking tea towel makes no sense, but it had been a long day.

"Good evening, Mrs. Rosen," I said. I stretched every syllable Tennessee thin to give myself time to cool down. It was the same as counting to ten.

"Sure, maybe for you." She turned to face me. "But it is not such a good evening for me, or for my Gabriel."

"Ma!" Gabe protested, but the old woman shot him down with a look that should be studied more closely by the Pentagon.

"I vas across the road cooking my boy a normal meal, and he gets this call from the little one asking what she should make for supper. Vhat was I supposed to do?"

"Alison called?"

"Nu, is there another child in this house?"

"But there's plenty for her to eat that doesn't require cooking."

Ida waved her spatula at the refrigerator. "You call that food? A dog should eat better than that."

"I'll pass that along to Freni."

"First you fire her, and now you vant to

hurt her feelings. Go figure."

"I did not fire her!"

"Ma!" Gabe complained, a convenient three seconds too late.

My future mother-in-law turned back to the stove. Looking over her head I could see that a frying pan and two large saucepans had been pressed into use. A little red light above indicated that the burners were on.

"That looks like an awful lot of food," I observed.

She waved the spatula above her head. "Just a nice brisket I brought over. And some potato pancakes, green beans, tzimmes, and a kugel."

"A what and a what?"

"A stewed carrot dish and a kind of noodle pudding," Gabe said, but he wouldn't look me in the eye.

"That's still an awful lot of food for one girl, even if she is a teenager." I stifled a gasp. "Unless you two are planning to eat with her."

"Ve already ate," Ida snapped. "At the proper time."

Gabe took a hesitant step in my direction. "Don't worry, hon. She said that with Freni being gone, and you unable to cook —"

"Say what?"

"Alison said —"

There was no point in hearing him out, not when I could hear it from the horse's mouth.

I found the horse's mouth alarmingly close to the pig's mouth. Alison was sitting on my bed, holding Babe in her lap, when I barged into the room. I think she'd been about to kiss his spouted little snout, because she flushed with embarrassment.

"Mom, don'tcha believe in knocking first?"

"Not when it's my room, dear."

"Well, before ya go ragging on me, he's clean. I bathed him, remember?"

"We'll talk about you kissing a pig later. I want to know what Mrs. Rosen is really doing in my kitchen."

"Oh that. Ya said if I made 'em supper," she said, referring to the guests, "that you would double my allowance."

"That, I did. But I didn't mention Ida Rosen."

"Yeah, I know, but I got to thinking. I could make them soup and sandwiches, or scrambled eggs or something — but that's kinda boring even for me. Besides, doubling my allowance ain't such a big deal, since ya don't hardly give me nothing to begin with."

"But there isn't anything in town to spend it on!"

"That don't stop you from wanting to make money."

"Yes, but I tithe. I give ten percent to the church, and a whole bunch more to charities."

"That's what I plan to do with my two hundred bucks."

"Your *what?*"

Alison grinned happily. Her pig appeared to smile as well. "I asked them guests if they had ever had authentic Jewish cooking. Guess what? They all said no. So I told them they could have a meal if they paid an extra twenty-five dollars, and they all said yes. Then I called Grandma Ida and told her I was hungry. She said she'd be right over to fix me supper on account of I'm neglected."

"But you're not neglected!" I wailed.

"Yeah, but she thinks I am. Anyway, ya know how she always cooks too much food? I asked her if I could keep the leftovers, see. And she said sure thing, seeing as how ya fired Freni and I'm likely to starve to death, on account ya ain't the world's best cook —"

"I didn't fire Freni! Alison, you have got to stop telling tales — wait a minute. Do you mean to say you're selling our guests leftovers for twenty-five dollars a head, and it isn't costing you a thing, *and* Mrs. Rosen is doing all the work?"

She nodded. "Ya ain't too mad, are ya?"

"Mad? You go, girl!" I said, and gave her the high five.

Of course, she wasn't expecting the gesture, but she's a quick study, and smacked her hand against mine. I yelped with pain.

"What's the matter, Mom?"

"Nothing permanent, dear. I'll be fine. By the way, where are the guests now? This place is as silent as the hospital morgue."

"Ah, they're taking a walk."

"A walk? Where?"

"Herniahenge."

I gasped, depleting the room of its oxygen, the end result of which was that Alison and Babe the pig gasped as well. Herniahenge is strictly off-limits to outsiders.

Lest you think that by now I have permanently flipped my prayer cap, please allow me to explain. Herniahenge is our equivalent of Stonehenge. Geologically it is a cluster of giant boulders, one almost as big as my inn, that some experts claim were pushed into place by advancing glaciers tens of thousands of years ago. Since the world was created no more than six thousand years ago, I find that theory highly unlikely.

More likely, if you ask me, is the growing speculation that these rocks were erected by aliens and serve as a navigational landmark of some kind. I know, many devout people deny the existence of extraterrestrials. But that's only because they have yet to meet the Mishler twins, who at age eighty-seven saunter naked around their yard (although in the winter there is really no point). Nor have these doubting Thomases met Wanda Hemphopple, with her potentially lethal hairdo that threatens to topple at every toss of her ornery head. Or what about Zelda Root, who keeps her face together with spackle and is the leader of a cult of Melvin worshippers? And speaking of the Stoltzfus, where do you think John Gray got his idea for men being from Mars?

At any rate, only we locals know about this unusual placement of rocks, and we want to keep it this way. After Stucky Ridge, this is our second favorite spot to picnic and cavort (not me, of course, since I am not the cavorting kind). Thankfully, this geological oddity remains hidden by deep woods — although we did come mighty close to sharing it with the world.

You see, the land upon which these rocks sit used to belong to Aaron Miller Sr., my pseudo ex-father-in-law. At one time he wanted to sell the land to the commonwealth for development as a park. He suggested calling it Herniahenge, or some such similar nonsense. A few of our wealthier citizens (need I say who?) banded together and made Mr. Miller an offer he couldn't refuse. But he was a cantankerous old geezer and did refuse.

Finally, when "Pop," as he still wanted me to call him, began to grope his way through the dark halls of dementia, he suggested that we play a game. If any of us succeeded at the game, we could buy the acreage in question for a dollar each. The object of this farce was to dislodge some smaller rocks that occurred naturally atop one of the tallest and steepest monoliths in the group. We were each assigned a small boulder, visible from the ground, but we were forbidden to use any sort of projectiles, such as catapults, slingshots, etc. Alas, none of us succeeded in getting our rocks off.

But neither could the commonwealth afford Pop's asking price. The situation might have become very interesting, probably even involved a lawsuit, had not Hermoine Liverbottom, an old flame of Pop's, shown up on the scene like an angel sent from heaven. She convinced Pop to sell her the property for a siren's song and a few thousand dollars. Hermoine was forced to make a verbal agreement that she would never sell the property to a resident of Hernia, but that turned out to be a moot point. Three weeks after the deed passed into her hands, Hermoine conveniently died. Shortly thereafter the townsfolk were overjoyed to learn that she had left her entire estate to the town — the only caveat being that the property be called, in perpetuity, Herniahenge.

"Alison," I said sharply, "you can't be sending folks to Herniahenge."

"But it's such a cool place. And anyway, I didn't send them — I led them. They paid me ten bucks each to be the tour guide."

When a smile and frown compete for face space, they can give the impression one desperately needs to use the bathroom. I was forced to look away from Alison, since she has told me on more than one occasion that I am full of it.

"Still, if word gets out — why, we could be overrun by tourists." Even worse, I thought, although I did not say it, my inn could accommodate only a small percentage of the influx.

"Ya worry too much, Mom, ya know that? I said I led them there. I meant that literally. I made them all wear blindfolds and hold hands."

My heart nearly burst with pride. I doubt if a flesh and blood daughter could have made me any happier.

"How will they get back, dear?"

"I'm supposed to pick them up — but of course, Grandma Rosen wants me to eat first." She set the pig on her bed and hopped to the window. "Holy guacamole, it's almost dark already."

"That it is. Look dear, you eat, and then get rid of Ida Rosen as fast as you can. In the meantime I'll lead the troops home."

"Thanks, Mom!" Not to be outdone, Babe squealed his gratitude as well.

I basked in the glow of combined filial and porcine love for a full minute. "Just one thing, dear," I finally said.

She skipped back to our bed. "Yeah?"

"Ida Rosen is not your grandmother. I'd appreciate it if you didn't refer to her as that."

Alison exhaled so hard Babe's ears blew back flat against his head. "Whew, that's a relief. 'Cause I already got me a grandma back in Minnesota, and I don't really want another one."

"Then why do you call her that?"

"She told me to, that's why."

"Well, we'll just see about that," I said, and turned on my narrow heels.

But Alison's role model is not as stupid as she looks. I had no intention of speaking with Ida Rosen until after my guests were fed.

There have been recent rumors of Bigfoot prowling about Hernia and environs, but since the tales were generated by Alison and are, in fact, based on yours truly, I don't put much stock in them. Still, I was somewhat startled to see three shadowy figures stagger out of the woods on the Herniahenge side of the road. Although I was carrying a flashlight, it wasn't so dark that I would stumble. Therefore I decided against turning it on. One must save energy whenever one can, right?

But it is always okay to pray. "Lord, if one of them wants to breed with me, please don't let him be too ugly."

Immediately one of the creatures broke ranks and advanced toward me at an astonishingly fast pace. "Miss Yoder, is that you?"

The voice was unmistakenly female in timbre, so even if it was an attractive Bigfoot bearing down on me, there would be no horizontal hootchy-kootchy in the vicinity of Herniahenge. I must say I was a mite disappointed.

"Miss Yoder, it *is* you!" Octavia Cabot-Dodge's assistant grabbed me by my right arm and pulled me down Hertlzer Road like I was her toy wagon. I tried to dig my heels into the asphalt, but it was a waste of good leather.

"Miss Miller," I protested, "I'm quite capable of walking on my own."

"Yes," she hissed, "but we must stay ahead of them."

"Oh, I get it. You want us to lose them — sort of like a game, right?"

"Don't be ridiculous, Miss Yoder. I have something to say to you that is a matter of life and death."

22

"I'm all ears," I cried. Now it was me who was pulling her. "What's this all about?"

"Your fleecing of America."

"I read that book!"

"I'm not talking about a book. I'm referring to all the ways you have of extorting cash from your guests. It doesn't seem at all like the Mennonite way to me."

I am the first to admit that I don't fit the profile of the typical Mennonite. That doesn't bother me. But there are areas in which I fit the mold quite well. Mennonites are supposed to be humble in their dealings with the world, and quite frankly I am proud of my humility.

"Man does not live on bread alone," I said, quoting the Good Lord himself, and then, because I speak to Him on a daily basis, I felt free to add a few words on my own. "And woman requires meat, fruits, vegetables, and a warm, dry place to sleep. That all takes money."

"Which my employer does not have."

"Get out of town! I mean, I knew Miss Cabot-Dodge is a has-been, but I thought surely she'd managed to sock away some moola in her heyday, brief though it was."

"She tries to maintain that image, but it's getting harder and harder. Have you looked closely at the limousine?"

"No, but if you've seen one, you've seen them all, right?" But even I knew that wasn't true. Colonel Custard, who had the unfortunate experience of dying in my inn recently, owned a limo, the seats of which were covered with the foreskins of stillborn whales.

"Miss Yoder, that limousine is twelve years old. It is in need of new tires. The dress my employer wore to dinner the other night — well, just between you and me, she bought that in a Hollywood thrift shop."

"You don't say. Well, you certainly didn't seem to be bothered by my rates when you booked the rooms."

"I was under orders to conduct business as usual. In the film industry image is everything. No one wants to hire a desperate actress — not one her age, at any rate."

"You mean she plans to make another movie?"

"Can you keep a secret?"

"Are my eyes blue?"

"I don't know, Miss Yoder. They just look dark and beady to me."

"Well, they *are* blue. Yes, I can keep a secret."

She glanced over her shoulder, but at the pace we were walking, there was no way her boss could be close enough to hear us. "Miss Cabot-Dodge is up for a part in a sitcom."

"You mean like *Green Acres*? Now that was a show worth watching."

Augusta Miller snorted, not the wisest way to express oneself on a road heavily trafficked by Amish buggies. There weren't any Amish out and about at that hour, but had there been, we both might have found ourselves behind traces.

"My employer's sitcom — and I have no doubt she'll get the part — is much more sophisticated than that. It's called *Clone on the Range*, and she'll be playing a wealthy widow on a Wyoming ranch who has herself cloned. But you see, the clone — and they're hoping to get Jennifer Aniston for the part — turns out nothing like the donor. That sounds like a winner, doesn't it?"

"Well, frankly —"

"But the thing is, she doesn't have the part *yet.* So all these extra expenses you keep coming up with are proving to be an embarrassment. She feels she has no choice but to say yes, in order to maintain her image as a star."

"Point taken," I said charitably. "I'll only pretend to charge her for the extra privileges. As for you and the chauffeur — well, I'll just say I've changed my policy and servants are no longer allowed to mingle with the rest of us."

"I am hardly a servant!"

I wrenched free from talons capable of eviscerating a marble antelope. "Now, if you'll excuse me, I was headed the other way. The folks at the rocks are going to need help getting back."

By the time I reached Herniahenge the woods were as black as Aaron Miller's heart. Fortunately my big feet knew every twist and turn in the path. When Aaron and I were courting we — never you mind. Suffice it to say, I reached the rocks without as much as stubbing my toes. Apparently, I was pretty silent in my approach as well.

"Of course it's a rip-off." Bibi Norton's voice boomed through the night air. "But Father and I were just saying that we really don't mind paying her exorbitant prices, because of the convenient location."

"They are not such high prices," Terri said softly. "In Japan many hotels cost this much. But Miss Yoder is so — how do you say — bossy?"

At least three people laughed. I couldn't identify the culprits in the dark, but believe you me, I was going to pay special attention the next time we were together in a well-lit situation and someone told a joke.

"She told me the place was haunted," Capers drawled, adding eight more syllables than were necessary. "But I still haven't seen her grandmother's ghost. Now, if she came to my house in Charleston, I could personally introduce her to several specters."

"You're joking, right?" If I hadn't recognized Chuck Norton's voice, I probably would have thought it was a barking dog I heard.

"Oh, no," Buist said. "In the eighteen hundreds a pirate was hanged virtually in our front yard. He had a peg leg, but they took it away from him before they strung him up. I guess it was an early form of recycling. Anyway, we've seen and heard him many times. Usually in the upstairs hallway."

"What do you mean you heard him?" Terri's voice had risen an octave.

"When you first see him he appears out of nowhere, leaning on a cane and asking for his leg back. Keeps asking for it, in fact, until you say 'here it is.' Then he turns and walks away, and you can hear both the cane and his leg clumping down the hall — but you can't see him anymore."

"You never actually see the peg leg," Capers said in a mere eleven syllables.

"There are many ghosts such as this?" Terri asked, now sounding properly terrified.

"They're everywhere," Buist said. "Walk down any street late at night, and half the people you think you see, aren't really there. At least not in a flesh and blood way."

"Remind me not to go to Charleston," Chuck said, and then laughed nervously.

"Oh, that one-legged pirate likes to follow us around. Once he even showed up in our hotel room on Maui. So much for the theory that ghosts can't travel over water."

"I'm not saying that I don't believe you," Bibi blared, "but if you ask me, Miss Yoder embellishes everything. Why, just look at those brochures we got in the mail —

'comfortable accommodations in a quaint, authentic Mennonite setting.' Ha! It wouldn't surprise me if those dowdy clothes she wears are just part of her act."

That did it. If the farmer's wife wanted to see acting, she was in for a treat. I played Brunhilde the Barbarian in a fourth-grade production, and everyone said I was a natural. I would have tried out for Ghengis Khan in the fifth grade, but that's the year Susannah was born, and I was forced to wash cloth nappies by hand while Mama napped.

The first thing I needed to do was to get my ungrateful guests' attention. I did that by moaning. My brief, but bogus, marriage to Aaron had honed both my acting and moaning skills.

Terri responded first. "What was that?"

"Probably just an owl," Buist said.

I moaned again. A long, low sound, quite unlike any owl I've heard. For Aaron it had been a signal that it was time to wrap things up and get the ordeal over with.

Southern owls must have their own vocabulary. "Yes, ma'am, that's just an owl," Buist said. "He's probably just upset that all our talk is chasing away his prey."

It was time to crank things up a notch.

"I want my peg leg."

"What was *that?*" Capers managed to spit that out in just four syllables.

Bibi grunted. "I didn't hear anything."

"I w-a-a-a-nt my p-e-e-e-g l-e-e-e-g."

I think it was Terri who screamed first, but if so, she was joined a millisecond later by the other two women, and at least one of the men.

"And I want it now!" I turned the flashlight on for the first time. I held it so that the business end was pointed up at the underside of my chin. No doubt my schnoz, silhouetted as it was, resembled a peg leg — of course one that hovered well over five feet above the ground. At any rate, the screams were practically deafening now, and involved both men.

A really rude person would have laughed far longer than I did. But really polite guests wouldn't have cursed me either. Eventually we calmed down enough to have a near civil discussion, and I informed them that I had been privy to the harsh comments about me. I'd been hurt to the quick, I said, and it would take me years of therapy to recover. There was no reason to add that the therapist's name was Mr. Hershey and that we had been having a bittersweet relationship for decades. Before that

I had been just plain nuts about him.

"I am so sorry, Miss Yoder," Terri said. In fact, she must have said it a dozen times.

I shone my flashlight in each of their faces by turn. The only one who didn't look at least a mite chagrined was Bibi Norton. She stared placidly at me, like a cow on antidepressants — not that I've seen many of those, mind you. Her brown plastic barrettes glinted like an extra pair of eyes. In a childish fit of pique, I wanted to rip the doodads from her hair and fling them among the scree.

Instead I prayed for patience. Imagine my surprise when I opened my mouth and discovered my prayer had been answered.

"Here, you take this," I said to Chuck, and handed him the flashlight. "A big strong man like you should be leading the way. Just follow this little footpath, and don't worry about getting lost, because I won't let you. And you others be sure to keep up right behind him — hold hands if you must. Mrs. Norton and I will bring up the rear, won't we, dear? We have so much to talk about, both being farm women and all."

Chuck didn't hesitate a second. That surprised me, although I can't say I blamed him. And once he was a couple of yards down the path, you can be sure the others fell right in behind.

Meanwhile I laid a hand gently on Bibi's arm, just in case she bolted. If it hadn't been for her skin temperature, I might have thought I'd grabbed hold of steel cable. You know, a thick one, like they use on the bridges in Pittsburgh.

"Miss Yoder —"

"Oh, you're perfectly safe with me, dear. We won't lag far behind. Besides I thought we might use this occasion to get to know each other better."

"But I suffer from night blindness. Miss Yoder, I could hurt myself."

"Nonsense, dear. Here, take my hand, and follow along right behind me."

This was, of course, a great sacrifice on my part. I eschew the custom of shaking hands, on the grounds that it is the number-one way in which the common cold is spread. And as if the mere thought of manual interdigitation wasn't enough to give me the heebie-jeebies, her hand felt exactly like a pinecone. Perhaps it was a pinecone she'd proffered me, but if so, it seemed to be attached to an arm. I made a mental note to examine the woman closer when we got back to the inn. After all, if pirates can have peg legs, why can't farmers' wives have cone hands?

"Now, dear," I said, when it seemed like we were making progress in our walking, "tell me all about yourself."

Bibi grunted. "Not much to tell. I'm just a simple farm woman from Inman, Kansas."

"What do you farm?"

"Mostly corn and hogs. Although Father put in a few acres of soybeans this year. Said he read in a journal that within ten years, everyone in America will have switched from cow's milk to soybean milk."

"That will never happen," I assured her. "Can you imagine going to your neighbor's house for tea, and they ask if you want lemon or beans in your brew?"

She grunted again. "Don't care for it much myself, but the small farm these days has to diversify."

"I'm sure that's the case. So tell me, Mrs. Norton — or should I call you Mother?" Okay, so that was wicked of me, but a gal can't be perfect, can she?

"Mrs. Norton is fine."

"Then Mrs. Norton it is. Tell me, dear, is this the first time you've been to Pennsylvania?"

"First time I've been west of the Mississippi."

"That would be east, dear — but never mind. Why did you pick Hernia?"

I can't say I preferred her snorts over her grunts. "Why, that ad in *Condornest* — the one I mentioned reading when I called for reservations. Father and I never had much opportunity to travel, on account our sons are too busy with their own farms to look after ours. But now that June Bug — that's Father's youngest brother — has been laid off from the Kmart, we finally have the time. June Bug is just itching to prove himself on Father's new combine, so bringing in the corn won't be a problem, and as for taking care of the hogs, well, Prissy Mae — that's June Bug's second wife, was raised on a hog farm over by Hutchinson. His first wife, Udmillia, lost her head in a threshing accident. Never could find it, until Horace Grubb — that's the man who bought the hay — opened a bale to feed his horses. Anyway, Prissy Mae was Miss Hog-Calling Champion of 1983. Both she and June Bug are like children to us. They didn't have any of their own, see, on account of Bug's sperm never learned to swim —"

I let go of the pinecone to clap both

hands over my ears. "T.M.I.!"

Perhaps it was my outcry, or the fact that I let go of her hand, but Bibi Norton was suddenly at a loss for words. That's not to say that she was silent. She thrashed about in the bushes like a spastic sumo wrestler. If there had been any bears in the vicinity, they were now halfway to the Maryland border. I hoped they remembered to take their provisions with them.

"Mrs. Norton, dear, give me your hand."

Groping desperately, she managed to grab my person — in a very personal spot. Had it been Susannah, no doubt Bibi would have had at least one finger bitten off. I managed to remove Bibi's hand before we had no excuse *but* to progress to a first-name basis.

"So," I said, just as smoothly as if nothing untoward had happened, "what are your impressions of Pennsylvania?"

"It's very hilly," she said, taking the smooth cue from me. "And there are so many trees."

"Actually, these are mountains, not hills."

"They look like hills to me."

"But you're from Kansas," I said. "I have wrinkles in my sheets that are higher than any hills you have there. So, what do you think of our Amish?"

"We have Amish in Kansas too."

"Any named Hostetler, or Hochstetler, or any variation thereof?"

"I'm sure I wouldn't know. I don't go around asking their names."

I pretended to think for a minute. It was harder work than I remembered.

"You look somewhat like my cousin Delphia Hostetler," I said. And that wasn't a lie, given that they both had the general human shape — Bibi more so than Delphia, I'm loath to admit. "Wouldn't it be interesting if you and I were related?"

"But you're a Yoder."

"Prick a Yoder and a Hostetler bleeds. If you have any Amish ancestors — any at all, you and I are undoubtedly cousins."

"Well, that isn't the case." She didn't sound the least bit disappointed.

"How about your husband? I know Norton isn't one of our names, but maybe through his mama — or his paternal grandmother."

"I think the Nortons were English all the way back. But neither my husband nor I are interested in genealogy."

"That's a shame, because you never know when a little knowledge of your family history can reap dividends. Take the

Hostetlers, for instance. There are family legends that mention a huge fortune, just waiting to be found."

"Ha, legends!" She lost her footing and thrashed a bit more. She was panting when she spoke again. "Every family has their legends, but I wouldn't bet the farm on any of them."

I was at my wit's end. "Are you sure you're not a Hostetler? You're just as stubborn as one."

"Miss Yoder, there is no need for you to be rude."

I gave up. "Fine. Then don't tell me anything about yourself. But you can't blame a hostess for showing interest in her guests. Why, even that nixnux Buzzy Porter was more forthcoming than you."

"Mr. Porter was no mere nixnux. That man had a mean streak a mile long. I couldn't stand him."

Shocked by what I'd just heard, I stopped dead in my tracks. Because I lack brake lights on my heinie, Bibi Norton rammed into me. They say the bigger they are, the harder they fall. Well, I may be tall, but I'm also rail thin, so I fell like a ton of feathers. I may even have floated to the ground, had not sturdy Bibi been determined to land on me.

"Ding dang," I cried as my probing proboscis penetrated the porous forest floor.

"You clumsy oaf," Bibi bellowed.

I didn't mind being called a name. At least now that I finally had a real suspect.

25

I thought of pinning Bibi to the ground while I interrogated her. But given her muscles, and my lack of them, physical restraint would be about as useless as it would be for me to enter the Miss America pageant. Instead, I decided to use the darkness that surrounded us to my advantage.

"What's that?" I gasped.

"I don't hear anything."

"It sounded an awful lot like a bear."

"Are they dangerous?" She sounded like she was already convinced this was the case.

Somewhere I read that grizzly bears — and we have no wild ones in Pennsylvania — are one of the most dangerous animals on the planet. Eastern black bears, on the other hand, would sooner run from you than attack. Of course there are always exceptions. I addressed the exception.

"Their claws could fillet you like a fresh salmon."

She pawed me with her pair of pinecones. She might be incapable of cutting open a fish with her nails, but I had no doubts she could mince meat.

"Come on, Miss Yoder, let's get out of here."

"In a minute, dear. Where did you learn the word nixnux?"

"I don't know what you mean."

"Just now, when I called Buzzy a nixnux — well, you knew exactly what I meant."

"It's an Amish word, isn't it?"

"Exactly!"

"So maybe I picked it up from our Kansas Amish."

"The ones whose names you don't even know? Look, Mrs. Norton — if that is indeed your name — we're going to stay right here, come hungry bears or high water, until you spill everything."

Thank heavens the woods are filled with obliging creatures who prefer to move around at night. The noise we heard next sounded like a large male deer crashing through the underbrush. Apparently they don't have many bounding bucks in the middle of Kansas because Bibi was all over me like gravy on Doc's mashed potatoes.

"All right," she screeched, louder than any owl I've heard. "I'll tell you every damn thing."

"Ah, ah, ah, no swearing, dear."

I doubt if she heard me, as fired up as she was to unburden herself of the truth. "My maiden name is Kauffman. Both my parents have Hostetler blood. And yes we have a family story about the Hochstetler treasure, but it isn't a legend — it's true!"

"And where is it supposed to be buried?"

"Buried?"

"Otherwise known as interment. Something that will not happen to either of us if that bear is really hungry."

"I know what the word means," she growled, "but the treasure isn't buried."

"It's not?"

"It's a city. You can't bury that."

"Ah, the Bern story."

"Zurich," she snapped. "Every last acre under that city is ours, and what's on top of it too. That includes the banks, you know."

I was tempted to throw my arms around her in the dark, but didn't want the gesture to be misconstrued. Here was a woman after my own heart — a woman who dared to think big. Who cared about Bern and its billions, when there was Zurich and its trillions to be had?

"Bibi, dear," I said, now that we were kissing cousins — just not in that way, "tell me something. Isn't there supposed to be a buried deed somewhere?"

An amateur might have thought hyenas had been imported to Hernia. "Haaaaa! The deed's not buried, it's in a Bible."

"It *is?*"

"The Hochstetler family Bible. The one that belonged to our Great-great-great-great-great-great-great-grandfather Jacob."

"Add a few greats for me, dear. I'm not quite as old as you."

"Anyway, by my calculations, that Bible is supposed to be here in Hernia."

"How do you know that?"

"I lied to you, Miss Yoder. I am into genealogy."

"No duh," I said softly.

"What was that?"

"Uh — I was just talking to myself. So, if the deed is in a Bible somewhere around here, what brings you into town just as we are about to unearth our time capsule?"

"Because the owner of that Bible is mentioned in a document that is buried in the time capsule."

Leave it to a relative to split hairs so thin they couldn't be seen on a bald man under a spotlight. "So you were after the time capsule."

Her anger emboldened her. Either that,

or her eyes had adjusted to the dark. At any rate, she pushed away from me. She even bared her teeth — unless a dozen fireflies, in an unprecedented act of cooperation, had aligned themselves in two straight rows.

"I did not kill Mr. Porter. I'm not saying I'm sorry he died, but neither I, nor Chuck, had anything to do with his death. Our plan was simply to buy the document. Barring that, just to get a good look at it."

"You keep mentioning this document. What sort of document is this?"

"A list of the founding fathers."

"What?"

"My grandmother was there when they buried the time capsule. She was just a little girl, of course. She said that she remembers there being an argument about whose name should be on this list. There was one person everyone wanted to omit, because his descendants refused to let anyone have a peek at their Bible — the one in which the deed to the Hochstetler family fortune is recorded."

I must admit that this particular family legend sounded more plausible than most. The Bibles of my ancestors were filled with annotations of a personal nature: genealogies, birthdays, even a hand-written marriage contract in my grandmother's well-worn tome. Why not a deed? Indeed, it made a great deal of sense.

"How old did you say your grandmother was when the capsule was buried?"

"Let's see, she was born in ninety-four — *1894*."

"But then she would have been only ten. How could she remember something so grown up as a list of founding fathers?"

"Oh, she didn't remember that. Her mother filled her in on that later. She remembered the fistfight."

"You're kidding!"

"The fight was quite famous. I'm surprised you haven't heard of it. One man had his jaw broken — by the one who kept insisting his ancestor should be included. Anyway, we already know — thanks to our genealogical and historical research, who all the founding fathers were. Now we just need to know who is *not* on the list. Then we can track down the Bible, buy it, and the fortune is ours." The last words were delivered as a sigh, the sort one might emit after a particularly satisfying dinner.

"Well, is that all?" I said. Yes, I was about to lie, and yes, I had a good reason. I also had enough of a conscience to recognize the impending error of my ways. "You should have just asked me for the list when you registered."

Her eyes glowed with greed. Either that, or there truly was a large wild animal in the vicinity.

"*You* have the list?"

"Of course." At least I had *a* list. Like any good Mennonite woman, I keep a pad and paper in the bathroom, in the little stand that holds my collection of *Reader's Digest.* Who knows when inspiration is going to strike or I might want to jot down a shopping list for my next trip to Mystery Lovers bookstore in Pittsburgh.

Her mission almost accomplished, Bibi wrenched herself free from my grip, ready to take on the monsters of the night if need be.

"Miss Yoder," she practically bellowed, "I'm sure we can make a deal."

In for a penny, in for a pound — of sin, I mean. Instead of answering her, I hauled myself to my feet and resumed my trek to the inn. Bibi crashed along behind me.

"So, do we have a deal?"

"Eighty, twenty," I said.

"Don't be ridiculous. I'm the one who did all the research. I'll give you ten percent."

"I'm afraid you have it wrong, dear. I'm

offering you the twenty percent."

"What?" she barked.

"Look, I have the list. And I have all the same genealogy books. I probably don't even need them, because all the founders are buried in Settlers' Cemetery up on Stucky Ridge. All I have to do is peruse the graveyard. Their headstones are specially marked. Anyway, it shouldn't take me more than a few minutes."

"Fifty, fifty."

"Hmm, that would make us equal partners."

"Not quite," she snapped. "Father and I have to share our half."

"As well you should. The two of you are married, after all. One flesh that no man should put asunder, or whatever the vows say. So, do we have a deal?"

She mumbled her assent. Still, it was loud enough to send roosting birds shrieking from the treetops.

"Good. But now that we're partners — fifty, fifty — we have to be absolutely straight with each other."

"I did not kill Mr. Porter, if that's what you're getting at. And neither did Father."

"You sure? I mean, if you did — well, what's one paltry human life compared to that much moola?" I tried to sound casual, but probably didn't. In our tradition there is no justifiable reason to take another human life. Our ancestor's wife was scalped because he refused to defend her when the Delaware attacked on the evening of September 19, 1757. Of course, Bibi's blood had been diluted — at least I assumed it was. She was clearly not of the faith.

"Miss Yoder, if we had killed Mr. Porter, we would have the list now, wouldn't we? There would be no use for this conversation."

I finally believed her. And if Bibi Norton was innocent, so was her husband, Chuck. That left just six suspects, five if you counted the Littletons as a unit. No doubt all five were now back at the inn with my precious Alison, who had only a pig to protect her — assuming that Babester and his meddling mama had gone home like they were supposed to.

"Come on, dear," I cried. "There's no time to waste!"

I charged down the trail with all the intensity of an infuriated rhino. These beasts, I am told, have difficulty seeing. Well, I couldn't see the trail either, and although my feet are used to it, they are also used to operating under much calmer circumstances. I made a few wrong moves, smacked into the odd bush or tree, but emerged onto Hertlzer Road without losing Bibi and having suffered only minor cuts and scrapes. Trust me, my engine was still only getting revved when I burst through the kitchen door.

"What do you mean she refuses to leave? She doesn't have any choice. This is my house, and I want her out — at least for now."

Gabe squirmed. "Shhh. Ma's in the kitchen. She'll hear you."

"Hear, schmeer. The two of you are supposed to be out of here. As in gone home."

"We couldn't leave when we found out about the pig."

"The pig isn't any of her business."

"Magdalena, you don't understand."

"Then enlighten me." I had already ascertained that Alison was safe in my room, trading swine-raising tips over the phone with Donna Wylie.

Gabe grabbed me by a narrow shoulder and tried to steer me out of the dining room, where we'd been standing, and into the parlor. The guests, thank heavens, had all gone upstairs to dress for dinner. I allowed him to pull me as far as the foyer, where I keep my little office.

"You see, Magdalena, pigs aren't kosher."

"I know that, but your mother doesn't keep kosher. And it's not like I'm asking her to eat it."

"Yes, but it goes beyond that. A lot of foods aren't kosher, but ham and pork have become symbolic of what is forbidden. Historically our enemies have used pigs to torment us. In some cases Jews have been forced to either eat pork or be killed."

"That's horrible. But I still don't see how I can ask Alison to give up her pet. She'll see me as a double-crosser."

"You can't be sure of that. She's a very bright girl."

"But I can't risk it, either. She's just now beginning to trust me — she's been betrayed so many times. Gabe, I just can't do it."

His fingers slid off my shoulder. They felt like icicles.

"Does this mean you're choosing a pig over me?"

"That's not at all what I said!" Gabe had taken my words and twisted them like a pretzel. A master baker couldn't have done a better job. And some women have the nerve to think of men as simple-minded creatures.

"Shall I take that as a 'yes'?"

"What does letting Alison keep her pet have anything to do with choosing, or not choosing, you?"

"Because I already told Ma that she could live with us. And I can't go back on my word, either, Magdalena. She's my mother — my *flesh and blood* mother."

That did it. That hiked my hackles so high they scratched my armpits.

"Are you trying to tell me that Alison doesn't count because she's not my biological daughter?"

"Don't put words in my mouth. But as long as you've brought the subject up, whose biological daughter is she?"

"You know the answer to that. She's Aaron's — and his wife's. His first wife."

"Enough said."

I had plenty more to say, and believe me, I would have said every regrettable word, had not Ida Rosen burst into the room. Pausing only long enough to look up and see where I was, she came right at me, like an angry pit bull.

"So now she stabs me in the back." Her eyes were on me, but her words obviously directed to her son.

"Ma, I told you I'd take care of this."

"Stay out of this, Gabey."

Gabey?

"Ma!"

Ida was all eyes and no ears. She glared at me as she poked me in the sternum with a finger no longer than a Vienna sausage.

"I make supper for your little one, and you vant to repay me by letting her sell the leftovers to your guests?"

"Who squealed?" I squealed. "Alison?"

"Don't blame her, Miss Yoder. But she is in the kitchen now, putting my leftovers into serving bowls. Big money, she says, she'll get for my food."

"Well, you are a good cook."

The Babester didn't poke me with a finger, but he glared at me as well. "How could you take advantage of my mother like that?"

"She wasn't supposed to find out," I wailed. "What she didn't know wasn't supposed to hurt her."

Gabe put a strong tanned arm protectively around his mother's shoulders. "Come on, Ma. I'll take you home."

"But vhat about my food?"

"Forget about it. You can make some more at home."

"Vhat? And let this gonef keep it?"

I stamped a long, narrow foot. "Take that back, Mrs. Rosen!"

"You see, she vants I should take it back, Gabey."

"I meant the name. I keep the food — rather, Alison does. You made it for her."

"I take back nothing, and *I* keep the food."

"She has a legal right," Gabe said. "She paid for it."

"But she gave it away. Besides, you're a doctor, not a lawyer."

"Yes, a doctor," Ida said, shaking her head like a terrier with a rat in its mouth. "He could have had his pick of women back in the city. Good Jewish girls too."

"Instead he retired to the country to become a paperback writer. And now he's engaged to a simple Mennonite woman. That must really get to you, doesn't it, Mrs. Rosen?"

"Magdalena," Gabe said sharply. "That's my mother you're speaking to. Your future mother-in-law."

"Not anymore," I said. I tried to wrench the football-size sapphire and diamond ring off my finger, but it wouldn't budge. Oh well, it was the gesture that counted, right?

"Yes," Ida Rosen hissed. If she got any

giddier, she was in danger of floating away, like a stubby helium-filled balloon.

Gabriel had nothing more to say. However, he did help his mother carry a small mountain of food back across Hertlzer Road. It took them three trips, and it wasn't until I heard the door slam for the fourth time that I realized the enormity of the situation. In the meantime, I sat in Granny Yoder's rocking chair in the parlor, my head in my hands, trying to look as dejected as possible (well, except for occasional peeks out the window). With any luck Granny Yoder's ghost would come to my rescue and knock sense into the Babester's head. Barring that, the Babester might stick his head into the room, and seeing me look so pitiful, send his mama packing and cleave to me, and me alone, like a proper husband was meant to do. At any rate, it wasn't until that final slam that I looked up to see Alison standing in the doorway.

"Mom," she said quietly, "was this all my fault?"

"Heavens no, dear. That woman and I — well, Gabe will see the light. Don't you worry."

"You mean you're really not breaking up with him?"

"Of course not, dear. He's breaking up with his mother — he just doesn't realize it yet. Men sometimes need a little push, that's all."

"Yeah, men. Go figure." She sucked in her lower lip. "Mom, I hate ta tell ya this, but we got ourselves a worse problem now than guys."

I smiled. "And what would that be?"

"Well, I just came to tell you that some of the guests have started to pack."

"They *what?*"

"They claim you're trying ta starve them. That stuck-up old movie star says she's already got herself motel reservations somewhere else."

"But that's impossible. Every motel in Bedford is booked up."

"Yeah, but she's willing to go all the way over to Somerset. She's dragging those slaves of hers with her. Some of the others said they'd be going too."

I stamped a long narrow foot so hard that I left a permanent groove in the floor. The entire house shook. If I didn't do something about reining in my temper, one of these days the roof was going to fall down around my head — a situation most likely not covered under my homeowner's insurance.

"We'll just see about that!" I roared. "Alison, call your auntie Susannah and tell her to get over to Freni's fast. Tell her she has my permission to drive like a bat out of — uh, a very hot cave. Have her tell Freni that the peasants are rebelling, and I need her help in the kitchen *now*."

"But Freni is really ticked at you, Mom. She quit, remember?"

"Details, dear. Tell Auntie Susannah to tell her that I apologize. That I'm down on my hands and knees begging."

"Cool. But why don't you call Auntie Susannah yourself."

"Because I'm going upstairs to put a stop to this nonsense. Guests checking out early, indeed!"

"Oh, Mom, can I watch? Please?"

"Sweetie, I'm not going to hit them or anything."

"I know, but ya do the best hollering in the whole wide world. If ya sold tickets, ya would be famous, ya know?"

I can't help it if my bony chest swelled with pride. My inflated thorax did not, of course, enhance my bosoms, but it did fill out my dress somewhat.

"Thank you, dear, for the compliment, but I'm not going to yell at them — well, I'm certainly not going to holler. Just the same, you go call your auntie Susannah and then you can come up and watch."

The girl moved like lightning. I did as well. Unfortunately I went straight upstairs like I said I would. A wise Magdalena, on the other hand, would have put her bony butt behind the steering wheel of her car and taken off for a week's R and R somewhere. Somewhere far away and really exotic, like Cincinnati, Ohio.

24

I rounded up all eight rats before they could jump ship and herded them into the parlor. If I were really a policewoman, and they were official suspects, I could simply have ordered them not to leave town. But I was only a pretend policewoman, and they were only pseudosuspects. My only power, as usual, lay in my lingua.

To my credit I didn't holler, but my frown muscles got such a workout that my forehead hurt as much as my hands. And with all that skin bunched above my eyes, there was hardly enough left on the lower half of my face to allow me to open my mouth. "You really don't want to book rooms in Somerset, dears," I grunted. "There's a tunnel between here and there. If it gets blocked — if there's an accident — well, it will take you forever to get to Hernia on the back roads. You'll miss out on some of the festivities to be sure."

"With all due respect," Capers cooed,

"the odds are against an accident in the tunnel."

"Tell that to Mama and Papa," I snapped. But then, because she had not meant any disrespect and was really a rather pleasant woman, I had to force my frown lines into a smile. "Whatever you think you'll find in Somerset, I'm sure I can provide for you here."

"How about some decent food?"

I wanted to wipe young Stanley's smirk off his face — with a piece of sandpaper. Instead I forced the corners of my mouth into unnatural positions. No doubt I looked like a constipated fox.

"That issue is being addressed as we speak. Mrs. Hostetler will be here momentarily to fix you an authentic Pennsylvania Dutch meal."

"Cold cuts and salads?"

So frustrated was I, that I actually thought of ripping out my own tongue and lashing the arrogant youth with it. But, of course, in order to do that, I would have had to open my mouth a lot wider.

"It will be a full, hot meal. I promise."

Octavia Cabot-Dodge cleared her throat to speak — eight times in all. "Miss Yoder," she finally said, "it isn't just the food — or lack thereof — that we find unsatisfactory. Quite frankly, we are tired of your games."

"Games?" I had yet to insist we play a rousing game of Scrabble or a death-match tournament of Chinese checkers. When it comes to games, with the exception of face cards, we Mennonites are known to excel.

"This A.L.P.O. nonsense and whatnot. The very idea of charging more to do janitorial work. These games might work on some of your unfortunate guests, but we do not find them amusing."

My face burned with shame. "That's because you are all descendants of Jacob — or else married to one, which is almost the same thing. Real English guests wouldn't have minded one bit."

Terri Mukai's face glowed. I'm sure she was quite pleased to be included unequivocally in my ancestral clan.

"Yoder-san, may we speak privately?"

"In a minute, dear. Just as soon as we sort out this silly little matter."

"Bilking the public is hardly trivial," Bibi burbled.

"Yoder-san," Terri said softly, "in my country, now would be the time to be generous."

"Generous?"

"Perhaps a reduction in price." She

whispered this time.

"Lower my prices?" I bellowed. You would have thought I was Bibi.

Fifteen eyes fixed on me. One of Stan's eyes remained on Terri. She was, after all, a rather attractive girl.

Buist Littleton is a very handsome man, except when he chooses to take sides against me. "The Wagon Wheel Lodge in Somerset," he drawled, "charges only fifty-nine ninety-nine for a double. And they have cable TV."

"Yes, but does that include meals?"

"Like your ridiculous fee does," Octavia Cabot-Dodge mumbled.

"It does in theory," I wailed. "I can't help it that my cook quits at the drop of a saucepan."

"I bet no one has ever been murdered at the Wagon Wheel Lodge," Augusta said.

Stan smirked again and held that look until I shot him a special look of my own — one that has been known to wither watermelons on a rainy day. "Mr. Porter was *not* murdered in this inn."

Chuck Norton, whom I almost thought of as an ally now that we'd chased pigs together, cocked his head. "But have there been other murders here?"

"No fair! The town is full of gossips, so

what? I'll have you know that lots of people have survived their stays here."

"Just how many murders have there been?" And I thought I could count on Capers!

"Your prices," Terri said softly. To her credit, the girl was just trying to be helpful.

I threw up my hands in resignation. "Okay, there is no need for anyone to get their knickers in a knot — and believe you me, you all better be wearing some. I'll cut my rates by a third, and you won't have to pay for the privilege of cleaning your rooms."

"Ridiculous," someone snorted. Had there been a collection of horses present, I would have guessed it was the Clydesdale. Under the circumstances I was forced to conclude that it was the diva who was still not satisfied.

"All right," I conceded. "You get fifty percent off, but count yourselves lucky. A lot of people are happy to pay big bucks to stay in a place where there have been so many — uh, I mean, where there is so much ambience."

"Ha!" Bibi put her hands on her hips, which is a very un-Mennonite gesture and was therefore a testament to her mixed blood. "Either you match the Wagon

Wheel's rates — including meals and maid service, or we're all out of here." She turned to the others. "Right?"

They nodded in unison, even Terri. And I thought the Japanese were supposed to be polite.

"But I have no maid to service you! I can't possibly ask a seventy-five year old Amish woman to do all that *and* cook."

"Then do it yourself," Augusta retorted.

"*Moi?* But I'm the proprietress!"

"You look sturdy enough to me — maybe a little on the skinny side. We're only talking about normal, everyday housekeeping."

For a soul-threatening second I had a vision of me mopping the floor, or perhaps scrubbing toilets, with Augusta Miller's graying locks, her head still attached. I took a deep breath, begged the Good Lord for forgiveness, and tarried on along that narrow, restrictive road of righteousness.

"I give up," I cried. "You have a deal. But you each have to sign a paper saying you'll never disclose these terms to anyone. If words gets out —" Too late I clamped a plate-size paw across the lips that had just sunk my own ship.

"Yoder-san," the Japanese Judas said, her voice still elegant and breathy, "perhaps you should let us stay for free. Otherwise there may be great temptation to — how does one say? — send you the dark mail."

"You mean blackmail, dear?"

"Yes. And Yoder-san, there is still the matter of my clothes."

"We're doing what we can to recover your luggage," I said, perhaps a bit too brusquely. "It is not my responsibility to reimburse you."

"I'm hungry," Stan whined.

"Supper's coming right up, dear."

I fled the room before I found myself in a situation in which I was supposed to pay *them*. Forget the waivers; my inn's reputation would survive somehow. Sometimes it is better to settle than to fight for one's rights. Besides, I'd fix their wagons with my chuck. I'm the first to admit that I'm a terrible cook. The only cook I ever knew whose food tasted worse than mine, died from eating her own grub. While my victuals are usually not lethal, they have been known to do permanent damage to unsuspecting taste buds.

Operation Gag was underway.

My scorched potato soup and rubbery grilled-cheese sandwiches would have done the trick nicely, had not Susannah taken me at my word. She must have driven a hundred miles an hour. Poor Freni was so shaken by her wild ride, that her knees buckled with every other step.

"Freni," I implored, "please sit for a minute and catch your breath."

"Ach, not if the English are revolting."

"I heard that," Bibi blared. The woman had the nerve to be eavesdropping on a private family conversation.

"Freni," I chuckled, "that wasn't such a nice thing to say, now was it?"

"Maybe. But that is what Susannah said."

My sister rolled her eyes. "I was just repeating Alison's message, sis."

I shook my head. "But what I said was — ah, yes. I said that the guests were rebelling, *not* revolting. Revolting has more than one meaning."

"English," Freni muttered, referring to the language that is not quite her mother tongue. "It has too many meanings, yah?"

"We'll discuss linguistics some other time, dear. Now, pop into the kitchen and work magic with those fingers of yours."

Her bottle-thick lenses magnified the horror in her eyes. "Magic? Magdalena, the Bible forbids us to practice this. It is a sin."

I sighed patiently. "I'm well aware of that. What I meant is that your fingers are capable of producing the best food in all of Bedford County."

She gazed with awe at her own stubby digits. "Yah? You think so?"

"Without a doubt." So perhaps it was a slight exaggeration. But what harm was there in that? The Bible also instructs us to encourage each other.

"These fingers," she murmured. "The best cook in the county — ach! Magdalena, you lead me into temptation."

"But you came willingly!"

"You people are weird," Bibi said. "No wonder my branch of the family moved West."

"Then keep moving," I said kindly, "like to your room or the parlor, so that our cooking whiz here can do her stuff."

Bibi's stomach must have overruled her tongue, because she actually cooperated. And while the meal Freni whipped up couldn't have compared favorably to one of Doc's worst creations, it was far better than anything I could have produced — even by accident.

Much to my amazement, all eight guests went to bed satisfied. The sound of their snores — audible even from the ground floor — confirmed that at least some of them had Hochstetler blood. If not diluted too much, the Hochstetler gene has the ability to induce such sound sleep, that more than a few of the clan have confessed that they are fearful of missing the Second Coming.

The Yoder gene, on the other hand, has the opposite effect. And by the way, this is the more dominant gene of the two. When they should be sleeping, Yoders tend to replay in their heads every conversation they'd had throughout the day. A few of us, due to excessive inbreeding, are capable of recalling conversations that may, or may not, have taken place twenty years earlier.

Alas, I am one of the unfortunate who suffers from diarrhea of the mind. What sleep I might have gotten was robbed from me by a pig and a hog. The pig had hooves and squealed when I accidentally rolled over on him. The hog was my foster daughter who, thanks to her Hochstetler blood, was sound asleep the entire time and continuously wrested the covers from yours truly.

I gave up on dreamland just after four a.m. My plan was to try and grab a few winks on the love seat in the parlor. What I did not plan on was an encounter with

Grandma Yoder. After all, the woman died when I was twelve.

But sure enough, there she was, sitting in a hardback chair, looking every bit as warm and welcoming as the statues on Mount Rushmore — which is about twice as friendly as she was in life. I know, you probably don't believe in ghosts. If, however, the vision was just the product of a fertile imagination, then my gray cells could make the entire Sahara desert bloom. That's how real she seemed to me.

"Sit down, Magdalena," she snapped. "I don't want to have to look up at you."

"I prefer to stand, Grandma."

"Then stand straight, with your shoulders back. But don't stick your chest out too much, because that would be immodest — well, I guess not in your case."

"Grandma!"

"It's true, child. You've got the Yoder mind, but not the Yoder bosoms. Must be that Lehman blood that found its way into your mother's side of the family. I told your father he should have married Rebecca Miller instead. Good bone structure, that girl had."

"There was nothing wrong with Mama."

"I didn't come to talk about your mama, child."

"Then what do you want, Grandma? I brush my teeth three times a day, just like you taught me, and I say my prayers every night before I go to bed."

"Not tonight, you didn't."

"That's because the English were revolting. Just ask Freni."

"Freni doesn't need me, child. You do."

"I'm not a child anymore, Grandma. In fact, I'm about to get married."

"Indeed you are. And for the second time, I might add."

"But I didn't know Aaron was married. Besides, since it wasn't legal, it doesn't count."

"Are you telling me it's all right to sleep with a man who isn't your husband? Why, Magdalena, soon you'll be telling me it's okay to dance."

"I never said that, Grandma!"

"Good, because it isn't, you know. There's a special place in You-Know-Where for folks who dance." Grandma sighed, and she sounded like wind blowing through the Allegheny tunnel. "There used to be lots of room in You-Know-Where. Now I hear it's getting filled up with Presbyterians."

"Are you saying that Hell is filled with —"

"Heavens, no, child. I'm talking about Mt. Olive Retirement Home. Used to be almost all shimmying Methodists and a few hard-drinking Baptists, but now the predestination crowd is taking over."

It was my turn to sigh. "Grandma, can we get to the point? Why are you here? I mean, don't you have a harp lesson or something you should be attending?"

"Been there, done that. Graduated from harp school with an A+ average. I don't start Cloud Making 101 until next week. We have plenty of time to chat."

Since Grandma Yoder never had a funny bone in her body — I think she even lacked a humerus — she was dead serious about the classes. But she still hadn't answered my question.

"What, specifically, is it that you want to lecture me about?"

"It's that Jewish man."

"Grandma, don't even start. Jesus was a Jew, you know."

"I know that very well. And what I've come to tell you is that you should marry this one. Don't let his mother stand in the way."

"But she runs his life. If I marry Gabriel, she'll not only run my life too — she'll ruin it."

"And if you don't marry him, will she ruin it then?"

"So what are you saying? I should make Alison give away the pig?"

"Don't worry, child. She'll give it away on her own account. Pigs and teenage girls weren't meant to live together."

"But, Grandma, that woman is domineering."

"So are you, child. Has no one ever told you that?"

"Of course not. True, I may have some strong opinions, but that's because I know I'm right. Take that time when Gabriel insisted that —"

But Grandma had vanished. Ghosts do that, you know. They appear and disappear at the most inconvenient times, and usually when I have a lot on my mind. Mama's ghost does that too. It's like they have a conspiracy to meddle in my personal affairs.

After waiting politely a few minutes, just to make sure Grandma wasn't roaming around the rest of the inn and planning to return, I curled up on the love seat. But sleep was not forthcoming, and after about an hour I gave up on this elixir altogether, dressed, and went in search of the one thing that was sure to see me through the travails of the coming day.

25

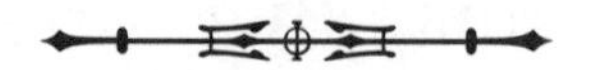

Grill-Broiled Green Tomatoes

4 medium or 2 large green tomatoes
Salt
2 tablespoons bacon drippings or
extra-virgin olive oil
Whole black pepper in a pepper mill

Prepare a grill with hardwood coals and light them, or position a rack about 5 inches from the heat source and preheat the oven broiler for at least 15 minutes before you are ready to cook the tomatoes. Cut the tomatoes in half crosswise, lightly sprinkle the cut side with salt, and invert them in a colander set over the sink. Drain them for 30 minutes.

When the coals are ready or the broiler is very hot, wipe the cut side of the tomatoes dry. Lightly brush them with the drippings or oil, then sprinkle them with several generous grindings of pepper. (If you are using the oven broiler, skip to step 3.) Put tomatoes on the grill cut side down and grill until they are lightly browned, about 6 to 8 minutes. Lightly brush them with more drippings or oil, turn them, and continue grilling until the tomatoes are tender, about 8 minutes more.

If you are using the oven broiler, put the tomatoes cut side up into a broiling pan fitted with a rack. Position the rack under the broiler within 6 inches of the heat source and place the tomatoes on it. Broil until the cut side is nicely browned, about 8 minutes. Turn them carefully, brush lightly with more drippings or oil, and continue broiling until the tomatoes are tender, about 8 minutes more.

SERVES 4

26

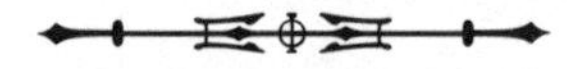

Doc opened the door even before I knocked. I have hard knuckles and he claims he's too old to refinish wood.

"Blue heard you again," he said, reading my mind. "I'm afraid I just got up myself, but if you don't mind watching, I'll make you a proper breakfast. If you're in a real hurry, there's a box of cereal somewhere around here, if you want to help me find it. Was Belinda's."

Since Belinda was Doc's wife, and she's been dead for over twenty years, I elected to wait. Besides, comfort food was what I'd come for.

Doc's idea of comfort that morning was broiled grapefruit halves oozing with melted brown sugar, Spanish omelets, genuine English-style kippers, lemon zest scones, and a large pot of homemade hot chocolate. Ignoring my protestations, he piled the latter high with fresh whipped cream, sprinkled with nutmeg.

Ever the gentleman, Doc waited until I was satiated before getting down to what he considered business. "So, do we have a dinner date every Saturday night until Christmas?"

"They're just dinners, not dates!"

"Aha! So I was right. Well, how many were there?"

"Too many. Even the Japanese girl, for crying out loud. And, Doc, if I keep my word, Gabriel is going to be really sore with me. It's bad enough the way things are."

"Problems in paradise?"

"Prob*lem*. In short, it's Ida, his mother." Under normal circumstances I would have laughed at my little joke.

"Ah, the woman you want me to date. Thanks to you, I took a second look at her. She's a stunner, all right."

"I beg your pardon?"

"A fine-looking woman."

"Very funny, Doc. Tell me another."

"I mean it." His expression told me that he did.

"But she's not your type!" An honest Magdalena would share that she was experiencing bizarre feelings of jealousy. But Doc was an eighty-six-year-old man for pete's sake. And I still had a shot at the hunky Gabe. What was there to be jealous of?

Doc grinned. "But you're exactly the same. Grant it, you don't look alike, but when you get to be my age it's what's inside a woman that stokes the fire inside a man's furnace. Sure, we still get turned on by the usual things —"

"No details, please!"

His grin widened. "But what you might think is a plain woman when you're young, can look mighty fine a few decades later if she's got that certain spark."

I knew he meant me. But as much as I love to talk about myself, I had to steer the conversation back to Ida. "Doc, you wouldn't mind it if I fixed you up with Mrs. Rosen?"

He didn't hesitate a second. "I'd like that mighty fine."

"But if I do, you have to let me out of my promise to have dinner with you every Saturday night."

Doc nodded vigorously.

"You don't have to agree so quickly."

Doc stopped nodding, but his eyes glittered. "Face it, Magdalena, you really wouldn't want an old codger like me. So, are you really going to fix me up with the Rosen woman?"

"If you let me have another scone and a little more hot chocolate. I'm supposed to meet Melvin Stoltzfus in a few minutes for some police work. We're hiking out to the base of Lovers' Leap. There's a cave there that might be important to the investigation. You ever been there, Doc?"

"Never at the bottom of the leap, only at the top," he said with a twinkle in his eye. "Been on top many times."

"At any rate, this may be my last meal."

"Then take a few scones with you. And a thermos full of chocolate."

"Thanks, Doc. I will."

"How long do you think you'll be?"

"I don't know. That depends on what we find. Shouldn't take us more than two hours, I'd guess."

"Stoltzfus is a nutcase. If I don't hear from you by noon, Blue and I are coming in after you. Where did you say this trail is?"

"I didn't. But it's behind the Block House. You know, the place with a zillion cats."

"Dang people should have been thrown in jail, letting them cats multiply like that. You know, Magdalena, I would have spayed and neutered them for free, but my eyesight is not what it used to be." He winked. "Except for a pretty woman."

I chose to interpret the wink as a compliment directed at me. Or it could have been merely a tic generated by his deteriorating eyesight. Whatever the reason, it was a high note on which to leave.

Melvin, as usual, was a low note. "Where have you been, Yoder?"

I glanced at my watch. "It's seven o'clock on the dot."

"It's eight, Yoder. I've been waiting here for half an hour. I was about to come and get you."

I grabbed his spindly wrist. "Melvin, *dear,* Mickey's thumb is on the seven. Pay no attention to the rest of that big fat glove. And if you've been waiting here for half an hour, then by your own cockeyed means of telling time, you're the one who is late."

Melvin can change subjects faster than a teenager. "Your sister is driving me crazy," he said, apropos of nothing.

"You mean this is the first time?"

"She can't decide what to wear to my inauguration."

We started into the woods. "I thought she had decided on fifteen feet of filmy fuchsia fabric. Isn't that what she always wears to any important occasion?"

"Until you talked her out of it. 'Be more conservative,' you said."

"Yes, and I suggested a nice opaque polyester."

"Exactly. But then she got to thinking —"

"Another first?" I know, that wasn't nice. And I owed Susannah, especially after what she did for me last night. But sometimes I just can't stop this tart tongue of mine.

"No, she's thought several times before this," Melvin said. *He* was dead serious, and there was admiration in his voice. "Anyway, she finally decided that if the material has to be opaque, she may as well wear body paint instead."

"Excuse me?"

"Are you hard of hearing, Yoder? I said paint."

"I know what you said, but it didn't make any sense. What do you mean by 'instead'?"

"You serious?"

"As serious as a hernia at a weight-lifters competition." I wasn't speaking from personal experience, mind you. This just seemed like a good metaphor.

Melvin thrashed on ahead, delighted to be in the position of enlightening me. "It's kind of a new fad. We get a lot of these pictures over the Internet. Anyway, instead of wearing real clothes, the person wears clothes that are painted on. You know, like a tuxedo, or a swim suit, or whatever."

"But over their sturdy Christian underwear, yes?"

"Over nothing, Yoder. Zip, zilch, nada."

"You mean they're naked?"

"If you don't count the paint."

The shock of his words was too much for me. Both knees buckled just as surely as if someone had punched them from behind, and I collapsed onto a tangle of blackberry brambles. The second flesh met thorns, I was up again, but my head was spinning like it does when I step off the Tilt-A-Whirl at the county fair. I sat down a few more times — once on Melvin, I believe. Finally I got to the point where I could lean against the fissured bark of a walnut tree while I tried to put a positive spin on things.

"But you said she's still deciding, right?"

"She's positive about the paint job. What she's trying to decide on is a pink outfit, or a yellow one. She's going to call it a gown designed by Sherwin Williams."

I took several deep cleansing breaths. There was no need to get my knickers in a knot over this nonsense. Melvin had as much chance of becoming President as I did at winning the International Patience Championships. And besides, there was always my not-so-secret weapon.

"Tell Susannah that if she wears anything *but* fifteen feet of filmy fuchsia, I'm cutting off her credit line at the Material Girl over in Bedford. I'll be calling all the paint stores too. If I have to, I'll cut off her allowance altogether."

"Gee, thanks, Yoder. I owe you one."

Melvin meant it. Between that point and the base of Lovers' Leap, he led the way. No blackberry bush was too mean for my protector, no sycamore sapling too savage. The stalwart Stoltzfus was unflappable — well, he may have flapped a few times, but after all, mantises do have wings.

Once we got to the cave, however, Melvin turned into Milquetoast. "Yoder, you have a flashlight. You look in there first."

"You have a flashlight too, dear. I think you should have the honor."

"Ladies first, Yoder."

"All right. All right." Fear, I have discovered, can make me a mite irritable.

I got down on all fours, then arching my behind like a puppy begging to play, I lowered my front half until I was leaning on my elbows.

"You see anything?" Melvin demanded.

"I haven't turned on my light," I snapped. "And if you even think of looking up my skirt —"

"Gag me with a spoon, Yoder. I'd rather rip out my own fingernails."

"Which of these two procedures would you prefer, dear?"

"Very funny, Yoder. Now turn on the light and tell me what you see."

I pushed the switch, but my brain lagged behind the beam of light. It took me forever to focus on what lay in a far corner of the cavern. In fact, I had to crawl all the way in to make sure that my peepers weren't lying to me. Alas, they weren't.

27

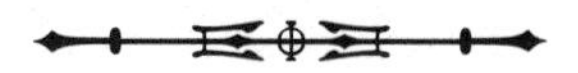

"It's Buzzy Porter," I said weakly. I'd backed out of the entrance and was sitting in the damp leaves. Who cared if bugs crawled up my skirt? In the grand scheme of things, what did that matter? They'd soon be crawling in and out of Buzzy until he returned to dust. At least I was assured of my salvation. As for Buzzy, I had no idea where he stood on that issue. For all I knew, by the time the worms played pinochle on his snout, his soul would be dancing with the Devil.

"Are you sure?"

"Don't be such a wuss, and look for yourself."

"I'm not a wuss. I need to stay out here and protect you."

"Then call for backup."

"Zelda?"

"No, Santa and his reindeer. Of course, Zelda. Tell her to get the Amstutz brothers out here. They can carry Mr. Porter out.

Heaven knows, they've carried enough deer out of these woods. And, of course, call the hospital and get that ambulance out to the Block House lickety-split."

"Don't be ridiculous, Yoder. The man is dead. He's not going anywhere."

"Don't be so sure. He's already done a fair amount of traveling in this condition. And this time have him taken to the county morgue."

"What about the sheriff?"

"What about him?"

"Yoder, if the sheriff gets involved — well, you know."

It is possible to be just too tired, too frazzled, to care anymore about the consequences of one's words. Trust me, I've been to that breaking point more than once. I think '83 and '96 were also watermark years.

"Enough about this stupid election, Melvin. You're never going to win, so put aside your pride and do your job for a change."

I could have knocked the Mantis over with one of the dead leaves I was sitting on. His mandibles moved mutely, while his entomological brain searched for words — any words.

Sadly, I didn't have the patience to wait.

"Face it, Melvin, there's no grain in your silo."

"Huh? I don't have a silo. But Mama does, and it's plenty full."

"Let me try again," I said kindly. "Your antenna doesn't pick up all the channels."

"That's because we have cable."

"Touché. Then let me put it this way, your belt doesn't go through all the loops."

"Yes, it does. Susannah looped it for me."

I was running out of analogies. "Your dogs aren't all on the same leash!"

He shook his head in pity. "We've only got the one, Yoder. And you know Susannah carries it around in her bra. As soon as the Amstutz brothers get here, have somebody drive you into Hernia so you can see a shrink. Personally, I recommend Dr. Frawd."

To my credit, I kept my cool. "For your information, it's Freud, not Frawd, and he's been dead for well over sixty years."

"Don't be an idiot. I see Dr. George Frawd every week."

That was jaw-dropping news, but I tried not to let even my teeth show. The Mantis in therapy? Perhaps there was hope for the world. But poor Dr. Frawd. I would definitely put him on my prayer list.

"Melvin, allow me to be as straightforward as possible. Nobody's going to vote for you — except maybe Susannah."

"Yoder, you're nuts, you know that?"

I saw that there was no point in continuing the conversation. What would Jesus do? I wondered. It seemed like he was forever breaking bread and passing it around. I didn't have any bread with me, of course, but I did have Doc's scones. And hot chocolate.

"Melvin, are you hungry?"

"Starved, Yoder. We ate all the cornflakes last night for supper. But what's it to you?"

Perhaps it sounds callous, eating and drinking, when Buzzy Porter lay moldering in a cave just feet away, but that's what we did. For the record, that was the first time I ever felt close to my bothersome brother-in-law.

Sheriff Hobson is a kind and competent man. He took over with grace and skill that amazed me. Melvin remained officially in charge of the case, but from now it would be the sheriff and his deputies that would do the actual work — the detecting if you would. Melvin would still get the credit when the case was solved. If there never was a resolution, my nemesis could blame it on the county. If not exactly a win-win situation, he certainly had nothing to lose.

Having turned the matter into Hobson's hands, I headed straight for the Penn-Dutch and Big Bertha. She's my one vice, now that I have given up sitting on my Kenmore. Big Bertha — that's her catalog name — is a 125 gallon, 30 jet-spray, whirlpool bathtub.

I know, a lot of people prefer showers, and 125 gallons is a lot to waste on a single bath, but I think the Good Lord wouldn't have allowed such a luxury to exist if he didn't approve of it. After all, this particular tub is practically deep enough for one to be baptized in — although we Mennonites prefer the more sedate method of "pouring."

I have only recently acquired this tub, and I had to send all the way to Sin City for it. Fortunately, the Philadelphia vendor was skilled in remodeling, because we had to rip out one of the walls to get the tub in. Susannah says it's big enough for six people — and not for a religious occasion either. Only a Presbyterian would think of such a thing.

At any rate, much to my relief, Alison was busy outside playing with her pig,

Freni was in the kitchen trying to decide if broccoli was a dairy product since she normally serves it with a cheese sauce, and the guests had all gone to the Blough farm to observe the hay-baling contest. At least for the moment, I was deliciously alone.

When I slipped into the swirling bubbles late that morning, it felt so good it had to be a sin. I turned the bathroom radio to a gospel channel, just to keep Big Bertha from giving me impure thoughts. As far as I'm concerned, the streets of Heaven don't need to be paved in gold, just as long as my suite contains a Big Bertha tub. And just for the record, it took only half the jets to make me feel this way.

Who knows how long my bliss would have lasted, had it not been for a hiss.

"Psst, Magdalena, are you decent?"

"What?" I jerked my sleepy head out of the suds.

"Ach, it's that Rosen woman," Freni said.

I turned off the radio and the jet sprays. "What about her?"

"She bothers me again. 'Make it this way,' she says. 'Make it that.' Do you want that I should quit, Magdalena?"

I sat ramrod straight. Thank heavens the tub was deep enough, and there were still enough bubbles, that my bosoms, such as they are, remained covered.

"Of course I don't want you to quit! I never want you to quit. Quitting is always your idea."

"Then you must make her leave. Magdalena, this woman is a horn in my side."

Freni learned Pennsylvania Dutch before she learned English, and her idioms sometimes need clarification. It is possible she meant that Ida Rosen was a thorn in her side, *or* she could have meant that Gabe's mother was goring her — metaphorically, of course. Either way, my kinswoman cook was not a happy camper.

"Give me a minute to get dressed, dear. Then I'll tell that buttinsky to get her buttocks back across Hertlzer Road."

"Ach!" By the gleam emanating from behind her thick lenses, Freni was both horrified and delighted by my strong language. "Yah, you tell her."

"Tell me vhat?"

I looked across the vast expanse of the tub, where my eyes locked on to those of Ida Rosen. Our peepers were on the same level.

"What on earth are *you* doing in my bathroom?" I demanded.

"Making sure she doesn't tell any lies."

"Ach, I do not lie!"

"Ladies!" I screamed. "Out, out, out!"

"I go nowhere until you tell me vhat you vere going to say."

"Yah, I stay too. Maybe she tells lies about me."

The two stout women glared at each other. Surely they were sisters under the skin. Put Freni's glasses on Ida, smear Ida's pink lipstick on Freni's pouting lips, and who could tell the difference? And both were equally guilty of violating the sanctity of my bath.

For a few very wicked seconds I fantasized about jumping out of the tub and throwing both uninvited guests in. I might even have done so, had I not remembered that Freni couldn't swim. And Big Bertha had a deep end. Also, I had no clue about Ida's aquatic skills. Although both women were blessed with natural flotation devices, if they found themselves floating on their stomachs, they might well choke to death on lavender-scented bubbles.

"Okay, ladies," I said, "stay. But at your own risk. I may get out of this tub at any minute, and believe me, it's not a pretty sight."

"Yah, I know. I helped raise you, remember?"

"So, vhat do I care either? You see one naked lady, you see them all."

"Enough! Okay, Mrs. Rosen, I told Freni I was going to tell you to stay away from the PennDutch."

"The buttocks," Freni hissed. "Tell her about the buttocks."

"Vhat about my buttocks? Yours are such a pretty sight?"

"Ach!"

"Just that you should keep them home where they belong," I hastened to explain. "I mean, what happens over here is really not your business."

"My Gabriel is my business, and if he changes his mind and marries you — oy, the heartache vill be too much."

"Marries me? Gabe and I aren't even speaking now — thanks to you. Besides, even if we do work things out, you wouldn't be losing a son, Mrs. Rosen. You'd be gaining a daughter. *And,*" I added, playing my trump card, "you could be gaining a boyfriend — well, a man friend."

Both elderly women snapped to attention. Surely they were once conjoined twins, separated at birth. Amish, Jewish, what did it matter? Both were descended from Eve and that apple-eating husband of hers.

"A man friend?" they said in unison.

"I happen to know that Doc Shafor wants to ask you out."

If Ida's beam was brighter it was only because she didn't wear glasses. "A doctor? Is he Jewish?"

"A chunk," Freni said, and licked her lips wistfully. A sin for a happily married woman, if you ask me.

"That's hunk, dear. And yes, he is a doctor of sorts — he's a genuine veterinarian. As for his religion, does it really matter? It's not like you two would ever raise a family together."

"Vhat does he look like?"

"A real woman-killer," Freni said. She licked her lips again.

"She means a lady-killer."

"So he's a looker?"

I don't find Doc physically attractive, but I know plenty of women who do. "That's the general consensus. Anyway, he wants to ask you out. Says he's had his eye on you for quite some time now."

"Vell then" — Ida patted her hair, as if it were possible that a strand had broken loose from the lacquered helmet — "perhaps I say yes."

"Ach!" Freni cried in distress, then clamped a stubby hand over a mouth that had betrayed her.

Ida Rosen smiled victoriously. Dating Doc was one thing that she could certainly do better than Freni. That smile, however, was directed at me.

"You see, Magdalena, how it pays to keep yourself up?"

"I think it's the aerosol spray, dear." Trust me, what Botox can't achieve, enough hair spray usually does. I see it in my guests all the time.

"Vhat is that supposed to mean?"

I answered her question with one of my own. "What time would you like Doc to pick you up Saturday night?"

"Seven thirty," she said without a moment's hesitation. "Tell him to make the dinner reservation for eight. And I do not like to be late."

"Uh — you'll probably be eating in."

"You mean he vants that I should cook for him?" She didn't sound the least put off by the idea.

"I think it's the other way around."

Ida recoiled — well, as much as it is possible for a woman of her stature to do so. "A man who cooks?"

"Not just cooks, dear. He lives to cook. What's more, he savors every bite he eats."

A fuming Freni flapped her arms futilely; she was never going to achieve liftoff.

"Ach," she squawked, "a sin!"

Ida did a little victory dance of a sort. She resembled a drunken chicken — not that I've seen very many of those, mind you. She too would never be airborne by her own power.

"Is it a sin to enjoy good food?"

"Like you should know," Freni said. These were strong words for a pious Amish woman.

Ida countered with even stronger words, but they came out in Yiddish. Freni must have understood them, because she lobbed them right back in Pennsylvania Dutch. Although separated by centuries of linguistic changes, both languages are based on German and bear similarities, enough at least to cause even further misunderstandings.

"Take it out in the hallway, will you, dears?"

They ignored me.

I stood up in the tub. "Get out," I bellowed in a voice worthy of Bibi Norton.

They stared at me for a second, and then turned as one. It wasn't a silent departure by any means. With every step the voices grew louder. Not that it mattered.

I turned the gospel music back on, even before getting out of the tub and locking the door. Then I turned on the jets. All *thirty* of them.

Refreshed and reattired, I wandered downstairs to see how lunch preparations were coming. Freni had wanted to make a pork roast, but I'd made her promise to hold off on hog until our little piggy went to market — so to speak. Instead, my stalwart cook made roast chicken and dressing.

"The hens are a little tough, yah? But I soak them in Vermont, so they get tender like pullets."

"Vermont?"

"Yah. It is a special recipe."

"It sounds special, indeed — given that Vermont is hundreds of miles away. How did you manage to pull that one off, and how does soaking them in another state make them tender?" I wasn't being facetious. The wonders of cooking — even Freni's — are beyond my ken.

"Ach, Magdalena, you talk such nonsense." She opened a cabinet, withdrew a tall bottle, and thrust it into my hands. "*This* is Vermont."

I reeled in shock. "That says vermouth, not Vermont!"

"But it also good for soaking chicken,

yah? Marionette, they call it."

"That's *marinade,* dear. And vermouth is anything but a state. It's a kind of — uh . . ." I bit my tongue. What was the point in telling a seventy-six-year-old Amish woman that she was cooking with alcohol? The shock could kill someone her age. Did I want to have her death on my hands as well? Besides, wasn't vermouth a kind of wine? And Jesus turned water into wine at the wedding in Cana, didn't He? Perhaps He turned it into vermouth. Except that when Reverend Schrock preaches on that story he is always careful to add that the translation must be in error, and that in his opinion the beverage served at that biblical wedding was really grape juice.

Freni was waiting for my approval. "It smells good, yah?"

"Delicious. Where did you get the vermouth?"

"That nice English woman, the one who speaks slowly. She gives me the recipe. And she brings me the bottle from a special store in Bedford."

I am certainly no expert on spirits. Before I lectured Freni on using ingredients supplied by guests, I owed it to the both of us to sample the contents of this bottle and determine if indeed it was prohibited by my faith. Yes, I know, there was a label on the bottle, but one can't trust everything one reads, you know. Why, just get on the Internet if you don't believe me; half the stuff on there is rubbish. Besides, the print on that label was so small I risked going cross-eyed, which would not be a flattering look for me, given my prominent proboscis.

Therefore, being ever the responsible daughter my pious parents raised, I filled a small glass with the amber liquid. It certainly smelled sweet and innocuous. Then, breathing a prayer for forgiveness, lest it turn out to be forbidden, I sampled the stuff.

Sweet, definitely. Perhaps a woody undertone — not that I chew on much wood, mind you. It didn't taste like I imagined wine to taste. But then how was I to know? And if it really was wine, I had better memorize that taste, so as not to inadvertently imbibe on some other occasion. It was practically my Christian duty to sample it again.

Due to the fact that I am an earnest woman, who really does try to do the right thing, I sometimes find it hard to make decisions. It was because I was trying to be fair that I drank the entire glass. In the end I concluded that the jury would remain out until I had the time, and was feeling well enough, for further sampling.

You see, the hot bath with the thirty jets had left me feeling a bit light-headed. In fact, I felt a definite need for fresh air.

"Hairy on," I said to Freni. "I mean, carry on. I'm going outside for a minute."

"Magdalena, are you all right?"

"I'm fine as frog chair, dear. Oops, make that frog hair. Although that expression has never made sense to me, since frogs don't have any. Hair — that is. Or chairs either, I presume." I giggled pleasantly. "At any rate, do what you do best."

Freni flushed. "Ach! What I do at home, with my Mose, is not your business."

"Cook," I cried gaily. "I was talking about cooking. Although, after all these years of marriage, if you and Mose are still doing the mattress mambo, then more power to you. Just remember — no dancing!" I chortled at my own wit.

"Dancing!"

"Yes, dancing, the worst of all sins." Feeling suddenly frisky, I grabbed a broom from the corner and pretended to dance with it. Having never seen the shameful act, I had no idea how to imitate it. But I shrugged my shoulders and waggled my hips in what I imagined to be lascivious gyrations.

"Ach!" Freni fled into the dining room. Who knew she could be so sensitive?

"It was only with a broom," I called after her. "It doesn't count. It's not like it was a vacuum cleaner."

By then I really did need fresh air. I dropped the broom and waltzed to the back door. Flinging it open, I shimmied into the sunshine.

"Woo-hoo, look at me, I'm dancing," I called to the world at large. And why not? Since everyone always thought the worst about me, why not enjoy the sins about which I had no doubt already been accused? Surely, the sharp-tongued Schrock had accused me of doing the hokeypokey before. And if not — well, this was equal to any two other sins on her list.

Alas, the world was not paying attention. While I shimmied and shook, Hernia was too busy watching sweaty farmers bale hay. Even Alison and her pig were too engrossed playing in a nearby field to notice me.

"This is your last chance!" I shouted to the sparrows in the trees. "If you want to see me shake my booty, you better look now."

That language, by the way, was courtesy of Susannah. To me a booty has always been nothing more than an infant's foot covering.

"And a might fine booty it is," one of the sparrows said in a surprisingly deep voice.

"Why, thank you — although it is a little on the skinny side, don't you think?"

"I like it just the way it is."

I whirled. That was certainly no sparrow. Not with that vaguely East Coast accent.

28

"Gabe!" My beloved stood not six feet away, a moon-size grin on his face.

"Hi, babe. Don't tell me you didn't know I was here."

"I had no idea! How long have you been standing there?"

"Long enough to see you strut your stuff. And you told me you didn't dance."

"I don't." The vermouth-induced feeling of liberation was now a distant memory. "This was the first time — and my last."

Gabe planted a long, lingering kiss on my lips. This is what Susannah calls getting to first base. I allow it because we are engaged. I don't know exactly what getting to second and third base entail, but I can guarantee that my fiancé is going to keep his bat in the dugout until after we're married.

"Hey," he said, finally pulling back, "I thought you were a teetotaler."

"I am. Totally tea!" What possible harm

could one more little lie do? It was basically the truth.

Gabe winked. "Tastes a little bit like you've been hitting the sauce as well."

"Marionette sauce," I explained quickly. "I mean marinade. Freni is roasting some old hens."

"What's in this marinade?"

"Well, I'm not really sure — okay, so maybe there's a little vermouth."

"Was it the sauce you sampled, or did you chug it straight from the bottle?"

"I didn't chug anything! I merely sipped. And does it matter? Because I'm never doing that again either. From now on, I'm flying straight as an arrow. Not that I'm flying now, mind you. Not high like a kite or anything. Definitely not high at all. Anyway, I promise never to do those things again."

His brown eyes twinkled. "Then that will be a shame. I was getting to like your wild side."

"But I can be wild in other ways. You should see me play Florida golf." I was referring to a Mennonite card game that is said to have originated in Sarasota, Florida, a long-time watering hole of Mennonite and Amish retirees. This game, by the way, uses Skip-Bo cards, and not the sinful face cards found in regular decks.

"I'd love to," Gabe said. His face became serious for a moment. "What's this I hear about you fixing Ma up on a date?"

"He's one of Hernia's most respected citizens," I hastened to explain. There was no need to mention Doc's reputation as a womanizer. If Ida Rosen was lucky, she'd find that out soon enough.

Gabe gave me a peck on the forehead. Believe me, not many men are tall enough to do that.

"My tone was supposed to be kidding. I think it's a wonderful idea."

"You do?"

"Absolutely. Mags, hon, I know how controlling she can be. Don't think I like it, because I don't. I put up with it because — well, I don't want to be disrespectful. And since Pa died, she doesn't have anyone else to order around."

"How about your sisters in New York?"

"Sarah and Dafna won't listen to a word Ma says. Never have. Ma needs someone to push around."

"Oops. I think Doc may be a pusher himself. He's definitely not a pushover."

"All the better. Neither was Pa. Ma likes to push just so hard and then get it right back at her. The trouble is, unlike my sisters, I go the opposite direction. Conflict avoidance, I guess you'd call it."

Too bad. Truth be told, I can be a wee bit pushy myself — well, not exactly pushy, but I do have strong opinions. That's what one can expect from someone who is generally right about things. It's not my fault I'm well informed.

"Gabe, you might not have noticed, but —"

"You're the pushiest woman, besides Ma, in Bedford County?"

"Hey, no fair! What about Lodema Schrock?"

"She's not pushy, she's merely obnoxious. Don't get me wrong, hon. I don't like it in Ma — too much history — but in you it's charming."

"It is?"

"You bet. Now, what the heck are you doing over there by the barn? Putting in a swimming pool?"

His words made no sense. Hernians don't build swimming pools. Our summers aren't long enough or hot enough to justify the expense. Besides, with a plethora of farm ponds and creeks about, why bother?

"Of course I'm not building a pool."

"Then why all the digging?"

I looked past Gabe's shoulder to the east

corner of the barn. To the left, where yesterday there had been nothing but a low, decomposing blanket of *haufa mischt,* there was now an immense pile of dirt. Anyone but a blind or very drunk person would have noticed the change in topography.

"Ding dang dong dung!" Thanks to an endless series of stressful situations, I could now swear like a trooper.

The Babester laughed. "Well, it was dung, wasn't it?"

Ignoring his crude remark, I trotted over to inspect the damage to my property. Believe me, by now any trace of the vermouth was well on its way to Vermont. I could think as clearly as Sean Penn.

And I needed every wit about me to process the awful sight. This wasn't just a pile of dirt; it was a wall of dirt that encircled what had been the perimeter of my manure heap. In the center was a hole, perhaps ten feet square and some three feet deep. As for the *haufa mischt,* it was scattered hither, thither, and yon around the farmyard. In fact, I was stepping in some that very moment. Thank heavens it was well rotted and beyond the smelling stage.

"Well, it looks like a good start on a swimming pool anyway," Gabe said. "Of course, it needs to be much longer if you plan to swim laps. And maybe another foot deeper. Plus, you'd do well to forget about installing a diving board, no matter how deep you make it. Private pools produce a lot of broken necks — even the ones that are supposedly deep enough."

"This isn't a pool," I wailed, furious at myself for not having figured it out sooner. "It's a treasure pit."

"Come again?"

"It's a family legend. The key to the Hochstetler fortune is supposed to be hidden somewhere in and around Hernia. Possibly buried. Only the descendants can claim it. Anyway, I cleverly planted the idea in two of my guests' heads — Capers and Teruko — that the treasure was buried under my manure pile. They obviously fell for the bait."

"Do you think they found it?"

A brunette can be just as dense as a blonde — which shouldn't be a surprise, I guess, since most blondes started out that way. I tried not to give my beloved a pitying look.

"Of course there wasn't treasure there, or I would have dug it up myself. I just wanted to get the manure turned over this fall, so I could have a nice fertile vegetable plot next spring. Carrots grown in well-rotted *haufa mischt* are the deepest orange you've ever seen. But my real objective to planting this idea was to see if either of these guests believed strongly enough in the legend to follow any lead." I peered down into the hole. Too bad it wasn't a lot deeper. How handy it would be to lower a long rope and hoist up freshly cooked Chinese food. Guests wouldn't rebel then.

"They may have fallen for the bait," Gabe said quietly, "but that doesn't mean they were the primary rats."

"I beg your pardon?"

"Your guest — Mr. Porter, right? — was murdered before this hole was dug. And he was found near another hole, from which the time capsule went missing. One can't make any reasonable conclusions from that. Different guests could have made different holes."

"Don't poke pins in my balloon," I wailed. "And anyway, Miss Mukai and the Littletons are awfully chummy. That very first night, when the taxi drove off with Miss Mukai's luggage, Capers Littleton offered to lend the girl some of her clothes. What do you make of that?"

Gabe shrugged. "That Mrs. Littleton is a gracious Southern lady?"

"Cahoots!" I cried. "They're in cahoots!"

Gabe threw up his hands. "You're the expert, hon. Whatever you say."

"Don't patronize me, Gabriel Ephraim Rosen."

"Oh, the full-name treatment, is it? Well, two can play that game, Magdalena Portulacca Yoder."

"Maybe, but my mother doesn't tuck me in at night."

"That's being childish," he had the chutzpah to say.

Well, I could be just as childish if I put my mind to it. Probably even more so. Instead, I put my hands on my hips and stamped a long, narrow foot.

"You're right, I *am* the expert. So just go home and do whatever it is you do to fill your days. Write those silly little mysteries, for all I care."

"Fine. In the meantime you can make this hole even deeper. Hey, I know, why don't you give it a name — like the Great Hole of Hernia? I bet you could charge admission."

"Just maybe I will. I'm sure I'll make more money from it than you will from your books — *if* you ever manage to sell one."

"That was a low blow." His voice was barely more than a whisper, but he may as well have been shouting. Without even giving me an angry glare, he turned and walked away.

"You idiot!" I said. "What do you know about relationships? Nothing, that's what. Don't be a total fool. Apologize this minute."

I was talking to myself. Gabriel Ephraim Rosen was the best thing that had ever happened to me. Okay, he was a bit of a mama's boy, but so what? Doc was going to take care of that. Why, then, was I so irritated with him? Because he had stated the obvious about my conclusions? That they were invalid? Did this mean I was no more competent than my nemesis, the Mantis?

Well, the truth hurts, as they say. In order that my ego didn't have to suffer alone, I kicked one of the mounds of dirt that surrounded the "Great Hole of Hernia." My toe hit a stone.

Angrily, I kicked a second pile with my other foot. Then another pile. There were eight piles in all — *eight* piles? I counted them three times. Sure enough, eight was the magic number. But that had to be a coincidence. Even if Capers and Terri had shared my misinformation with Octavia

Cabot-Dodge — well, a woman her age couldn't possibly have dug a hole this large by herself. And if by some miracle she had, surely there would be another clue.

I circled the pit like a hawk over a field fire, one intent on catching mice. What was I missing? Nothing, that's what. There was nothing untoward that I could see about that pit and the eight piles of dirt — well, except that one was a tad smaller than the others. Wait, a minute. One was also considerably larger than the others. But they all had stones.

Stones! That was it. The dirt on my farm does contain stones, but it's not like I live in a gravel pit. Yet each pile appeared peppered with stones. My heart raced as I began to count the stones on the nearest pile. Just as I suspected; there were eight on the first pile. Eight on the second. Eight on all eight piles, and not a stone more.

"Aha," I said, as the lightbulb went on in my otherwise empty head. Given my pale eyes, it probably shone right through them, bestowing on me the look of one possessed.

"Mom!"

Bless Alison's heart. I hadn't seen the child approach. But to be fair, I was every bit as startled by her sudden appearance as she was by my glowing peepers.

"Not to fear, dear," I assured her. "Your old mom just had an epiphany."

"Mom, do we have to talk about religion now? Babe just ate my hair."

"What?"

"My hair!" she shrieked. "What's the matter, ya blind?"

When the girl first came to live with me, her head was decked out in spiked hair the color of a ripe eggplant. The first thing I made her do — after losing the body-piercing jewelry — was to undo the spike and get her locks back to their original color, a rich shade of chestnut brown. Over the past eight months it had grown to the point where it no longer attracted undue attention.

"Alison, I don't see —" I gasped. A huge chunk of hair from the left side of her head was missing.

"Ya see now, don'tcha?"

"The pig did that?"

"Yeah, and I was just getting to like my hair that way."

"Why did you let him — I mean, how did that happen?"

"Well, I kind of fell asleep out there in the meadow. And the next thing I knew he was chewing away. Mom, I hate him."

At least there was a bright side to this catastrophe. "As a matter of fact, dear, I was just about to suggest that we reconsider —"

"And he peed in your bed."

"*What?*"

"When I woke up this morning you were gone and the bed was all wet. I know I didn't do it, so it had to be him." She put her hands on hips that were just beginning to round. "Unless it was you."

"*Moi?*" I put my hands where my hips should have been. "I'll have you know, young lady, that I haven't wet the bed since high school."

"See? So it was him. Mom, I hope ya don't get mad or anything — like holler real loud — but I'd kind of like to . . . well, get rid of him."

"Oh." It was all I could do to not jump up and down with joy.

"Actually," she said, averting her eyes, "I was more like hoping you would let me sell him."

"Child of my heart!" I cried and clutched her to my bony chest.

She pushed out of my embrace and then glanced at the road behind me. I turned just in time to see two cars, the Littletons' and the Nortons', pull into my driveway. Heaven forbid anyone saw a kid being hugged by her mom — even a foster one.

"Ya don't have ta get all weird on me."

"Sorry. It was probably just an electrical impulse beamed down on me from a satellite. Where's the little monster now?"

"In the barn. So, it's all right with you? Selling him, I mean."

"Sell away," I said happily.

"And I get to keep the money, right?"

"Right as rain. Unless you want me to invest it for you."

"Nah." It was obvious she couldn't wait to get into the house and start making her calls. Not that she would get a lot of money for a single piglet in a farming community, but knowing Alison as I did, I had no doubt the critter would fetch a lot more than it was worth.

I would have insisted that Alison stay long enough to hear at least the short version of the "saving money speech." But before I could open my nagging trap, the most incredible thing happened.

29

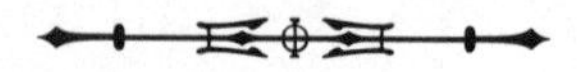

"Will you look at that!"

Alison was already halfway to the house and the nearest phone. No doubt visions of a shopping trip into Bedford danced through her head.

Never mind. I don't mind talking to myself. After all, I find that I am my own best listener. And rarely do I interrupt myself.

"What on earth is that down-on-her-luck diva doing with the Littletons? She has her own chauffeur, for crying out loud. Well, she doesn't look too happy, that's for sure. Then again, when has she looked happy? Slap that woman's mug on a jar of pickles, and it will sell itself. Now there is a business opportunity I should seriously consider. I could call the company Cabot-Dodge Dill Pickles. My slogan could be 'The taste so tart it's guaranteed to wipe the smile off your face.' Should go over well at church suppers across the country. And if dour diva refused to sell rights to her likeness, I could always try one of my own photographs."

Although I rather enjoy my private conversations, seldom do my questions get definitive answers. Therefore, I trotted over to greet my guests to give them the third degree. Unfortunately, they saw me coming and all but one of them hightailed it into the house. The only reason I was able to catch the diva is because she was trapped in her stair-counting ritual.

"Miss Cabot-Dodge," I said, mustering the fake cheer that comes with years of inn keeping, "where are your staff?"

"Ha!" she barked. "Staff. That's a joke if I ever heard one." Then, because she'd lost count, she retreated to the bottom step.

"They are planning to show up for lunch, aren't they?"

"Whether or not they miss lunch is not my concern, Miss Yoder."

"But it is mine. If I have to throw away a lot of food —"

"Well, I paid for it, didn't I?"

"Yes, but —"

"The nerve of those two, after all I've done for them. Always complaining that their wages are too low. But where would they be if I hadn't supported them all these years, tell me that?"

"Somewhere different?"

"Ragsdale to riches, that's what she thought it would be." The diva sat to deliver the rest of her diatribe. "But she didn't have the talent. I did. And she certainly didn't have the skills to be my manager. Kept saying the parts weren't coming in, but a good manager would have known how to bring them to me. At least get me a competent agent. But no, not Augusta. Like Jacob and Esau, Mama always said. From the very beginning I had a hunch that things wouldn't work out. I should have followed my instincts and gone it alone. Now look where I am."

"Sitting on my front steps?"

"Blood may be thicker than water, Miss Yoder. But at least you can drink water."

My legs were shaking so hard I found myself forced to sit on the opposite side of the steps. "Where are they now?"

"Running their own errands — and in *my* limousine."

"Miss Cabot-Dodge, are you and Augusta twins?"

It's a good thing the Good Lord created cartilage, because her reworked skin could not have held those jaws together by itself. That's how wide her mouth opened. For the record, Octavia Cabot-

Dodge has had her tonsils removed.

"How did you know?"

"That Jacob and Esau reference. Plus the fact that you were obviously both born in August. You know, Octavia — Augusta."

I slapped my forehead, but gently of course. My hands may be bony, but they can deliver quite a punch. Plus my palms still hurt. But why hadn't I seen that connection before?

"Ha! For all you know, I was named after Mark Antony's wife."

"Yes, but in Hernia that would make you Elizabeth Taylor. We're not the most sophisticated folks, you know."

"What makes you think I'm from Hernia?"

"You just said you were. 'Ragsdale to Riches' you said."

She glared at me. "Ha! You must think you're really clever, Miss Yoder."

"Only some of the time. Right now I'm having a hard time coming up with a reason for your visit. Nostalgia, I can understand. But if that's it, why not be open about your roots — small town girl makes good, that kind of thing?"

"Coming here was my sister's idea, not mine. She thought it would make me grateful for how far I've come."

"Has it?"

Her glare intensified. "Surprisingly so. I'm grateful to have left this narrow-minded community behind. And you know as well as I do, Miss Yoder, that Hernians do not consider being a movie star a badge of success."

"Narrow minds keep the devil away," I said, quoting my mother. I didn't agree, but Mama's mind was so narrow, she had room for only one thought at a time, and I'm sure it was never put there by the man with the pitchfork.

"Ha!"

"Miss Cabot-Dodge, did you drive all the way from California?"

"Of course not! My chauffeur did. Airline fares are ridiculous these days."

"You could have flown by yourself."

"Ha! You don't know Augusta." She had nothing further to say. And although it must have been humiliating, especially under the circumstances, she completed her ritual and climbed the stairs.

I turned away to give her privacy. Besides, now that all the pieces were finally falling into place, I was back on the job. But before I rolled up my sleeves (to a modest elbow length) I had to run my theory past the person in Hernia who was best suited to answer my one remaining question.

* * *

Doc put the plate in front of me almost shyly. "It's not much, I'm afraid. Blue's radar must be down. Anyway, it's just some chicken and walnut salad with a bleu cheese dressing. Avocado wedges and ripe tomatoes — those are late tomatoes from my own garden, by the way. At least these," he said, placing a basket of crescent rolls in the center of the table, "are made from scratch. Not out of those tubes. I know, folks say it's a lot of trouble to make fresh ones, and you can't tell the difference from the tube ones, but I say they're wrong. Take one — tell me what you think."

I voted by taking two. That was just the first round. Altogether I had six rolls and three helpings of the chicken salad, but just one slice of the quadruple chocolate cake with mocha icing, and real chocolate-covered coffee beans on top for decoration.

"You should enter that cake in the Bake-Off, Doc."

"I plan to. Got to be there at two sharp. That's why lunch isn't anything to write home about."

"But it's really good, nonetheless. This is the tastiest chicken salad I've ever eaten. Really moist."

"That's because it's beer butt chicken."

"I beg your pardon."

"Grilled it this morning. You see, you stick a can of beer up — never mind. I'm sure the only thing you need to know is that the alcohol cooks off."

Like it did with Freni's Vermont chicken. But if I'd drunk the beer straight from the can — well, there was no point dwelling on past sins.

"Doc, you know a lot about human diseases, don't you?"

He cocked his head. "Not as much as that handsome young stud of yours. Why don't you save your question for him?"

"Because Gabriel and I —" I sighed. "Because we're not communicating well at the moment, that's why."

"How about his mother? Did you communicate with her?"

"The woman is hot to trot," I said, borrowing one of Susannah's seemingly meaningless phrases.

Doc rubbed his hands together. "Excellent!"

"Glad to be of service," I said, as I swallowed more irritation than salad. "Now that I've gotten you lined up with a date, how about answering my question."

"Which is?"

"What do you know about Obsessive-Compulsive Disorder?"

"So it's finally gotten that bad, has it?"

"I beg your pardon?"

"Don't worry, Magdalena, your secret is safe with me."

"But I don't have a secret," I wailed. "I'm not talking about me."

He smiled encouragingly. "Let's pretend you're not. I just want you to know that they have ways of treating this disorder these days. Some of those antidepressant drugs are said to be very useful, especially in conjunction with talk therapy. It's certainly nothing to be ashamed of. You come by it honestly, you know."

"I do? I mean, I don't — because I don't have it."

"Your mama — now there was a fine specimen of a woman — always had to put her right stocking and shoe on first."

"How on earth do you know that?" I clapped my hands over my ears, dreading the answer. But not so tight that I couldn't hear it.

"Because your papa was always teasing her. Also said she had to check the gas stove ten times before she left the house."

"Well, I'm not Mama, and I only check it twice. I asked the question because of one of my guests, not me."

He took a sip of coffee and leaned back in his chair. "I'm listening."

"Her name is Octavia, because she was born in August, and apparently she has this thing about the number eight. Especially when it comes to stairs, but I've seen her doing it at other times as well."

"Go on."

"Well, I planted a false clue — to two other guests, not her — about the Hochstetler treasure being buried under my manure pile."

Doc's coffee exited in a fine spray. "That's my girl. Magdalena, I sure as heck hope this Rosen woman is half as interesting as you."

"Thanks — I think. Anyway, this morning the *haufa mischt* had been scattered and the ground beneath it dug up. Into eight piles. And each pile had eight stones pressed into it."

"Were the stones randomly placed, or in recognizable groupings?"

"Random. I didn't notice them at first. And what's more, Doc, the piles weren't all the same size. Close maybe, but not the same."

He dabbed at his shirt with a crisp linen napkin. "Well, like I said, I'm not a people doctor, but if you want my guess — for what it's worth — it looks like a setup. Anyone who was compulsive enough to put the dirt in eight piles would make them as even as possible. As for that stone bit, it's over the top."

"That's what I thought. It's like someone is purposely calling attention to the eight piles. To direct suspicion away from themself."

"Exactly."

"Ah, so you know who it is?"

"I have my theory."

"But you're not going to act on it alone, right?"

"Absolutely not. Trust me, Doc, I've learned my lesson."

He sighed. "Yeah, I bet. Promise me that if you get in over your head, you'll call the sheriff, not the dummkopf."

"Aye, aye, Captain — I mean Doc."

But if life throws you a curveball, and you don't have any of your own — curves, that is — you take what you can get. I was on my way to the inn, fully intending to give the sheriff a call if things got out of hand, when I spotted Octavia's limo. It was headed not back to PennDutch, but in the other direction, toward the road that leads up Stucky Ridge. It was my duty to follow it, at a discreet distance, of course, to see if the occupants were up to any mischief. They were, after all, on the wrong side of town for both the hay-baling and the Bake-Off.

When they turned on the winding lane to the summit, I stuck with them. Yes, I know it should have been the sheriff I dialed on my cell phone. But in my defense, Melvin does live on this side of town. Besides, I still had no proof.

"What now?" he snapped. I was right to assume that our Chief of Police would take the day off when the town was overflowing with visitors. There were probably a million — okay, maybe half a dozen — fender benders, and no one available to write up citations. Not unless Zelda could be convinced to give up her vacation. Perhaps I should give her a call next and entice her with the probability that at least one of the fender benders was going to result in fisticuffs. Breaking up a fight was an activity she was bound to enjoy.

"I think I know who did it," I said calmly.

"Don't tell me, you idiot. Unless, of course, it was Erica Kane."

"Are you watching that soap opera again?"

"It's not a soap; it's a televised drama. So you don't know who, do you?"

"Augusta Miller and Stanley Dalrumple. She's Octavia's twin sister. I'm not sure what Mr. Dalrumple's connection is, other than chauffeur."

"Don't be an idiot, Yoder. They're not even in the story line."

"Listen to me you — you —" Fortunately I sputtered out of steam before I called him a name. I took a deep, cleansing breath. "I'm talking about the murders of Buzzy Porter and Ron Humphrey."

"Yeah, those names I recognize."

If my arms were skinnier I could reach through a phone line and grab Melvin by his equally scrawny neck. I was, however, on my cell phone.

"Melvin, dear," I said dripping so much sarcasm I feared for the floorboards of my car, "if you can't remember the last several days, then perhaps you should indeed consider the presidency. Or maybe big business."

"Thanks, Yoder — hey, that wasn't a compliment, was it?"

I watched the limo make the last turn before reaching the summit. "No, it wasn't. But if you want a chance to exercise your strongest muscle — maybe even redeem yourself — meet me up on Stucky Ridge. Pronto."

"I'm a married man, Yoder."

I considered the source. "The suspects are in the limo. I'm pretty sure they don't know they're being followed. Meet me just before the top, at the last bend. We'll go the rest of the way on foot."

"Okay, Yoder, but you better be onto something. *One Life to Live* comes on next."

"Summit!" I hissed and then hung up.

30

Author's note: Pious people should avoid this recipe, which involves both alcohol and the business end of a chicken. However, yielding to temptation does reward one with a delectable treat.

Jim and Jan Langdoc's Beer Butt Chicken

Hickory- or mesquite-scented
  wood chips
1 can beer
Commercial or homemade "rub."
1 whole chicken, thoroughly washed
  and patted dry
Vegetable oil as needed

Homemade Rub

1/4 cup salt (sea or kosher)
1/3 cup brown sugar (light or dark)
1/4 cup paprika (sweet or hot)
3 tablespoons freshly ground pepper

Soak hickory- or mesquite-scented wood chips for 30 minutes in half of the beer, leaving the other half of the beer in the can. Spread soaked chips over hot coals in the grill (or if using gas, put in smoker box).

Sprinkle 1 teaspoon of rub into cavity of chicken. Oil the outside of the chicken and sprinkle with 1 tablespoon of the rub. Rub in well.

Put about 1 1/2 tablespoons of rub directly into tab opening of the beer can. Punch 2 additional holes in the can, using a sharp object (such as grilling fork). Insert the beer can into the cavity of the chicken.

Place can and chicken on grill, so that the legs and can form a tripod to support the chicken. Cook until meat thermometer reaches 180 degrees without touching bone (between 1 and 1 1/2 hours). The steam from the beer keeps the bird moist and succulent, as well as giving it character. Let the chicken rest 5 minutes before serving.

31

The limo stopped soon after it reached the summit, which surprised me. It did not surprise me, however, to see both Augusta Miller and Stanley Dalrumple hop out. Stanley was carrying a coil of rope over his shoulder. Augusta had a pair of binoculars hung around her neck. I was able to spot these accouterments because I keep a pair of binoculars of my own in the glove compartment. Don't ask me what I use them for, and you'll be spared an answer that might embarrass you.

At any rate, neither of them glanced my way, and if they had, they probably wouldn't have seen me anyway. I'd stopped my car the second I saw their brake lights come on, and had advanced on foot. Now I was hiding behind a tree trunk, which is yet another advantage of being rail thin.

I could hear their conversation, thanks to a gentle breeze that was blowing in my direction. Still, it was faint, so I cupped both hands behind my ears.

"You should have marked the spot where you threw the shovel over." At that distance Augusta's voice sounded identical to that of her sister. Why hadn't I noticed that before?

"But, Grandma," Stanley whined, "it's not like I had the time. That jogger was onto us, and my prints were all over the handle."

Grandma! So that was Augusta's relationship to the boy. I crept closer.

"You should have worn gloves, Stanley, like I told you."

"So I forgot them. You didn't remember either, and this whole damn thing was your idea, not mine."

"Don't you swear in front of me," Augusta snarled. "And switching the bodies at the morgue was most certainly not my idea."

"You got to admit, that was brilliant thinking on my part. Kept them confused long enough so that we could dispose of Buzzy."

She sighed. "It wasn't supposed to turn out this way. Buzzy was my grandson too. But oh no, he had to jump the gun — get all the treasure for himself. Didn't I tell you from the beginning that he was high-risk? Just like that no-good magician father of his, who sold my youngest daughter off to Vegas."

"Yeah, but Grandma, you said yourself that Buzzy probably heard the treasure story a million times before Auntie Vera and Uncle Ray died in that accident."

It was a bizarre time for her to laugh, but that didn't stop her. "I guess we should be glad that my dotty old sister has been too stuck on herself all these years to see the boy even once. She didn't even blink when they were introduced Sunday."

Stanley snickered. "You can bet the cops would have blinked if they'd had more time with his body. I look just like him when I take off my glasses."

"Don't flatter yourself, Stanley. Just thank your lucky stars I remembered that little cave at the bottom of Lovers' Leap."

"Yeah, but I had to lower his body through these trees and then push all them leaves up against the cave."

"Well, I couldn't exactly get down there myself now, could I? I'm not a spring chicken anymore, you know."

"You were supposed to run over the jogger, but you didn't. So then I had to shoot him."

"Stanley, are you getting cheeky with me?"

"I'm just saying, seems to me I've had to do all the work. So what if I had a little fun along the way?"

"You're just like your cousin, Stanley. You know that? You could have been caught, and that would have been the end of everything."

The lad giggled. "Yeah, but Buzzy is dead, and I'm not. Man, I'd give anything to hear what went on in that rinky-dink morgue when they discovered the switch. But you can bet it wasn't one of the staff. They were as dumb as bricks."

Augusta snorted. "They couldn't sew shut a Thanksgiving turkey if their lives depended on it. No, it had to be that busybody, Ms. Yoder."

"Needle Nose?"

Needle Nose? Why, the nerve of that boy! And she was no better — busybody indeed. I crept closer so as not to miss a disparaging word. Unfortunately, it is hard to put a size eleven shoe — even a narrow one — down on any surface without making a noise. It is especially hard to do so when skirting a woods. The branch that cracked under my foot must have been as dry as tinder, because the report was as loud as a sonic boom.

Stanley and Augusta wheeled in unison,

as if they had choreographed the scene. He was holding a gun, which appeared to be aimed right at me, and she already had the binoculars pressed to her face.

"It's her," she said. "Needle Nose. Under that sycamore."

Intellectually I knew that small handguns are notoriously inaccurate, especially at a distance. If I ran, particularly in a zigzag pattern, my chances of escaping unharmed were good. And since I stood at the edge of the woods, they were, in fact, excellent. Alas, my brain refused to communicate this knowledge to my legs, which had suddenly become columns of overcooked pasta. Mountains of mushy macaroni. Rebellious rigatoni. Spastic spaghetti. Limp linguini. Choose your carbohydrate, but you get the picture.

This cowardly reaction is quite unlike me, I assure you. Under normal circumstances I might well have charged the deadly duo and then nudged them off the cliff with my infamous schnoz. These were not normal circumstances, however, because when I stepped on the crackling branch, I had placed my tootsie no more than an inch away from a snake.

It was a small snake, not more than a foot and a half long, but from the pattern on its back, not to mention its telltale tail, I could see at once that it was some form of rattler. It was coiled when I first saw it, but almost immediately it began to unwind in a quest to slither away to safety. It was, however, directionally challenged, and in its haste to escape, slithered directly over my foot.

I can't blame the poor thing for mistaking my black brogan for just another boulder. I'm sure it was as confused and scared as I was. It took only a second or two for the reptile to cross my foot, but those precious seconds were all Stanley Dalrumple needed. As the snake disappeared under the litter of leaves that blanketed the ground, the chauffeur and would-be heir closed the gap that was my margin of safety.

"Take one step, Miss Yoder, and I'll blow your refrigerator head off." He actually used a far cruder expression, one that bears no repeating.

My legs were still not under my command, although my tongue was. "Your grandmother should wash your mouth out with soap."

By now Augusta was close enough to hear what I said. "My grandson's language is none of your business, Miss Yoder."

"Some grandmother you are. You don't seem the least bit saddened by your other grandson's death. That bogus fortune means more to you."

"It isn't bogus," Stanley snapped. "Tell her, Grandma."

Augusta's face, when viewed closely, was not a pretty sight. Please don't misunderstand, there is nothing wrong with wrinkles. Her skin, however, was so dry and so crisscrossed with creases, that it resembled the soles of my feet in the dead of winter.

"We found a map in the time capsule."

"Map?"

"Don't pretend you're stupid, Miss Yoder. It's a map that shows where the Hochstetler family treasure is buried."

"I honestly don't know anything about a treasure map. If anything, the capsule was supposed to contain a list of the founding fathers. Sort of a code as to which family Bible to look in."

"Ah, Bibi Norton's theory. Well, she's wrong. As simple as that. It's a map, and we have it now."

"Get out of town!"

"We plan to, just as soon as we figure out how to read it."

"Show it to her, Grandma."

I was dying of curiosity. "Yes, please show it to me."

To my astonishment Augusta reached into the front of her dress and withdrew from her bosom an ancient piece of paper. Mama used to keep a clean handkerchief in her cleavage, and Susannah keeps a dog where her bosom should be, so this was definitely a family trait. It's just that I didn't really expect there to be a map.

"You help us find it," she said, "and we won't kill you."

"But she'll squeal," Stanley squealed. He sounded just like our soon-to-be-ex-pet pig.

I shook my head vigorously. My legs had regained their strength and I was feeling feisty again — well, at least foolish.

"Split it three ways, and I won't tell a soul."

"Why, the nerve," Augusta said, but her eyes shone with admiration.

"Show me." I held out my right hand.

Augusta opened the document with great care. "I remembered the cave, but not all the area landmarks."

She wouldn't let me touch it, but she did let me get close enough to get a good look. It was all I could do to keep from laughing. In fact, a sort of bray escaped my lips before I could will them closed. The map, you see, was not a treasure map at all, but the siting plan for an outdoor toilet. An outhouse, as we used to call them.

This particular sketch was not for your run-of-the-mill outhouse, but the famous six seater that Great-grandpa Milo Yoder built on the family farm. It was hailed as the largest outhouse east of the Mississippi, and some wag on the Bedford newspaper even dubbed it the Eighth Wonder of the Underworld. I know it must sound ostentatious to have such a grand bathroom, even if it was detached from the house and lacked plumbing. But you see, my great-grandparents had eleven children. An ordinary two seater just wouldn't do. Besides, Great-grandpa Milo was of the philosophy that the family that sprayed together, stayed together. Trust me, I hadn't an inkling that the plans for this incredible structure (which was sadly destroyed by fire in my lifetime) had been deemed important enough to be included in Hernia's time capsule.

"Is something funny, Miss Yoder?" Stanley looked like he wanted to snatch the map from his grandmother's hands and away from my mocking eyes.

"Oh, nothing in the least," I managed to say with a straight face. "It's just that I recognize everything on this map." That, incidentally, was the truth. The large rectangle was our barn, the square was our house, and the long narrow rectangle with the row of small circles in it, the famous six seater. There were even two scalloped circles to represent the pair of large maples that still stand in my front yard.

"Okay, you're in," Augusta said. She handed me the map.

I shall always regret what I did next. I honestly believe I intended no harm to these killers, merely a way for me to escape so that I could be reunited with my loved ones. And anyway, we were a long way from Lovers' Leap, and the drop-off wasn't more than thirty feet at that point. Besides, the ledge below the cliff was covered with small trees and bushes, so that if anyone did go over, they might be badly scratched and break a few bones, but they surely wouldn't die from the experience.

"That," I said, pointing to the rectangle that represented the barn, "is Murphy's Mountain over there to the southwest. And that" — I pointed to the box that marked my house — "is Buffalo Mountain, which is behind us."

"Don't look like mountain symbols to me," Stanley said.

I flashed him a smile, which, if genuine, would have rotted his teeth in a nanosecond. "That's because in those days a triangle was considered vulgar, imitating as it does the female bosom."

Augusta nodded, as if she remembered "those days." Perhaps she did.

"And what about these two scalloped circles?" she asked.

"Ah, well, this one is the Neunschwander farm, and the other one is the Berkey place. They're just on there as points of reference. What's important is this long narrow rectangle with six circles in it."

They stared at the design for great-grandpa's outhouse. "What does it mean?" Augusta demanded. Her breath was as hot as any August day, although not nearly as sweet.

"You see," I said, praying for inspiration, "this long skinny rectangle is Stucky Ridge. That, of course, is where we're standing right now. The circle on this end is the cave just below Lovers' Leap — but you already know all about that one. There are five caves just like it, only they're harder to find. Now this" — I tapped the slanted line that indicated the location of the outhouse door —

"tells us which cave contains the treasure."

"You said there wasn't a treasure map," Stanley said. The boy was far smarter than I gave him credit for. "Now you tell us you know where the treasure is buried. Grandma, I think she's conning us."

Where in tarnation was the Stoltzfus? What were the chances he'd sneaked up on us and was lurking in the underbrush, just seconds away from being my hero? Frankly, it was about as likely as Charlie Sheen joining the NRA. No doubt Melvin was still at home, lollygagging about in his La-Z-Boy recliner, watching *One Life to Live*. If I got out of this predicament alive, I would pull strings with the finance company he used and get his TV repossessed.

However, now was not the time to appear anything but serene. I tapped the map again.

"This circle is right below a rock feature we call The Old Man. If we get closer to the edge you can look down and see his nose. It's almost as big as mine."

"I don't remember a rock called that," Augusta said.

"Well, it has other names as well. But look, there it is."

I'd been stepping sideways toward the

cliff, and they, unwittingly, had been moving with me. Just a few more steps and I might be able to trip or push one of them, and send him or her crashing into the foliage below.

"I don't see a nose," Augusta said, craning her neck. "Do you, Stanley?"

"Maybe it's because I'm taller than either of you," I said, "but I can see it. I'm sure you will too, if you get closer."

They each took a couple of steps forward. In fact, they were now nearer the edge than I was. When opportunity knocks, you either open the door or rue the day you didn't. This was my opportunity, so I took it.

32

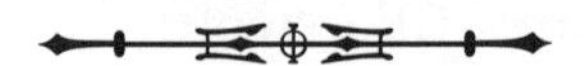

I pushed Stanley. Because of his youth and testosterone, he was the biggest threat to me. Besides, he was the one holding the gun. And it was Stanley who had shot Ron Humphrey when Augusta found herself unable to run the jogger over with her car.

Alas, the youth had the reflexes of a cat. One foot went over the edge, but he managed to whip around and grab my left arm. Using me as a fulcrum, he pivoted so that both his feet were back on the cliff. Then, instead of being generous of spirit, he pushed *me* off the cliff.

"Sayonara," I heard him say, as I sailed out over the abyss.

Okay, so it was a rather short cliff, but you try falling thirty feet, even if there are trees in the way to block your fall. To this day I thank the Good Lord that I have never given in to the temptation to wear slacks. My broadcloth skirt contains almost as much material as your average parachute. And in addition to my sturdy Christian underwear, I am never without a slip. These modest garments saved my life.

To say that I floated into the trees below would be an overstatement, but at least I didn't crash. In fact, I never even made it to the ground. The hem of my frock caught on a bare branch, in two places, and just feet below the ledge. I continued to fall a couple of feet more, so that when I jerked to a stop, both skirt and petticoat were up around my face.

I saw this as God's mercy. If I was to be shot at close range, at least I would not have to see the actual pulling of the trigger.

"Thank You, Lord," I said. "Thank You for all the blessings You've given me throughout my life. I truly am grateful. But please don't let this be a painful death — although I probably deserve it for grilling my guests like weinies. I'm not really big on pain, you see. Even if it hadn't been against Your will, I still would not have pierced my ears. And whenever the dentist works on my teeth, I make him use laughing gas — oops, that's not a sin, Lord, is it? Well, I guess I better sign off and let the Angel of Death do his stuff. Oh, just one more thing, please tell Mama and Papa I'll be seeing them real soon."

No sooner had I finished my brief prayer than the gun fired. In fact, it fired several times. There was nothing I could do but close my eyes and try to relax as much as possible while the bullets zinged through me. Perhaps they wouldn't hurt so much if my flesh was pliable. I was, after all, a sitting duck — make that a hanging woman. Cooperation with my killers would well be the last gift I gave myself.

There was shouting as well, but I did my best to tune it out. The quicker I left this world and its concerns behind, the quicker I entered Heaven. In fact, I was starting to get excited. What fun to be fitted for my celestial robes. I sure hoped we got fitted for halos as well, because it would be hard to find a ready-made halo my size. And I could hardly wait to see my mansion. Just as long as I wasn't expected to play a harp. I tried playing Susannah's guitar once and got blisters on my fingertips. Perhaps St. Peter would issue me an oboe instead.

The gunfire ceased. Well, now that was a big surprise; dying wasn't half-bad. I mean, it hadn't hurt at all. My wedding night with Aaron — well, never you mind. Trust me, dying was a lot more pleasant.

I opened my eyes. What on earth was my skirt still doing in front of my eyes? And why weren't my feet resting on golden streets? Metallic avenues had always seemed a mite dangerous to me, but I was willing to give them a try.

"Help me, Lord," I implored. "Help me to at least die right."

The Good Lord had a surprisingly high-pitched laugh. "I see London, I see France, I see Yoder's underpants."

"Don't tease me, Lord — hey, you're not God at all! Are you?"

"Your sister seems to think so."

"Melvin Stoltzfus!"

"Quit horsing around Yoder. Get back up here and give me a hand."

"If I could get back up, I'd give you a flock of birds, Melvin." You see what having a trash-mouthed sister has done to me?

"Then go hang yourself," he said.

"I did *not* say that." Melvin punctuated his statement by giving me the evil eye with his right orb. Meanwhile his left eye was surveying the Founder's Day Picnic, which, I shudder to mention, had hastily been renamed Melvin Stoltzfus Day.

The mouthwatering smells emanating from dozens of portable barbecue grills did nothing to ameliorate the bitter taste of jealousy. I had done all the work, and now the Mantis was reaping the glory. How fair is that? The time capsule, which truly did contain nothing more interesting than the oversized outhouse plans, had been safely returned from the trunk of Octavia's limo.

"You left me hanging, Melvin, and you know it."

Susannah, who was standing next to me, and whose fifteen feet of filmy fuchsia fabric was flapping in my face, had to open her big yap. "That's because my Babykins had to drive the two killers, which he handcuffed all by himself, down to the jail. Really, Mags, you should be grateful."

"Well, he wouldn't have had to do it all himself if he'd come straight up here when I called for backup."

Melvin forced his left eye to leave the crowd of picnickers and focus on me. "I already I told you, I had just gotten the call from the Harrisburg police."

"Right. But *they* caught the cabdriver who stole Miss Mukai's clothes; you didn't have anything to do with it."

Gabe's fingers encircled my biceps. "Hon, can I speak to you for a minute?"

"Yes, but first —"

My on-again, off-again, fiancé pulled me away from my family's grill. Melvin couldn't boil water if given written directions, yet he somehow manages to excel on a grill. It must be a guy thing — one that includes male mantises. That day he was cooking a side of ribs that smelled so delicious, half of Hernia was leaning our way, inhaling the breeze.

"I'm sorry," Gabe said, without a preamble. "From now on I'm putting you first."

"I'm sorry too. And you don't *always* have to put me first. After all, Ida is your mother — I mean, Alison is my daughter, and there might be times when I —"

You should have heard the collective gasp as hundreds of Mennonites and Amish assembled on that ridge saw the Babester silence me with a kiss. On the lips, no less. First base, right out there in the open, in broad daylight. They could have been more shocked only had we broken into a jig. Or maybe the highland fling.

"Ooh," Susannah squealed, "how come you never kiss me like that, Babykins?"

"But I do, Sugar Poodle."

"I think I'm gonna be sick." I recognized the voice as belonging to Alison.

"Hon," Gabe said to me, "do you want me to do it again?"

Of course I did! Just not in front of the entire town.

"Yes, let's talk."

Gabe grabbed my hand and ushered me through the gaping crowd. Neither of us said anything until we reached the cemetery. This was, incidentally, the least populated spot on the ridge. The wooded area in which Buzzy was found dead was full of teenagers. Because of their youth, no one cared if *they* got to first base. And believe me, Cornelia Unruh and one of the Bontrager boys (they all look alike) had just rounded second and looked eager to press on to third. But the cemetery, for the most part, remained the domain of its long-term residents.

My beloved knew me well enough to keep away from my parents' plots. We sat on the grass next to Ebeneezer Schrock's headstone. This man, by the way, was no relation to Lodema or her husband. Ebeneezer Schrock was an itinerant preacher who had no business being buried on Stucky Ridge. This unfortunate event happened well over a century ago, and nobody alive is quite sure of the circumstances. My point is that since Ebeneezer has no descendants in Hernia, his plot is seldom visited.

"Hon," Gabe said, when our privacy was

assured, "for your own sake, you have got to let go of this."

"But it's Melvin," I wailed. "For years I've done all his work for him, and now, suddenly, he gets lucky and ends up a hero."

"He did single-handedly apprehend Augusta Miller and her grandson."

"He shot her in the toes when his gun accidentally discharged!"

"Nevertheless, this is his shining moment, and you're a big enough person to let him have it."

"But I'm not! And it just isn't fair."

"What's not fair," Gabe said, his lips so close to mine that I could feel their heat, "is that I didn't meet you twenty-five years ago."

"But I —"

I fully intended for Gabe to silence me again with a kiss. He seemed happy to comply.

About the Author

Tamar Myers, who is of Amish background, is the author of the Pennsylvania Dutch mysteries and the *Den of Antiquity* series. She lives in South Carolina with her husband. Visit her on-line at www.tamarmyers.com.

The employees of Thorndike Press hope you have enjoyed this Large Print book. All our Thorndike and Wheeler Large Print titles are designed for easy reading, and all our books are made to last. Other Thorndike Press Large Print books are available at your library, through selected bookstores, or directly from us.

For information about titles, please call:

(800) 223-1244

or visit our Web site at:

www.gale.com/thorndike
www.gale.com/wheeler

To share your comments, please write:

Publisher
Thorndike Press
295 Kennedy Memorial Drive
Waterville, ME 04901